About the Author

Karen Angelucci is an author, realtor, and mom thriving in the heart of Kentucky, USA. With a love for nature, a thirst for history, and a zest for culture, she embodies the essence of living life to the fullest.

Francesca's Story

Karen Angelucci

Francesca's Story

Vanguard Press

VANGUARD PAPERBACK

© Copyright 2024
Karen Angelucci

The right of Karen Angelucci to be identified as author of
this work has been asserted by her in accordance with the
Copyright, Designs and Patents Act 1988.

All Rights Reserved

No reproduction, copy or transmission of this publication
may be made without written permission.
No paragraph of this publication may be reproduced,
copied or transmitted save with the written permission of the
publisher, or in accordance with the provisions
of the Copyright Act 1956 (as amended).

Any person who commits any unauthorized act in relation to
this publication may be liable to criminal
prosecution and civil claims for damages.

A CIP catalogue record for this title is
available from the British Library.

ISBN 978 1 83794 141 4

This is a work of fiction. Names, characters, businesses, places, events and
incidents are either the product of the author's imagination or used in a
fictitious manner. Any resemblance to actual persons, living or dead, or actual
events is purely coincidental.

*Vanguard Press is an imprint of
Pegasus Elliot Mackenzie Publishers Ltd.*
www.pegasuspublishers.com

First Published in 2024

**Vanguard Press
Sheraton House Castle Park
Cambridge England**

Printed & Bound in Great Britain

To my daughters Sarah and Rachel,

In your laughter,
I find the melody of life;
You are the joy that fills my every day.

Acknowledgements

I extend my sincerest gratitude to J.D. Lester, a remarkable friend, and invaluable collaborator. Grateful for your humor, artistry and writing skills - couldn't do it without you!

Chapter 1

Italy—March 1917

On a lovely spring morning in the remote Italian village of Castel Frentano, Francesca Viviano prepared to leave her life, family, and most that she knew.

After six long years, Antonio Bucci, Francesca's husband and father of their two children, and love of her life, had finally sent for them!

Life had changed since Antonio had left for America, but Francesca's devotion never wavered, and she longed for her children to know their wonderful papa—the man she remembered and still adored.

Francesca was to travel on a large seagoing ship most unlike the small fishing vessels her papa's brother, *Zio* Pasquale, owned. She had never been on a large ship, but she had fond memories fishing with her papa, and she loved swimming in the sea. Would America, and this body of water called the Atlantico, dim her recollections of Castel Frentano, her lifelong ancestral home?

Growing up in the village, Francesca gardened, cooked, sewed, and was especially gifted in the creative art of embroidery. Her skill allowed her to help her parents and even put away a few liras over the years. She knew she'd be fine in America as long as she had her children, embroidery tools, and Antonio, with his head for numbers, to provide.

Antonio had gone ahead to establish a career and make a home for them in a small town in Kentucky. Francesca was relieved he'd settled in a small town. She had heard enough about the brutal hardships that existed in the larger American cities. Her papa said the rats in New York were as big as dogs!

To Francesca, family meant everything; to leave her parents and sisters was inconceivably difficult. The children were happy and healthy here in Italy, and uprooting them seemed cruel. Even though Antonio had been long away, she knew where her loyalties ultimately lay, and now he had called for her to follow his path. She knew what she had to do.

Just when it was becoming nearly impossible to imagine his face, or remember his touch, a letter with his familiar handwriting arrived from America. He had a fine job, Antonio wrote, and a home two stories high made of clay bricks. He wrote of electric lights, a front porch with a swing, a *cucina* with a stove that lighted with only a touch. He'd prepared a small garden with vegetables and herbs, a few grape vines, and even had neighbors from the old country who looked after him. I miss you and the children, he'd said. As excited as Francesca was to hear at last from her love, her heart was full of apprehension. How could she leave her home?

"Antonio has sent for me and the children," Francesca broke the news to her mamma. "The letter came yesterday, and I've been in a daze. You must know how much I love and miss him."

Her mamma placed a warm hand on Francesca's shoulder. "I know you miss your love, cara, but you must stay here. It is too dangerous to travel with the war going on."

"In his letter," Francesca replied, "Antonio says we will be safer in America, and that I must board a ship at the end of the month." She realized it was already the Ides of March, and she felt the pressure double. "He regrets that he could only acquire steerage tickets, as second-class was not available. He feels certain the journey has improved in six years. We will be okay, Mamma, you will see."

Francesca went to her papa the evening before they departed for America, and they cried together.

"Papa, I don't want to leave you, but I long to see my Antonio."

"You must, cara, Antonio needs you, and the children need their papa," Signore Viviano soothed, wiping his daughter's tears with a handkerchief, just as he did when she was a young girl.

Even if she did return someday, this was to be a most heart-wrenched farewell. She knew her sisters could manage without her, but their parents' age and declining health concerned her greatly. To leave them behind was almost more than she could bear.

Her papa tapped urgently on his forehead. "*Cara*, don't waste time looking back; your eyes are in the front of your head." Francesca grinned at Papa's familiar words, and she vowed to herself to remember to look ahead.

After a restless night, Francesca awoke early. She gathered up her things, slipping the whole of her life into small packs and bundles. She could only carry so much to America, so she made emotional choices. She layered on skirts and petticoats, wearing as many as possible, allowing her to fit more necessities into her bundle. She included a small sewing kit with embroidery needles, one hoop, and her favorite colors of floss. She covered her dark brown hair with a light blue scarf, and tucked it into a marine blue cloak. To her parents, she looked like the *Adriatico* surf, gathering itself for departure at low tide, and they knew she was as unstoppable.

The children each had a small waxed canvas rucksack in which they put only their most prized possessions, such as stuffed animals, balls, special pebbles, a bow and arrow—until Francesca repacked and put in changes of clothes and snacks instead.

Francesca's mamma, already in the kitchen with fresh coffee and a plate of almond biscotti, had prepared a basket and filled Francesca's favorite pottery vase with food to take on their voyage. Her mamma knew there were challenges ahead for her beloved *figlia* and young *nipoti*. She busied herself with maternal tasks to shake the fingers of dread from her heart. Inside the food basket, she tucked away Rosa's favorite *bambola* named Lu Lu and a toy horse for Raffaele—she hoped these might ease the long journey.

The thought of a trip to America had the children bewildered. Raffaele, almost seven years old, was sure to be a handful all by himself, but Rosa—well, she was already eight years old now and had had her first Communion. Why, she was practically a lady, and ready to help Mamma with the child.

With a thudding heart, Francesca looked around and breathed in the last scent of home. Heavy with the fragrance of lilac and sun-baked honeysuckle, the air felt warm and fresh. Her sisters, Bianca and Adriana, as well as a few friends and neighbors, had come to say goodbye. Pink azaleas in full bloom lined the cobbled walkway as Francesca and her children turned to wave one last farewell. Backlit by blazing sunlight, her family already appeared as dim, faceless figures, and Francesca choked back the urge to run to them.

Signore Viviano helped the voyagers into a simple carriage and drove them to the *Madonna delle Piane* train station. Francesca sat alongside her papa, as she had done hundreds of times. Would this be the last? They both silently pondered the same question, troubled because no clear answers came.

Along the way, Francesca took in every tree, shrub, and flower, seeking out pretty shop windows and favorite landmarks—anything to help retain the sights and memories of home. Her breaths were heavy and deep, her entire body taking in the salted, precious breeze. The children rode quietly, not really understanding the enormity of the moment.

At the station, her papa bade them farewell and bon voyage. His words, typically, were few - just a tender embrace, a kiss on the forehead, and a whisper to each of them, *"il mio sangue"*—my blood.

The train ride to Naples took better than three hours. The passing mountain range opened to green valleys, and Francesca continued to absorb the view from her window. This was the first train ride for Raffaele and Rosa, and they were fascinated by every detail of the train, the sounds, smells, and textures. Francesca quietly feared for the journey ahead, but knew her capability as a mother. She rode on in silence, with one hand pressed to the window, and the other to her heart.

Once they departed the train at the Bay of Naples, Francesca opened her bundle and removed a patchwork quilt. In it, she recognized a checkered tablecloth scrap, a piece of Communion lace, an old pair of her papa's rough work pants, a patch pocket from *Nonna's* herb gathering apron, and a bit of salvaged sailcloth. Her entire life was in this well-loved quilt. Not even Queen Elena of Montenegro possessed such a priceless *famigila tesoro*.

Francesca carefully spread the quilt out under a shade tree high above the dock to rest. She unpacked pears and cured meat from the food basket. The toys for the children that her mamma packed brought a smile to Francesca's face and she hid them for later. As they snacked, they watched the crowd creeping and lurching along, as if it was one living thing with many eyes and many boots.

Port of Naples – stunning even with the ominous presence of Mount Vesuvius grumbling across the bay – teemed with travelers and onlookers alike. Lovers, loners, grandparents, and entire families lined up to board the vessel. Many passengers waited on the wharf below, elbow to elbow, in the shade of the towering ocean liner.

Francesca gathered the remaining snacks and repacked the basket. Rosa tenderly folded the quilt and settled it back into the top of the bundled pack as they prepared to board the *S.S. Giuseppe Verdi* headed to America.

"Mamma, why do we have to leave *Nonna* and *Nonno*?" Raffaele, wailed, balling his little fist to rub his eyes—and Francesca knew he had grown tired. "Will Papa know me? I am so tall now!"

"Si, let's stay here—*Zia* Bianca wants to teach me how to quilt!" Rosa pulled at her mamma's arm, already tired of being a grown lady.

"Children." Francesca smiled with more confidence than she felt. "We will go see Papa in America—he misses us terribly. Then, we will return home for lots of visits with presents for everyone."

They made their way through Piazza della Borsa and passed a large circular fountain with a sculpted likeness of Neptune, the Roman god of the sea, powerfully rising from the center. Neptune was surrounded by leaping dolphins as he held his gleaming trident aloft. A few ominous sea monsters caught the eyes of Raffaele, as they spurted endless streams of water into a large shell basin. Francesca pulled out her rosary and said a quiet prayer of thanks for the spectacular distraction from their weariness and fears.

As they approached the funneling crowd, Francesca quickly released her hand from Rosa's, made the sign of the cross, and blessed her children. Naturally, she thought of the Roman goddess Diana, protector of children, and Saint Andrew, patron saint for men at sea, and asked for their protection.

The seagoing vessel loomed large and imposing before them, glinting like a small city in the sun. She took hold of Rosa's hand once more and they trudged onward, consumed now in the shuffling crowd, each passenger with their own bundles full of hopes, misgivings, and mementos from home.

Francesca and the children stared up in astonishment at the two vast red smokestacks capped with black bands that seemed to reach all the way to the sky. Each smoke funnel displayed a large five-pointed white star, and two huge billowing masts towered at the stern and bow. An awed Raffaele thought the steamship could be one of Neptune's sea pets, emerging from the lapping waves.

The *Verdi* would transport over twenty-two hundred passengers to the new world on this voyage. Named for Giuseppe Fortunino Francesco Verdi, a Milanese composer who was criticized by the elite for catering to the taste of common people, Verdi's work was a favorite of Francesca's. She was honored to share his name and now to board his namesake. Francesca secretly hoped the coincidence might bring them good luck.

One hundred of the most privileged passengers would travel first-class on this voyage, and close to two hundred in second-class. The steerage, however, later called third-class, held nearly eighteen hundred passengers, by far the vast majority of those onboard. Only around two hundred passengers planned to vacation in America with no intention to stay, while the rest hoped and prayed for new lives of promise on new land.

When Francesca discovered the cost of the first-class ticket compared to hers, she understood why she was at the bottom of the ship. Each ticket in steerage cost about twenty-five American dollars. For Francesca's family, this equaled about two month's pay. She heard some of the staterooms in first-class went as high as two thousand American dollars! She couldn't fathom that amount of money. Who could pay such a kingly amount?

Francesca led Rosa and Raffaele down the dock to board.

"Welcome aboard, *Signora*. Watch your step, *per favore*," the helmsman held out a hand and greeted them at the end of the bobbing wooden gangplank.

"*Grazie Signore.*" Francesca made the sign of the cross as their feet left the last of dry land.

Since each class was kept separately on the ship, it came as no surprise that their 'cabin' turned out to be one large, open area in the hull of the ship. Dark, damp and already reeking of mingled human odors, the steerage area had previously been used as a large hold for seagoing cargo, including exported livestock, before the immigration boom. Now the cattle were immigrants willingly pushing themselves forward into their dreams of a strange land.

Francesca furrowed her brow, momentarily annoyed that first and second-class passengers were referred to as 'ladies' and 'gentlemen' while steerage passengers were simply 'males' and 'females.'

First-class guests would enjoy beamed ceilings and polished brass lanterns, and stately rooms filled with the rarified scents of ladies' perfume and fine imported cigars. Francesca could only imagine how luxurious it must be.

With Raffaele resting on one knee, and Rosa pulled close to her side, Francesca sat on a worn wooden bench on the lowest deck, alongside the interlocking controls that would steer the ship. The incessant thrumming of loud engines did little to drown out the pressing noises of all the people, perhaps not all that different from how unsettled livestock must've echoed off hull walls in years past.

They sat and watched the crowd file in, wearing clothes much more like their own. Soon elbow to elbow with strangers, they gripped their possessions all the more tightly. Hoping for fresh air, Francesca, Rosa, and Raffaele made their way to a less crowded steerage promenade deck where they found a few more wooden benches filling with travelers. Well-wishers filled the queue, tearfully waving their hats and handkerchiefs to bid a final farewell to their loved ones.

Francesca imagined Papa, Mamma, Adriana, and Bianca back at home, and wondered if they missed her and the children as much as she missed them. "Eyes forward, Francesca! Eyes are on the front of your head for good reason!" she could hear her papa gently urging. There was no room for looking back, self-pity, or heavy sentiments on such a crowded ship, where even every breath was taxed.

Francesca watched as the first-class passengers embarked the ship from a different ramp, while their many leather steamer trunks papered in exotic stamps were stowed safely by ushers into their staterooms. They carried themselves with erect confidence and looked to be dressed in royal finery.

Dazzling in both design and color, the ladies' tailored wool and serge jackets with draped bustle skirts captivated

Francesca. The collars, made of stiff lace, were worn high to elongate the feminine neckline, and many of the women wore silk and suede gloves embellished with colorful and intricate embroidered designs that captured and reflected every flattering slant of sunlight.

Francesca's wide eyes soaked up every stitch of the needlework. The fanciful costumes reminded Francesca of when she and her sisters played dress-up at home. The memory of her oldest sister, Bianca, covered from head to toe in mantillas and petticoats they had spent hours designing and sewing as young girls, brought a needed smile to her face. Francesca had the patience and rich imagination—and her handiwork on napkins, handkerchiefs, linens, and Christening gowns had grown popular in the village.

Sadly, the austerity of the war had dulled the obsession with fashion. The short-lived Beautiful Age - La Belle Epoque - had gradually waned, until only the very affluent could maintain wardrobes full of carefully tailored velvet, fur, and silk.

Rosa spotted a few chic women who sported the new hobble skirts with flares made of Middle Eastern influence and colors that had made their way to Europe. Their shoes appeared to be studded with glittery marcasites and silver filigree.

"How does she walk in that dress?" Rosa asked her mamma, pointing across the crowd.

Francesca lowered Rosa's hand and replied, "I've heard that some women actually tie their legs together so as not to take too large of a stride." She looked down at Rosa with a smile. "That can't be any more comfortable than wearing all your skirts at once!"

From the air above, a powerful steam siren blew, causing the three of them to startle, and signaling the time for departure. This same siren would blast in the event of danger, so one never knew for sure what the blaring meant. The high-pressure steam boilers engaged and rumbled below, and Francesca's stomach churned almost as forcibly.

As the ship departed, the sun was climbing high and steady over Vesuvius. The zephyr and waves were reassuringly gentle, and the sky, a perfect, cloudless blue. St. Christopher, Diana, and the Blessed Mother must be looking down as they embarked for America.

Francesca had overheard elders in Castel Frentano speak of harrowing stories of the journey to America. Knowing all this, she had tried to steel herself – but nothing could have prepared her for the journey ahead. She peered out across the expanse of aqua blue water, and marveled that it could ever end. Her last view of land gradually faded and uneasiness gathered uncomfortably around her, heavier even than her thickly layered petticoats.

Francesca felt like she could see both the sun and the moon in the sky at once. She willed away threatening tears for her children's sake, as the final view of Italy burned into her memory and slid out of view. They now belonged to the whims of the sea.

Many new sights and choice words abounded onboard, many that Francesca preferred the children not to see or hear. "Children, please stay close to me. We will be in America soon."

"I want to go home!" Raffaele kicked the side of the ship with his foot.

"We will," Francesca soothed. "We just have to see Papa first."

Francesca stared at her children and prayed that her decision was the right one. She looked at Rosa, who was beautiful with her brown curly locks and coal-black eyes. She was a petite child with freckles and a bright smile. Raffaele, fiery and stubborn at times, looked just like his papa. He had Antonio's dark brown hair, and short bangs that exposed dark amber eyes, inky eyelashes, and a mischievous smile.

He stood there in long shorts and knee socks, looking sadly at his mamma. "Why did we have to leave?" Her heart squeezed in her chest, and she realized once again that she did not really want to leave either. Even with war rampant across Europe, Francesca still felt that Castel Frentano was the only home for her.

"Will Papa know us?" Rosa stared out into the ocean.

"Papa hasn't even met me," Raffaele complained bitterly, kicking a barrel.

"Of course he will know you, you are his *bambini!*" Francesca pulled her children to her and hugged them tightly.

Antonio Bucci, Francesca's husband of nine years, was from the same village. They had played together as children, and their marriage, as most others, had been arranged. It had been almost too easy for them. They fell fast in love and never looked back.

After a few years of married life, Antonio had grown anxious to leave for America. He was impatient to create a better life for his family. So in 1911, at twenty four years of age, and with five hundred and eighteen lira in his coat pocket, two hundred and ten of which covered the cost of the ticket, he crossed.

In the six years he had been away, more than distance had come between them. Francesca had even accepted that he might not send for her. The letters, once as regular as the tide, came less and less. She had a life now, a life preoccupied with small children who needed her—and a life without a husband. Would Francesca even know him? Rosa had just turned one when he left, and Raffaele was born just six months later.

The three of them made their way back to the hold, amid the many other passengers scurrying around, looking as disoriented as Francesca felt. The ship's hold had been divided into two halves, one half for men and one half for women and children. Francesca was more than happy to spend time with women and children rather than to be surrounded by a group of strange men. Her beauty sometimes attracted the eyes and unwelcomed utterances of coarse men, which always made her wince and gather her arms more tightly around herself. Instinctively, she touched the silver band of promise on her left ring finger, as though touching it could summon Antonio to their aid.

The steerage accommodations were barely tolerable, and Francesca chose to live through the voyage minute by minute. Only a few gas lanterns illuminated the large cell. At one end, a large skylight centered on the deck above allowed for scant sun and even less ventilation. The air in the hull grew thick with a variety of rancid odors, and Francesca covered her face with a handkerchief, trying to pray the smell away. Ironically, she had embroidered the linen square with Italian lilac blooms and bright rays of spring sunshine—things that seemed suddenly very far away.

Each passenger was issued a metal berth, a frayed canvas mattress stuffed with straw, one thin worn blanket, and a life preserver. The preserver also served as a pillow, something that disguised its intended use. Fortunately, Francesca had brought heavy woolen blankets and a crocheted shawl. Passengers also received a tin pail and blunt eating utensils. The bundles and packs that Francesca and the children brought had to fit on their berths since there was no extra room. She directed the children to share one berth, and the third held their meager, though precious, belongings.

Francesca could wait no longer, and anxiously peeled the layered garments from her body and stashed them away. She felt lighter and was relieved to be unbound, though she wrang wet to her undergarments with perspiration.

The berths, if one could call them that, were two tiers high, side by side, and only eighteen inches wide. As more passengers found their way to the hold, the conditions became even more crowded and noisy, and the foul smells only continued to intensify.

After a few passengers became seasick, a chunky film of vomit soon covered the iron floor, making the journey to and from the outside deck dangerous. But Francesca kept her thoughts forward and her eyes on her children.

With no hot water in steerage, Francesca was told she could wash clothes and dishes with cold, salty water from the sea. A shipmate rigged a wooden bucket tied to a rope that allowed passengers to bring up briny water to wash and clean. The ship supplied only limited fresh water to drink and cook.

For those who had brought food, the ship was equipped with stoves for cooking. Others lined up twice daily with their tin pails to receive the usual meal of thin lentil soup, boiled beef, herring from salt water barrels, hard stale bread, and boiled potatoes. One could only imagine what the first and second-class passengers had to eat.

"This food stinks so bad, Mamma." Raffaele covered his nose. "I want *Nonna's* ravioli."

"Now, Raffaele, you must eat and be thankful for the food we have," pleaded Francesca. "It will not be long, and Mamma will cook you everything."

"Where are the tables, Mamma?" whined Rosa, beginning to understand how trapped they were.

"We don't need a table—we can have a picnic on our berths!" Francesca enthused, glancing quickly away from the putrid floor, their only alternative.

On the berth next to them sat a petite lady with an open smile and one arm protectively draped around a girl who looked exactly like her. "Well, I see we have finally made it to first-class," the lady said with a laugh. "*Ciao, amica mia,* my name is Silvia Tenaglia, and this is my daughter, Ella."

Silvia was a short, thin lady with long black, braided hair that was wrapped neatly on top of her head. Ella, strikingly beautiful and vivacious at thirteen years of age, had the same bright smile as her mother, and her face was framed in two, neat long braids. Silvia was traveling to reunite with her own husband in America—and seemed just as reluctant to leave her family in Sicily.

Francesca introduced herself and the children.

"You have your hands full with Rosa and Raffaele," Silvia said frankly and empathetically.

"They are good children, but already they are tired of this unbearable hull." Francesca dipped the bread in her soup to see if it made a difference.

Several berths over, a woman angrily spanked a boy who had pushed his little sister. He screamed over and over as she punished.

"I am sorry, Mamma! I am sorry! I will be good!" cried the stricken boy.

Silvia looked at Francesca and rolled her eyes, and Rosa and Raffaele looked on in horror as she pulled them to her.

Rosa and Raffaele took to Ella right away because she was older. To them, the ship was a daring adventure; to the mothers, it was a rocking, stinking, and hopefully temporary hell to be survived.

"Ella is wonderful with children," Francesca observed, and Silvia nodded warmly.

"When we get to America, she wants to become a teacher!"

"Oh, Ella, I think that sounds wonderful!" replied Francesca. "I am sure you will make a fine teacher, and how rewarding that will be."

After they had eaten the barely edible rations, the women and children went topside to find fresh air. They wove their way through the mass of women and children, huddled together in their respective berths.

"I'm surprised they let us outside," Silvia snapped. Francesca liked her new friend because she held nothing back - harsh, funny, kind, or otherwise.

The freight deck was yet another challenge, covered with ashes that rained down from the smokestacks overhead. The steerage passengers had to dodge hot falling cinders, but the fresh ocean air, after the stench of the hull, was so worth it.

While on deck, the women became friends with Olga Rossi from Sicily, a ship maid that Francesca had seen at the ticket office before they sailed. Olga was as tall as a man, and just as burly. She took charge on the ship with brazen authority, and wasn't afraid of much, that was clear. She would turn out to be a very valuable ally while at sea. From time to time, Olga slipped down with extra food for the children—rich treats and rolls with butter that had been tossed away by the first-class passengers.

Olga taught them a lot about the vessel. Apparently, they were on a ship, not a boat, and it was considered a she, not a he. Olga was very kind and never upturned her nose with disdain like many of the first-class passengers sneering down from the upper spar deck.

Francesca never let their obvious scorn bother her. Her parents had always told her that people were creations of their environment, and they just couldn't help the way they turned out. "Everyone is equal in the eyes of God, *cara*."

Olga led them to a narrow wooden bench away from the masses. The women and then children piled onto it and watched the clouds meet the water. Since they had nothing else to do, this bench became their precious respite from the stinking hold while on board.

"Hey, Fran!" exclaimed Silvia. "What do you think our *antenati* might say if they could see us now? They actually stood on the decks of ships and sent crews to find the new land. If Columbus, Cabot, or Vespucci had any idea how their descendants were to be treated in steerage, they'd be appalled!"

"I'm sure they only thought of riches and glory," Francesca mused, recoiling as she flicked a stowaway roach off the side of the bench with the back of her hand.

The friends remained on deck until darkness came, admiring the bright stars and the ship's great funnels against the night sky. The sky was growing black and the breeze, while invigorating, was salty and cold. The *Verdi* was undeniably impressive. But as night fell, the decks began to fill with men seeking companionship. Francesca and Silvia knew they'd be safer inside.

Back at their berths, the children fell fast asleep. Francesca and Silvia slept in shifts, allowing them to watch out for each other and their belongings. They had heard worrisome stories about rapes and thieves, and all they wanted was the assurance of morning light.

Each evening after the children fell asleep, Francesca pulled a rosary from her skirt pocket and prayed. She kissed it and repeated the prayer until her eyelids felt heavy. She asked over and over for a safe and quick voyage.

Each day the friends tried to manage their children's necessary tasks. In steerage, there were fewer than ten bathrooms to accommodate the eighteen hundred passengers. Trips to the bathroom were the most dreaded and most revolting efforts of the day. Between Rosa's complaints about the smell and Raffaele's flat refusal to enter the small compartment, Francesca had to bribe the children with a few bits of remaining torrone candy she had stashed away.

Over the next few days, they noticed fewer people lined up for food. Seasickness had taken its toll on many passengers with the continual rock and crack of the ship. The days merged into disheartening sameness: crying children, and mothers with thinning patience and ready backs of their hands. Although eager for something to break the horrible monotony, they were nevertheless not at all pleased to see a bank of dark storm clouds aggressively rolling in on the seventh day.

"The skies don't look very happy," Rosa observed, anxiously covering her head with her scarf and settling in more closely to her mother.

"I am sure it will be fine, *cara*," Francesca reassured. "A little fresh water rain will do us all some good."

Francesca reached out her hand to touch the lacy mist. But, within moments, the deck beneath their feet had grown slick with beating rain, and passengers began to dart inside. Rosa eyed the furious clouds over her shoulder and began to cry.

"Hurry, let's get back to our berths, I have a story for you." Francesca tried to console her children. By the time they arrived at the berths, the ship began to rock on ever growing waves. They hunkered down to brave the storm.

"Mamma! I am scared!" cried Raffaele, clutching her skirt.

Francesca thought it was the perfect time, so she brought out the children's favorite toys that their *nonna* had hidden in the picnic basket. Their eyes lit up as they reached for the comfort of their familiar friends.

"Shh, quiet now, and I will tell you a story." Francesca pulled the children in closer to her. "Ella, come hear my story?" she asked.

Feigning fearlessness, Ella managed to say, "Yes, that sounds nice." Ella and Silvia moved closer as the rain began to pound the surface above. Silvia lifted her crucifix out of her blouse, brought it to her lips, and kissed it.

Francesca pulled Raffaele in close and wrapped her shawl around him. She stroked Rosa's bangs away from her face as the child lay shivering like a frightened puppy in her lap.

"In the city of Marostica, in the foothills of the Asiago plateau where forget-me-nots grew, lay a pristine castle and a story of love and mystery." Francesca blew a kiss toward Raffaele and he blushed, momentarily forgetting the ocean waging war above them.

"In the thirteenth century, long, long ago, Lord Taddeo Parisio was in power. His servants advised him that his lovely daughter, Lionora, had stolen the hearts of two men. They were not just ordinary men, they were brave and capable knights who were most dedicated to Lord Parisio. Every day the loyal knights, Cavalieri Rinaldo D'Angarano and Vieri da Vallonara, did all they could to win Lionora's heart." Francesca stopped to hug the children after an especially alarming crack of lighting reflected off thousands of terrified eyes in the echoing hull.

"In those days," she continued. "Men usually fought other men to the death for the simple amusement of the kings and queens. Cavalieri and Vieri were both too important to Lord Parisio to forfeit either of them, so he came up with a plan for a winner that would spare the life of the loser. Lord Parisio declared that the winner won Lionora's hand in marriage, and the loser would win the hand of the lord's younger sister, Oldrada. This clever plan of marriage kept both loyal knights in the family."

Francesca raised her voice above the noise of the raging sea and the wailing, tearful women and children surrounding them. "In the town square in front of the lower castle, Lord Parisio called upon the townspeople to create a large chessboard on the street. In a pageant of medieval society, the lord appointed villagers to play the pieces of a chess game. He made them dress appropriately in his noble ensigns of white and black before they enacted this life-size game of chess."

The ship began to tilt and buck harder, like an enraged swordfish at the end of a hapless fisherman's line. Francesca swallowed a frightened cry rising in her throat and continued, "As each knight called out in turn to the king and queen, rook and knight, bishop and pawn, each actor moved respectfully to the chosen square." Francesca cowered down after a nearby explosion of thunder, instinctively pulling her children to her. Silvia did the same, and Ella did not resist.

Francesca regained her composure and continued, "Now, what few in the crowd knew was that Lionora already had her favorite knight, and she secretly longed for him to win. She told her footman that if her true love won the duel, the lower castle tower was to be illuminated with white light. When her love prevailed in the match, joy came to this village, and now the white lights shine from the lower tower every night."

"Who won Lionora's hand?" Ella asked from her mamma's protective arms.

"Well, that's the mystery in the story! I don't know who won!" Francesca tried to laugh to ease the tension reverberating among them.

By the time the story ended, torrential rain and ruthless gales battered the helpless ship, tossing Francesca, Silvia, and their children into the foul slurry of waste on the floor, where they went sliding and screaming.

The steerage took hard slaps from the waves, sounding as though the riveted iron sides were snapping like sticks of dry kindling with each successive punch.

Francesca pulled her terrified children back into the berth, held them with all the strength she had, and prayed to God, Mary, Uranus—to anyone listening. She thought of her parents and sisters in Castel Frentano, and of Antonio waiting for them in America—and she prayed simply for survival.

Open my heart,
and you will see,
Graved inside of it, Italy

– Robert Browning

Chapter 2

Atlantico Oceano, April 1917

Like a child exhausted by a tantrum, the black storm clouds eventually thinned and the turbulent waves slowly calmed. Stunned and bleary-eyed passengers greeted the first glimpse of the reappearing sun with relieved cheers. Strangers hugged and wept. After cleaning up and sorting their possessions in the hull of the *Verdi*, Francesca noticed that peevish mothers weren't quite as impatient, and the children were a bit better behaved.

Many slowly made their way topside for fresh air and to reassure themselves that the ship had truly held. Shouted praises of thanks were carried on updrafts straight to heaven. Still afloat, they were not yet at the bottom of an unforgiving ocean. The *Verdi* had taken fierce blows, but the crew encouraged everyone not to worry as they set about needed repairs, and swabbed away evidence of violent seasickness. After Francesca noticed one or two missing railings, she steered the children clear of that side of the ship.

Francesca and Silvia were both near the point of delirium—neither mother had slept soundly the entire trip.

Silvia noticed the bags under her friend's eyes gathering like bruises and urged Francesca to nap. "I will take this shift to care for the children," Silvia offered, and Francesca gratefully accepted.

In a semi-lucid daze, she drifted back to memories of when she and Antonio were first married and worry-free. She could almost feel the waves of the *Adriatico* gently lapping at her bare feet, and she could nearly see the foam that lingered as the sea receded. The air that day would have been crisp and the breezes full of salt spray and wild roses. She felt the sun beating down on her shoulders, and suddenly heard Antonio laughing.

Antonio took her hand in his and led her to a tiled terrace lavishly lined with a profusion of pastel blooms. She breathed in the bright, tangy air surrounding the lemon trees along their path. They spread a quilt under a pergola dripping pale and fragrant purple wisteria blooms. As Francesca started to unpack a special picnic, Antonio cupped her face with his hands and gently kissed her lips. His eyes burned into her as she welcomed him to lean in for another…

"Mamma! Mamma!" Raffaele cried as he tugged on her sleeve. "I am hungry! It is time to go eat."

Jolted from her reverie, it only took Francesca a second to remember the waterborne hell still pressing against them from every side.

"Mamma, please, we are hungry!" Rosa groaned, rubbing her belly.

"Okay, yes, let's head that way." Francesca stood in a daze, and led the way to the food line.

"Come on, Fran! You don't want to miss out on today's meal! I think it is the same thing we had last night and the night before," Silvia laughed wearily. "I can't wait."

Francesca filled her plate and ate quickly before the evening activity: sit on a wooden bench, look for familiar objects in the clouds, watch the now monotonous waves, and count the minutes.

"Fran, I'm exhausted and dizzy. I feel like I should get some water and lie down," Silvia yawned.

"Of, course! I will watch the children first tonight." Francesca waved her away.

"*Grazie.*" Silvia kissed Ella on the forehead and left the deck.

"Mamma, Mamma, look at the dolphins!" Raffaele screamed as he pointed to what appeared to be three dark gray porpoises. "They are chasing us!"

"Maybe they hope to catch a ride to America and can be our pets!" Rosa leaned over the rail a little too far for Francesca's comfort, and was yanked by her skirt waist back to the bench.

"Let's find Olga and see if she has located any extra blankets." Francesca gathered up small hands and shawls.

As they walked the deck to find Olga, they passed by a young boy of about ten years old and his younger brother who looked to be about seven. Francesca wondered to herself where their parents were. She walked over to the youngest child and handed him a piece of torrone candy. She then handed the older brother one as well. *"Grazie,"* the boys said together, beaming.

After Francesca found Olga and learned that there were no extra blankets to be found, they returned to their berths and were surprised to see Silvia's straw mat empty.

"Ella, please stay here with Rosa and Raffaele. Try to get some sleep," Francesca said. "I will find your mamma."

After a frantic half-hour of searching, Francesca found Silvia, cornered by a violent man in the dark shadows of the ship's deck.

They should not have separated, her mind screamed. They should have stayed together! "A woman is never safe alone," she heard her *nonna* saying in her ear. "To vile men, women are no more than prey. You must always be careful!"

With all of her strength, Francesca managed to tear Silvia free of her attacker, and led her, weeping, back to the safety of the hull. It had been a night of terrors and Francesca worried deeply about her friend. Brimming with adrenaline and revulsion, the rest of the moonless night passed without the relief of sleep.

The following day, Silvia lay on her berth staring up at nothing. Noticing the agony haunting Silvia's face, Francesca told the children that the seasickness had taken hold of her. They had all seen countless passengers lie in extreme distress, moaning and whimpering for relief. They offered Silvia fresh water and bread, but she refused everything with a listless wave of her hand.

"Silvia, you must eat something," Francesca pleaded.

Silvia closed her eyes and rolled silently towards the wall.

"You rest, then. I will take the children up to the bench for fresh air." Francesca covered Silvia's body with a blanket. "Everything will be fine. You will see, my friend." Francesca wiped her brow with a dampened cloth and said a prayer for mercy for her friend.

Francesca watched over the children all day while Silvia rested. The children were easy to handle with Ella around. With the kindness and patience of a good teacher, she had already become like an older sister to Rosa and Raffaele.

When they returned to the berths, they found Silvia in the same motionless position as though life and will had passed from her. Ella whispered comforting words about how many kisses Silvia would receive from Papa when he arrived to meet them. I bet he buys you the prettiest dress he can find!

Rosa and Raffaele quietly played a finger game called *morra* to pass the time. Raffaele, as usual, fell asleep first.

He was the youngest, and most adaptable. Despite the offending smells, he mostly found the ship to be an adventure. He always found the best spots for hide and seek, and had even made a few rambunctious friends in the berths close by. Rosa soon fell silent as she, too, gave in to the night. Francesca and Ella stayed awake and talked about Ella's papa.

"My papa is a carpenter. He can build anything," Ella explained with a proud smile. "He made me a real carriage pulled by a donkey when I was a little girl. He left for America five years ago when I was eight. I have changed since I saw him last." Ella grew silent then to be alone with her swirling worries, until sleep arrived at last to relieve her from duty.

Francesca watched over them all from her berth. In the night, she saw Silvia begin to stir. She stood beside Ella, for just a moment, and then walked away without a word. Concerned for Silvia's safety, Francesca slipped into her shawl and followed. She had moved quickly through the crowd of snoring and tossing people. Francesca passed Olga in the dark narrow hallway that led to the upper deck.

"Olga! Have you seen Silvia?" She reached out to Olga as if she could help.

"No," Olga answered with concern. "What is she up to?"

"I am very afraid for her!" Francesca cried.

"Of all people, you should know not to go out on deck alone, *Signora*," Olga warned. "I will go with you."

The two made their way to the deck. It was very dark and only a few passengers roamed around. "No one should be out here at this time of night." Olga looked around warily. They turned the corner and to their horror, they saw Silvia climb the metal rail under the starless night. Without a glance back, she was gone. At the sight of Silvia's floating green dress and billowing, undone braids disappearing into the dark, Francesca ran to the rail, hollering out to her friend, running to the rail. Hearing Francesca's shouts, two crewmen raced to help. But it was too late—Silvia was somewhere in the churning, deadly dark waves below.

One of the men threw a life preserver attached to a long rope. After what seemed like forever, the man pulled up the empty ring as Francesca fell into Olgas's arms and sobbed.

Francesca's mind rushed to buffer her from the horrible truth. Silvia must have slipped on the salt-sprayed deck! Surely, she did not just jump! She would not leave Ella!

It had happened so fast, and Silvia had disappeared into the darkness as quickly as a hungry seabird diving for its dinner. Only she never came back up. Francesca stared out into the black void, with the blur of horror looping in her mind, over and over, until she was finally able to understand. How was she to explain this to Ella? She was just a child, and she needed her mother.

Olga put her arms around Francesca. "I am so sorry, my friend. But it is not safe out here. We must go inside!" Olga turned Francesca away from the dark, empty space.

"What do I tell Ella?" Francesca cried. "She is only a child. She will not understand how or why this happened."

"You tell her the truth. It is a dangerous place out here, especially at night." Olga stroked her back and offered solace. "I can tell her, if you want?"

"No! I need to tell her." Francesca's voice suddenly sounded much older, and infinitely weary.

The path back to the berths took an eternity. Francesca rehearsed in her mind how to break the tragic news, but she knew nothing was right. The girl had just lost her mother, and she was now traveling alone to a strange land to meet a papa she hadn't seen in five years.

Shaking from nerves, Francesca stopped in a stairwell to cry. She pinched her arms to make sure she knew what was real, and slowly made her way back down to Ella. She approached the berths as though in a somber trance. Ella was still awake and saw that Francesca was upset. "*Signora* Viviano, what is the matter? Where is Mamma?" Ella asked quietly, as to not wake the children.

"Oh, Ella." Francesca held back the tears and drew in a deep breath. "I am so sorry. I don't know how to tell you. A terrible, terrible thing has happened. I wish I could take it all away, but I can't," she cried and held Ella tightly.

"Your mother has had an awful accident." Ella covered her mouth in horror and waited for whatever came next.

"It was dark outside, and your mamma lost her footing on the deck. The brace that secures the railing gave way and she fell." Francesca blotted the tears with her sleeves. Though she was sure in her heart that Silvia took her own life, she concealed the truth and made it easier for her to say, and for Ella to hear.

"You're wrong! Where is she?" Ella ran to the stairwell. By that time, Olga had returned to check on them.

"Olga, I must go after her. Please watch over my children! *Grazie*." Francesca ran after Ella.

"I will stay with the children, go!" Olga said.

Francesca found the weeping girl in the dark hallway that led to the deck. Francesca approached and hugged her from behind. "Ella, I am so sorry. I wish I could have been there to save her."

They stood in the darkness and cried. Ella pulled away and walked toward the steps to the deck. "Ella, you mustn't be out there, it's too dangerous." Francesca reached for her arm. "Besides the slick deck, there are dangerous people out there for no good reason," Francesca pleaded. "Please come back to the berth with me."

Francesca guided Ella back to the berth and held her. "Ella, your mamma loved you, and so does your papa. I will take you to your papa. I just want you to know that I will take care of you no matter what."

"Why? *Signora*, why did this happen to us? I need her. I barely know Papa, and he will not want to take care of me alone," Ella cried.

"Hush now, your papa loves you. He sent for you and your mamma. He will no doubt be devastated, but you are your mamma's image and that will comfort him. Come with me. You can stay close to me tonight," Francesca said quietly.

Ella was young and very impressionable. Crossing the Atlantico should have brought her family joyfully together. How could things go so wrong? Ella wanted only to return home to the warm, comforting arms of her *nonna* in Italy, but that was not an option now.

The next morning, Francesca told Rosa and Raffaele about Silvia's fall. The children wept and clung to Ella tightly. They tried to comfort her, but Ella fell away from them, as though she, too, was following her mamma to the black depths of an endless ocean. She just stared ahead, lost in a dawning world of worry and inescapable grief.

As the journey wore on, many of the passengers grew more restless. The days were excruciatingly long, and the nights brought little relief.

Francesca now found herself with three children to tend to. If it were not for Olga, she'd certainly have failed. Olga came around as often as she could to relieve Francesca and take the children for walks on the deck. Every evening when darkness set in, Francesca made sure that the children were tucked in safe and sound before she fell wearily asleep at their feet. Fear and nightmares plagued Francesca's nights and she slept very little. She found she now hovered in a state of dread over the children, with few breaks from her deepening anxieties.

Ella grew ever more withdrawn and refused to leave her berth, and Francesca had to beg her to eat even small amounts of food. The next day was to be their last on the ship. This long nightmare surely had to end?

"Not like the brazen giant of Greek fame,
With conquering limbs astride from land to land;
Here at our sea-washed, sunset gates shall stand
A mighty woman with a torch, whose flame
Is the imprisoned lightning, and her name
Mother of Exiles. From her beacon-hand
Glows world-wide welcome; her mild eyes command
The air-bridged harbor that twin cities frame.
"Keep, ancient lands, your storied pomp!" cries she
With silent lips. "Give me your tired, your poor,
Your huddled masses yearning to breathe free,
The wretched refuse of your teeming shore.
Send these, the homeless, tempest-tost to me,
I lift my lamp beside the golden door!"

— The New Colossus, Emma Lazarus (1883)

Chapter 3

Ellis Island, New Jersey 1917

Francesca's first sight of America was overwhelming—like a thousand prayers being answered at once. After the passage that had stolen so much from her, Francesca was certain that once she touched *terra firma*, she didn't want to board another ship as long as she lived. This realization broke her heart, for it meant that she might never see her parents or sisters again.

Francesca directed the children, as well as Ella, to wash up and change into the cleanest clothes reserved for this occasion. She tidied herself as well, and slipped on a pale violet dress, Antonio's favorite color. Francesca rolled, folded, and pushed with all her might to stuff belongings back into their packs and bundles. She solemnly gathered Silvia's things, as well.

As though they had merely been on a pleasure cruise, the ship sailed serenely into the New York harbor. Lower Manhattan appeared to hover on a thin bar of land. Standing shoulder to shoulder, passengers crowded the rail to watch as smaller tugboats approached the *Verdi* to escort her to the pier. Men put small children on their shoulders to see America coming into view, and everyone cheered at the sight of dry land. They had made it!

"Look, children, there is Lady Liberty on the horizon!" Francesca pointed. "The French gave her to the United States to honor the friendship between the two nations. She's become a symbol of hope and opportunity for all immigrants because look! She is welcoming us!" Francesca held back the tears. Whether they were happy or sad tears, she did not know. Francesca wanted more than anything to see Antonio, forget the horrible journey, and start their married life anew. She stared up at Lady Liberty, and hoped she was indeed holding a hopeful lantern of welcome for Francesca's little family.

"They say her index finger is eight feet long!" Ella spoke up suddenly, her finger out, as she gestured with her hand to Rosa and Raffaele.

Just to have Ella in conversation was some relief. The sight of land had lifted Francesca's flagging mood, and perhaps Ella's, too. Francesca picked herself up out of grief and exhaustion, and pressed on. Eyes forward, *mi sangre*, eyes forward. The children seemed very happy to leave the ship, and Raffaele ran about excitedly, whooping. His knee breeches, Francesca noted, hung off his newly slim hips.

After a total of seventeen grueling days that had tested each of them, the *Verdi* finally docked at pier number thirty-three in Hoboken, New Jersey. The steerage passengers were transferred to a large flat-bottom barge that hauled them en masse to Ellis Island to be processed. Anxious to be free of the ship, passengers jostled each other as they disembarked, each trying to recover equilibrium on wobbly sea legs.

To ensure speedy processing, all immigrants wore small landing cards pinned to the top of their shirts and dresses. Each small card listed an immigrant's name, destination, steamship name, and manifest number. For all Francesca knew, the strange scribbled words could have said she was Queen of the Nile. Or a monkey from the zoo.

Some cards simply stated W.O.P., which Francesca later learned stood for without papers. Francesca also carried medical cards issued by the ship's physicians for check-in.

As the barge approached Ellis Island, the building seemed to float on water. And sadness swept over Ella like rolling fog. She should be entering with her mamma, but her mamma was gone, swallowed forever by that cruel sea. Looking lost, Ella reached for Raffaele's hand. Francesca took his other hand and then Rosa's, and they moved forward, foot by foot, to be poked, prodded, and interrogated by strangers in a strange land - the price of entry.

Without warning, Raffaele began to cry. He was tired, hungry, and angry about leaving Italy.

"Shh, we are almost there," Francesca soothed. "You will see Papa soon!" Francesca, with children and bags in tow, made her way off the barge and up a steep flight of stairs. A large canopy extending from the turreted, ornate red brick and limestone building sheltered them from the hot midday sun. Two large sculpted stone eagles looked down upon them with somber expressions. In a single file, they ascended more steps to the Great Hall, where the real inspection process began.

When they finally had their turn, Francesca presented their medical cards to the team of inspectors. Each of them was then subjected to a six-second physical that Antonio had warned her about in his early letters.

All immigrants were examined for signs of physical and mental illness. Many received chalk marks on their sleeves to identify those who were blind (B), mentally challenged (X), pregnant (PG), and so forth. It didn't take long before immigrants realized that the chalk marks revealed a lot about who they each were.

Then came the dreaded exam. A physician used a cold metal buttonhook or hairpin to pull back the eyelids of each passenger to search for signs of trachoma, one of the very contagious diseases everyone wanted to avoid. Hair and fingernails were inspected, and if approved, the newcomers pressed forward in a single file line, spaced a few feet apart.

Since Antonio had warned Francesca about his experience, she was not too dismayed by the buttonhook peeling back her eyelids. But she was not prepared when a young doctor with red hair reached for Raffaele and sought to take him away. At first, she bellowed in maternal distress, but an interpreter informed her that the doctors meant no harm. They thought her young son might be contagious, and they needed to take him for further examination.

Francesca pleaded with them not to take her son, "He is fine. He only cries because he is tired and scared!"

Nurses peeled Raffaele off his mamma's leg, and he let out a blood-curdling war cry. Although Francesca tried to console him from a distance, he did not understand what was happening. "Raffaele, the doctors will just look at your eyes. Mamma, *sorella* and Ella will stay right here!" she called out to him, trying not to choke on the sobs that wanted to be set free in her throat.

"Mamma! Mamma!" the boy cried.

The image of her thrashing and screaming son as he was dragged away from her was torturous. The medical staff took Raffaele immediately to a holding room. If he had trachoma, he faced quarantine for up to twenty days.

Against Francesca's wishes, the line continued on. They proceeded to receive mandatory vaccinations before registration. Distraught, Francesca was desperate to know where Raffaele had been taken, and she was nearly as eager to find Antonio so he could help locate their son.

Francesca and the children endured the same bewildering procedures that all immigrants faced in the chaotic registry room.

Large American flags hung from a vaulted, terracotta-tiled ceiling. Francesca noticed a wrap-around balcony that overlooked the teeming room, and recalled Antonio's description. She had expected to see something like a stockyard with iron bars and mazes of railing. Instead, the years had relaxed Ellis Island and the maze of iron had been removed. In its place were long wooden benches where immigrants sat until they were called on to proceed. Off to one side, they saw cages that detained immigrants. To Francesca, they looked like jail.

"Will they put us in those cages?" Rosa asked, eyeing the enclosures suspiciously.

"No, no!" Francesca hugged Rosa. "Everything will be fine, you will see!"

At that moment, a young girl was pulled from her mother by what appeared to be an older sister. They watched in terror as the girl's screaming mother was dragged to the caged holding area for quarantine. Fear, confusion, and tension intensified, permeating the room. How much more could they be expected to endure?

While they waited on the hard wooden bench for their turn, Francesca's eyes swept over the large arched window at the top of the room. Warm sunlight streamed in on the new arrivals, and she prayed that it might inspire a sense of hope and renewal. Beyond that arched beacon, she knew, was a new life. It was her choice to survive and thrive. Eyes ahead! However, one thing was certain: she was not leaving that room without her son.

When Francesca's name was called, she approached the tall wooden desk.

"Are you Francesca Viviano? Are you married? Who is your sponsor? How much money do you have? Are you skilled? Can you read? Do you have a place to stay?" Francesca knew she had to answer all the routine questions or face deportation. She relied on an interpreter to translate her answers.

One man who had sat next to Francesca on the bench quickly hid some of his money to avoid disclosure. Francesca feared for him and thought that he should enter honestly. Besides, she did not have much to report. She had been told that, a few years earlier, the United States had made it mandatory that all immigrants had to have at least twenty-five American dollars to enter.

Antonio had written to her about the spotters. Sure enough, a spotter saw the man hide his money, and then he promptly searched and humiliated him. "This is the land of the free, not a free land," the spotter huffed after he pulled the man aside to confront him.

"*Signora* Viviano, what if they don't let me enter without Mamma? I can't get back on that ship!" Ella stared at her, fear clouding her eyes.

"You call me Francesca, *cara*. We are forever friends. And everything will be fine. I have your travel papers, as well as your mamma's, and I will tell them you travel with me." Francesca put an arm around her.

"I am scared. What if Papa doesn't want me without Mamma? I barely know him. How will I recognize him?" Ella's voice quivered as she finally gave voice to her deepest fears.

"Everything will be just fine, Ella, I will see to it." Francesca gave the girl a hug and smiled despite the nervousness in the pit of her own stomach.

Thirty passengers at a time came forward to answer the battery of questions. Then, they were led to the currency exchange counter. Francesca reached into her blouse and pulled out a small burgundy velvet pouch on a string from around her neck. Antonio had warned Francesca of the corrupt currency exchange officials, so she asked a translator to assist her. She exchanged her liras for unfamiliar American dollars and coins, and tucked the pouch back safely into her blouse.

Officials then directed Francesca and the children to the Central Railroad of New Jersey Terminal to be taken off Ellis Island to the mainland. Determined not to leave without Raffaele, Francesca demanded to stay until Raffaele had finished his examination. "He must be scared and confused," she pleaded to the officials. "Please, let me see him!"

"It won't be long, *Signora*." A man pointed to a long wooden bench loaded with others who waited in anguished uncertainty. Another kindly man approached and offered them food. Francesca knew the children must be starved, and she too, felt on the verge of collapse from malnourishment and stress. They were led to a cordoned area lined with long wooden tables and benches, and were encouraged to eat while they waited. They gulped fresh fish, bread, and milk—the best food they believed they had ever tasted. Francesca filled her pocket with bread for Raffaele.

As Francesca looked around the room, she was humbled and shaken. She wondered if she carried the oily odor of the hull. How did she look? She was sure that her hair must be badly matted, and she had difficulty recalling her last real bath. The children looked worse for wear, but they didn't seem to care.

What if Antonio no longer recognized her former beauty in her disheveled state, with torn stockings and shoes caked in only God knows what? She flicked her tongue repeatedly across her teeth and twisted her wedding ring nervously.

For three long hours, they waited fretfully, until the doctor had cleared Raffaele of any diseases. When Francesca saw him running toward her, she fell to the ground and kissed him from head to toe. "My baby, are you okay? Mamma was so worried. Did they hurt you?" Francesca rubbed her hands around his face and looked for any signs of abuse.

"Mamma, I am okay," he reassured her. "They gave me a piece of cinnamon candy and said you were just outside, and you waited for me. It's okay Mamma, they said I am a big boy." Raffaele straightened his shoulders and smiled, looking exactly like a small replica of Antonio. On the voyage, Raffaele had also left behind a sizable piece of childhood and innocence.

"You certainly are a big boy, Raffaele!" She hugged her brave little man tightly.

"*Signora*, are you ready to board the train?" asked an officer. "If you are, I will escort you and your family to find your husband." My husband! Francesca flooded with emotion, even though she could not bear any more. "Come with me, and I will get your travel card," he said. The travel card read: To the conductor, this person does not speak English. Please show her where to change trains.

After they paid a head tax of four dollars each, they boarded the train to the city.

"Now we get to meet your papa, the carpenter!" Francesca forced an encouraging smile for Ella. Ella thought of her papa, Donato Tenaglia, and wondered if he was already there. What if he had made a beautiful carriage for them pulled by a horse, not a donkey? What if the horse was to be hers? She would name it Liberty and help Papa with his carpentry, if he allowed it. She was sure she could learn to cook.

A whistle blew and the train began to make its way across the harbor, with its stunning backdrop of multi-storied buildings rising to the sky. Francesca's amazement was simultaneously spiked by bursts of adrenaline and blunted by deep exhaustion. Holding fast to her children, she could barely focus on everything speeding past outside like a feverish dream.

Antonio also felt pulled in two as he waited at the train station to receive Francesca, Rosa, and baby Raffaele. He had been there most of the day, pacing back and forth and smoking. The longer he paced, blisters began to form inside his hard shoes, and the more impatient he became. He hoped and prayed to see them soon so the agony of worrying about tragedy at sea would at last end.

Little did he know there would be four of them to greet. Much had changed since he had last seen Francesca, and he was unsure how to feel. Time had faded his memory of her. Would she still want him? He had a bit of gray at the temples, and a little paunch. Even so, he couldn't wait to see her and Rosa, and the boy he hadn't yet gotten to hold.

People bustled in every direction around the station. Cabbies held signs in strange lettering and yelled out foreign sounding names. As Francesca emerged from the building, she spotted Antonio from the corner of her eye, and a much-needed smile lit her face. Antonio looked heavier and older, but he was very much the same handsome man she remembered.

She noticed he was smartly dressed, a starched collar stiffly around his neck. Crisp cuffs revealed themselves beneath the sleeves of his neat suit jacket. He looked clean and well-kept, unlike Francesca, who had made it through the last two weeks with only four dresses. Her unkempt hair must look like a tangle of seaweed, and she must surely smell like a barrel of old mackerel. She suddenly felt very shy before this polished stranger. When Antonio spotted Francesca, he hurried to her and pulled her into his arms. There were no words for this occasion. It had been six years.

He took her hand and raised it to his lips. He ignored all the unsavory evidence of the long journey, and saw only the beautiful girl he had once loved, and loved still. He stared into her eyes until he was able to find his voice. She noticed his hands tremored as he whispered, "Francesca, my Francesca, my love, I am so happy you have arrived! Thank you for coming!"

He made the sign of the cross and then bent down on his knees. He hugged Rosa and kissed her forehead over and over. "My little Rosebud, you have grown so much, and you are just as beautiful as your mamma!" Antonio smiled then and looked at the young boy standing stone still beside Francesca.

Francesca held Raffaele's hand out to take his papa's, and the tears filled his eyes when he took his son's soft, little hand into his own.

"Antonio Bucci, this is your son, Raffaele Bucci." Suddenly the horror of the journey seemed somehow a bit further away, and Francesca swelled with emotion to see her family reunited.

"It is very nice to meet you, Mr. Bucci, I hope you like it here in America." Antonio hugged and kissed the boy on the forehead. Raffaele touched his papa's nose and smiled. Antonio pulled Rosa into his other arm, alternating kisses on the tops of their heads.

"Antonio," Francesca gently interrupted. "Antonio, I'd like to also introduce you to my dear friend, Ella Tenaglia, who has been invaluable help with the children! Ella is from Sicily, and plans to be reunited with her papa today," Francesca said. "We can discuss it later," she added. The look she gave Antonio let him know something serious had happened.

While the children took turns scrambling into their papa's arms, and looking for candies hidden in his pockets, they all waited together for Ella's papa. Slowly, daylight faded away, taking Ella's hope. In the travelers' aid office, Antonio tried his best to learn the whereabouts of Ella's papa. But, there was no word. "Sometimes, the fathers do not come. It is a sad thing for the children," Antonio was informed.

Antonio had already traded their tickets for the afternoon train, the last train to Kentucky, but departure time had drawn near.

Antonio pulled his wife aside and whispered into her ear, "Francesca, we must leave. We can leave Ella at the office to wait for her papa."

"No! I will not leave her! She will stay with us." Francesca fixed him with a firm gaze. "I made a promise to her that I will look after her until she finds her papa, and I must keep my word."

Antonio nodded his understanding and went to the ticket window to purchase a fifth ticket. Ella remained dry-eyed and mute, her face still and stony as Neptune's marble façade, the one she had pointed out to her smiling mamma just two weeks before.

*...the long journey is over, the new life begun.
Those who have no friends run the gauntlet of the
boarding-house runners, and take their chances with the
new freedom, unless the missionary or 'the society' of
their people holds out a helping hand.
For at the barge-office gate Uncle Sam lets go.
Through it they must walk alone.*

— Jacob Riis, *Century Magazine,* 1903

Chapter 4

En route to Lexington, Kentucky, April 1917

Francesca's land legs had barely steadied when she boarded the passenger train headed to Kentucky. The journey would take one day and a half. A loud steam whistle blew as the train slowly chugged away from the station. The five of them crammed into one small Pullman car. Rosa and Raffaele crowded closely on either side of Ella, and she was grateful for the warm squirming bodies.

The scenery across the land faded to pink, then lavender, and then to black as night finally arrived, and the children fell asleep. Francesca waited not a second more and then she, too, gave in to the night. With Antonio's arm around her, she could finally rest. Antonio waited until all eyes were closed before he fell asleep upright, never letting go of Francesca.

Francesca slept soundly, and soon her mind wandered through dreams of home. Verdant Castel Frentano gardens, full of roses and amaranth, cascaded down the cliffs. Lush foliage appeared to drop into the turquoise water of the *Adriatico,* whose sea air was pure and alive. The sun warmed her skin, and she could hear the familiar sea grass rustling in the breeze as the foam from the receding waves cooled her bare feet. She could see Antonio's face, she could smell him next to her. He slid his arms around her, kissed her lips and stroked her lower back. She murmured appreciatively and let him pull her closer.

The lurching train abruptly awakened Francesca. Daylight had broken on the horizon. Francesca looked at her sleeping family, and said a quick prayer over their angelic faces. Next she disentangled from Antonio's protective arm, and wiped the dusty film off the window with her sleeve. She could see the dark outline of the distant trees that came into view. Patches of thick fog shrouded the emerging silhouette of the countryside. She suddenly longed for life with Antonio back in the comforting familiarity of home, *Italia.* She peered out thinking of Mamma, Papa, Bianca and Adriana, and wondered were they thinking of her?

Antonio was slouched uncomfortably against a thin partition; he had barely dozed in the night. He opened his eyes and smiled at Francesca. He reached for her hand and said, *"Buon giorno, Madre,* how did you sleep?"

With a sigh, Francesca managed a small smile, and whispered, "I'm just happy to see your face. The journey was as difficult as you said."

"*Madre,* you are here with me now. Safe. You must be starving, I will see if I can find some food." Antonio kissed her brow and exited the sleeping car.

Francesca found a small mirror on the wall. How many days since she had last seen her reflection? When she finally did, she put her face into her hands and cried—she looked like *Nonna!* She ran her hands through her unkempt hair, tidying the wispy strands that hung in her eyes. She secured a loose bun at the base of her neck. It was the best she could do.

When the children awoke on a train, they squealed with excitement. The endless ocean was far behind them! Ella, however, seemed especially quiet.

"Children, come and look at the beautiful countryside!" Francesca noticed Ella's silence and said, "This land is full of surprises. Unlike the ocean, I see something brand new every time I look out. Have you ever seen a deer? I saw a family of five. The papa was huge!" The children crowded around the dusty peephole, and made little squeals of wonderment. Even Ella looked out in awe, and seemed to momentarily forget her cares.

"After breakfast, your papa will take you on a tour of the train," Francesca promised them, and Raffaele jumped up and down, just a little boy who loved trains once again.

The long ride, however, soon grew tiresome. They fidgeted on the hard wooden benches trying to find comfort. Francesca noticed a cockroach scurrying across the floor, and she quickly tucked her feet. "One thing you can count on anywhere, *scarafaggi!*"—she could hear Silvia's teasing voice, and suddenly Francesca felt a deep pang, desperately missing her friend's wry observations and quick humor. She stole a glance at Ella, and her heart lurched like a train inside her. Poor Child!

Antonio returned then with the only provisions he could find, a biscuit for each of them, water for the children, and one cup of tepid coffee. Francesca tried the thin brew and shook her head. "Well, it is not Mamma's coffee, that's for sure," she grimaced.

Antonio laughed, "Your mamma's coffee could wake the dead and I'm pretty sure it's also why I have so much hair on my chest."

After a small bit of breakfast, Antonio took the children for a tour around the train and they reported back that there were stoves to cook within the lead car. They first visited the rear of the train where they had found the refreshingly clean toilet the night before.

Francesca could tell that Antonio's sweet temperament had not changed. For a man to have lived so long alone and now have two, possibly three, children to raise, might prove challenging to another man. But he made the train ride with the children an adventure all by itself. Even Ella seemed to warm to his silly jokes and kind questions about her family in Sicily.

When a trainman allowed them to step out onto the platform for fresh air, Francesca gasped in delight. A multitude of trees in all shades of vibrant green surrounded each cleared meadow. Wildflowers blanketed the open fields like a giant box of spilled paints. The April air in America was surprisingly cool, and smelled like a fertile, wild world just being born.

Back inside, Raffaele had found an old issue of *The Saturday Evening Post* on the floor. He was locked on the image of an old man at bat while a young boy played catcher. The girls busied themselves with games of *morra* and peeked from time to time out at the scenery from the window. Ella mostly remained quiet and reserved, revealing little about how she felt.

When they had a private moment alone together, Francesca told Antonio about Silvia's death, and he held her while she cried. However, she could not bear to burden him with the sad truth. Antonio hugged his trembling wife, saying, "We are partners in everything - even tragedy." He promised to try to locate Ella's papa. He had made friends in New York City and he just had to reach out to a few. Francesca suddenly remembered her papa and uncles who talked about the *mafioso* in New York. She privately hoped Antonio's New York connections were men of God, not crime.

The small windows continued to reveal more unspoiled countryside with expansive hills that rolled into farmland filled with grazing cows and horses that ignored the distant whistle of the train as it passed.

With spring in this land came freshly plowed fields furrowed with dark, churned soil and emerging cool weather crops. Endless clouds of pink and white billowed past on the limbs of blossoming redbud and dogwood trees. Painted, dusty wooden barns and white farmhouses with wide porches intermittently dotted the landscape, while farmers in caps led horse-drawn farm machinery. Everywhere in the world, Francesca mused, people coax both beauty and survival from the land.

Although the scenery that passed took Francesca's breath, it surely could not compare to springtime in Castel Frentano, though she refrained from saying so. As the train pushed on through towns called Cleveland and Cincinnati, she felt sure she would never see her homeland again and would never bury her toes in the fine sand of the *Adriatico*. Sadness, dread, homesickness, and excitement warred inside Francesca, as persistent and rhythmic as the chugging train carrying them into the unknown.

As the children played, Francesca recalled her adventures with Antonio in Italy, their intoxicated love, their day trips to the coast, and the picnics they shared among the pre-Roman tombstones at Madonna del Casale.

The hillside and ravines on a clear morning came into sudden focus in her mind. The scene looked like a freshly painted watercolor with sun-washed hues ranging from butter yellow and periwinkle blue to ripening peach. She loved Antonio still, but… did she really know him any more?

"Francesca, the train station is just beyond the horizon, we must prepare the children," Antonio interrupted her faraway thoughts and stood to put on his jacket and gather their belongings. As the train approached the Lexington terminal, Francesca readied the children. For what, she did not know.

As Francesca stepped down onto the platform of the bustling Union Station on West Main Street in Lexington, she saw a well-dressed lady staring at them with a wrinkled nose, muttering under her breath.

"What did she say, Antonio?" Francesca looked at her husband with concern.

Antonio translated for her, "The poor lady said she stubbed her toe." He spared her feelings and did not tell her the truth that the lady said, "Filthy foreigners!"

Francesca smiled with warm concern at the lady's disgusted expression. Perhaps her pale skin bruises more easily?

An older man in denim coveralls sat on a bench outside the station strumming an instrument that Francesca later learned was a banjo. The children jumped and swayed to the energetic tunes and watched in amazement as he picked the instrument with calloused fingers. His smile radiated kindness and welcome. Serenaded by music of the Kentucky mountains to the east, lovers and families reunited just as joyfully.

Rosa pointed to a little girl and her eyes lit up when she saw the beautiful soft pink serge dress with rounded collars trimmed in white daisy guipure. Antonio noticed Rosa as she looked down at her plain dull blue cotton dress.

Antonio smiled at his child, "I will buy you one even prettier as soon as possible, my little Rosebud. And Ella, too!" Rosa's face nearly cracked, and she hugged her papa long and hard. Ella looked shyly away.

As they departed the station, Antonio picked up a copy of the *Lexington Leader* that read *EXTRA* across the top, with headlines on the front page that screamed *WAR!* He looked at Francesca and said, "While you were on the ship, the United States declared war on Germany. I am sorry, Francesca, but I wanted to get you and the children away from the war. The Germans torpedoed a luxury liner full of innocent people off the coast of Ireland, some of whom were Americans." Francesca made the sign of the cross, and felt her knees giving away, thinking it could have easily been them sacrificed to the war at sea.

Antonio steadied his wife, clarifying, "The rumors were that England intercepted a telegram from Germany that was intended for the Mexican government. The Zimmerman telegram stated that if Mexico joined the Germans, they were to repay them with American territories of Texas, Arizona, and New Mexico. I presume America had to join the war, since Mexico is on the southern border."

"So, the entire world is at war—what madness!" she said sadly.

Antonio, now proficient in English, translated many of the conversations from the people at the station to Francesca. The station buzzed mostly with talk about the Great War, and the draft. Francesca made the sign of the cross and thanked God that Raffaele was too young to be drafted. Antonio held back the fact that even though he himself was not yet a naturalized citizen, he still had to register. He had learned this when he went to apply for his American citizenship.

"Wait here, and I'll be right back!" Antonio disappeared into the crowd, a large smile on his face.

Francesca and the children stood with arms around each other while Antonio went for a horse and buggy. To their amazement, he drove up instead in an automobile.

He pulled up beside them and said politely, "May I offer the Bucci family and honored guests a ride?" Everyone laughed and even Ella smiled. "This is a Model-T made by the Ford Motor Company," Antonio said excitedly. "What do you think about this horseless buggy?" he asked excitedly. "I call her Donna Bella. Isn't Donna fancy?"

"Antonio, she is wonderful and so are you!" Francesca said, smiling as she climbed in.

"Donna is mine when I need her, my boss calls her a company car," Antonio said as they piled into the machine. "Don't worry—she is very safe!"

"I want to drive, Papa!" screamed Raffaele.

"Soon, *bambino*, soon," Antonio laughed and handed the children three red and white striped boxes of caramel-coated popcorn. Raffaele was delighted to find a small, plastic dog figurine inside.

The engine of the wheeled machine drowned the sounds of carriages as they passed, and the drive through the new town had them all sitting up straight, heads swiveling to take it all in. The brick streets were lined with three-story buildings, many in the Federal and Colonial Revival style. Francesca especially liked the Greek Revival and Italianate structures that boasted fabulous façades. She noticed they were not as ornate as the buildings in Italy, but they had wonderful corbels and columns nevertheless.

Even carriage houses and stables reflected the wealth of their owners. The wide diversity of architecture revealed multitudes of cultural influences converging as a beautiful, complex mosaic in Lexington. The mild spring weather welcomed them, and she realized with a grateful smile that Kentucky also belonged to God. Maybe Kentucky could also one day belong to them, as well.

To ward off darkness of night, black lamp posts topped with white globes lined both sides of the street. The scene buzzed with horse-drawn wagons, bicycles, pushcarts, and several automobiles used as taxis. The occasional backfire startled them all, and spooked work horses had to be calmed. They passed seed stores, hardware and dry goods stores, and Francesca saw what were surely three banks and two balconied hotels. The churches were ornamented with tall steeples enclosing sonorous brass bells. At first glance, her new home was exploding with vitality and beauty, and for the first time since leaving Castel Frentano, Francesca drew a deep breath. For the first time, hope outweighed fear, and the tension in her brow eased, making it easier to smile.

Nearby, a bearded man standing on the top of a colorful horse-drawn buggy shouted at onlookers and waved amber bottles in the air. Francesca was equally enthralled and concerned. His voice lacked the natural lyricism and poetry of spoken Italian, although he certainly had plenty of passion! Antonio explained that the man was a salesman for Rawleigh & Watkins Company. From his buggy, he peddled household products, baking aids, tonics, and flavorings to anyone who would listen, and stop to buy. Francesca noticed that Ella was also focused on the man and his dramatic spiel to those gathered around his buggy. The English language sounded harsh and unfamiliar to their ears.

The women they passed were smartly attired in long skirts that gathered at the waist, paired with blouses with long sleeves, many delicate buttons, and high necks. Rosa pointed to a girl with a large floppy bow in her hair and smiled. Women and children wore black heavy leather ankle boots, and the men wore vested suits, many with black bow ties. Almost all the men sported hats, as well as mustaches that grew bushy and thick. This explained why

Antonio's mustache looked so much larger than Francesca remembered. Those not dressed in suits were casually clad in denim coveralls. Francesca assumed they were farmers or laborers who had no need for fussy suits.

"What is that, Papa?" Rosa pointed up to a gray limestone building that towered overhead with Romanesque arches and outstanding dormers in a multi-sided dome copper roof, oxidized to a glowing weathered green. At the very top, a cupola held a copper weathervane shaped like a horse.

"That is our courthouse! And this is Cheapside Park. That tall building right there is a bank." Rosa tilted back her head all the way to admire the towering structure, taller than even the *Verdi*!

Reassured by the view from the Model-T, Francesca smiled as Antonio proudly drove his family to 246 Lexington Avenue, where a two-story red brick house awaited them, standing proudly in the middle of other beautiful, well-tended homes. The front porch was large and supported by white, fluted columns on sturdy brick pedestals. On the front porch hung a white wicker swing. Lavender lilac bushes lined the outer perimeter of the property.

"Antonio! Your home is beautiful, and the lilacs are especially lovely," Francesca smiled as she reached over to touch her husband's arm.

"It is *our* home," he corrected with a small kiss on her nose. "And I planted the lilacs last fall when I bought the house. I knew they were your favorite, and the same color as the ribbons you wore for me when we were courting." He looked suddenly as shy as a teen boy, hoping she would approve of the home he had prepared for them.

Talking all at once, they scrambled out of the sleek automobile. Neighbors standing on their own porches called out warm greetings in Italian, and Francesca touched her heart and smiled at each of them, up and down the street. Ella smiled at the familiar Italian words and ran to touch a mailbox on the porch. She was just happy to have an address for her papa to find her.

Francesca walked into the house and hugged Antonio. "It is *perfetto!*" And for the first time in six years, he kissed her. His kiss was soft and warm as she had remembered.

"I hope you like your new home," Antonio spoke softly as he held her. "Please let me know what you and the children need, and I will do whatever I can. I am happier than I can say to have you here with me."

As Francesca perused the rooms, she stared at the bare mantle of the fireplace, wondering in amazement how men could live without personal touches in a home. The furnishings were modest and simple in design—not like home, where most of the furniture was handed down, but more artful. A crucifix hung over the doorway that led out of the foyer.

"Antonio, this is… far more than I expected! You have prospered in America!" Francesca gazed around the spacious room with molded wood trim and gleaming wide-plank floors.

"I am afraid I did not expect Ella, "he reassured, "but it will be no trouble to pick up another bed and linens tomorrow. We have plenty of room." Antonio touched Francesca's hand, and went to unload their packs and bundles.

"Ella, you and Rosa can have the room upstairs to the right. Raffaele, you get the room to the left of mine." Antonio corrected himself and said, "Well, I mean, your mamma's and mine." The children ran up the stairs and took most of the afternoon to explore their new home, surely a mansion.

Antonio then took Francesca on a tour. He led her through the *salotto*, the dining room, and an indoor *bagno*. He had taken a spare room, and converted it as soon as he moved in last spring. He then led her to the most important room in the house.

La cucina was painted a pale yellow with clean white lace curtains in the windows. "What is this?" Francesca ran her finger over the square cast iron gas range. "Is this for cooking?"

"*Si*, you will not find an outdoor oven in all of Lexington," Antonio watched Francesca's face as she discovered the flat iron on top of the range. "The oven comes in very handy if you need to iron. I can press a shirt on the kitchen table while I wait for the kettle to boil!"

Antonio looked out the kitchen window and smiled again, "You will not find chickens that run around town, either. I buy them already plucked at Murphy's, down on the corner of High Street and Woodland Avenue.

"When the Farmer's Market opens, I will take you for the freshest tomatoes, corn, and green beans. I get fruit at the Phoenix Fruit Store down on East Main Street. My good friend Baldasarre Amato owns and runs the store." He handed her a pear from a basket on the table and continued, "Our neighbor *Signore* Ginocchio is a butcher, and he has a market over on Limestone Street. His backyard garden is amazing! He sells produce from his garden at his market and just outside on the street. Most days, he has a good selection of fruits and vegetables. Every Monday down at Cheapside Park, almost anything can be bought or sold."

Francesca took a bite of the sweet pear, walked to the kitchen window and smiled at a miniature statuette of the Blessed Mary. She walked to the back door and looked out at her new home. She thought about the fruit and vegetable stands in Lexington and knew she would surely miss walks to the market with her papa and Sugo.

Seeing her faraway look, Antonio continued, "You don't have to walk to town to get water from the well any more! I hope you will love it here, Francesca. I have stocked up and prepared the house for you. I think you will find everything you need." With that said, he left the room to check on the children and see how they were settling in.

In an alcove near the back door, Francesca found a cupboard full of preserved foods and tins of salted anchovies, which she detested, but Antonio loved. Shelves were lined with ceramic jars of green and black olives. Cans and tins with unfamiliar names like Del Monte, Nestlé, Borden, Crisco, Rawleigh's Spices, and Hills Brothers Coffee neatly lined the shelves. Beautiful pale blue Mason jars capped with zinc lids held what appeared to be fresh whole tomatoes. From the rafters hung dried cheese, sausages, and cured salami. Crafty weaves of coupled onions and peppers dried in swags hung from the top of a kitchen cabinet.

She found a heavy oak ice box lined with zinc by the back door. Antonio had already informed her that deliverymen from Lexington Creamery and Lexington Ice delivered blocks of ice every morning, as well as butter, milk, and cream to put in the icebox for the day.

Antonio had, in fact, thought of everything. She couldn't wait to thank him with a home-cooked meal. Francesca knew the children must also be ready for a nourishing dinner, so she washed her hands and arms and asked Antonio to light the stove. She found the largest handled pot, and laughed as water poured out of the *cucina* sink faucet. The simple act of boiling water for pasta to feed her family helped her gain her bearings.

Humming, Francesca walked out the back door of the house and noticed that Antonio had maintained a small kitchen garden. This brought another smile to her face. She was delighted to find a few of her favorite herbs such as thyme and oregano in the neatly kept plot. At the back of the property, grapevines scrambled across a lovely wood and wire arbor.

"Ahh, I see you found it," Antonio said, reappearing with a shy grin. "In a few weeks, it will be warm enough to plant sage, basil, rosemary and several vegetables, especially tomatoes. I'm not the best gardener, but Uncle Sam has requested that all homes with yards produce their own vegetables, so the surplus can go toward the war effort." Antonio handed her a colorful poster of a woman in a dress decorated with white stars on blue fabric, and red and white stripes. The patriotic lady sowed seeds from a woven basket with a swoop of her hand. It said, *Sow the seeds of victory! Plant and raise your own vegetables!*

"I love it! Let's put her on the wall in the kitchen, and we will help grow a victory!" Francesca smiled up as she hugged him.

Directing her to the back fence, Antonio showed off his vines, "These make pretty good table wine. The tiny, black fruit of the 'Virginia Norton' has a nice, bold, fruity flavor. Though not as tasty as your papa's, of course, the vines grow well here. Louis Ginocchio, next door, has mastered making table wine and he will help us bottle our own. He and his wife, Maria, have a *cantina* in their basement with a press and grinder. They will harvest about 500 lbs of grapes this year, and are happy to help us cut grapes."

Remembering the boiling water, Francesca gathered ingredients to prepare dinner. Antonio stoked the coals in the stove before he left to check on the children again. Francesca found a large rolling pin in the top drawer and wiped the cool, metal countertop that was just perfect to roll and cut pasta.

While she waited for the pasta to cook, she examined the cabinets below the sink. She found unfamiliar lettering on bottles and boxes with names like Palmolive and S.O.S. When Francesca learned English, she would discover S.O.S. stands for 'Save our Saucepans.'

She cooked a simple sauce of tomatoes she found in one of the blue jars. It would be months before the market carried fresh tomatoes. She added in dried garlic cloves and herbs she found in jars, using her nose to direct her. The sauce was served over thin-cut noodles accompanied by herb roasted potatoes and aromatic pork sausage.

This meal brought appreciative murmurs and smiles from all around the table. For the past few weeks, she and the children had lived on meager provisions that hardly deserved to be called food. The meal that Francesca had lovingly prepared was much more than they all expected. After they ate, Ella and Rosa helped clean the kitchen, which was to become their new evening ritual.

Raffaele helped his papa boil more water for the desperately needed baths. Raffaele would be first in the tub, but he didn't know it.

The day was drawing to a close and Francesca knew her body and mind were spent. Antonio reintroduced the *bagno* to his family and they each took turns soaking in the steel-cased tub lined with copper. It was such a guilty pleasure after weeks of a rag moistened with salt water and only occasional fresh water. She felt truly reborn when she stepped out of the luxurious tub and swaddled her body with a soft cotton towel.

The children fell hard into their beds. Rosa and Ella slept together in Rosa's room while Raffaele slept alone in his room, but they called out jokes to one another, giggling. Exhaustion soon won out, and the house fell silent.

Antonio approached Francesca who had slipped on one of his shirts. "Antonio, I will do the wash tomorrow. I had to borrow a shirt; all my clothes are so filthy from the journey."

Before she could say any more, Antonio took her into his arms and kissed her. It had been years, but the awkwardness of the reunion vanished. His intense kisses were hungry for her. He unbuttoned the shirt she had just put on and it fell to the floor. He kissed her neck and shoulders as his fingers remembered the curves of her body. He whispered in her ear how much he had missed her. They made love under the darkness of the night and fell fast asleep in each other's arms.

Within days, just as the family settled into new routines, young men across America were drafted to serve in the war. Francesca thought worriedly about home, but busied her mind and hands creating a home for her family. "Eyes ahead! Eyes ahead!" her papa called out reminders to her from across the great ocean.

Ella's eyes, however, were firmly in the back of her head, still mourning the loss of her mamma and feeling ever certain that her papa did not want her. He had been gone for years, but Ella wanted her family. The shame of abandonment was eased by the Buccis loving acceptance. *Signore* Bucci bought her pretty dresses, included her in every family discussion, and talked to her about enrolling in school. Francesca hugged her and fussed over her like one of her own, but Ella missed her *nonna* and *nonno* in Italy. She was loved, but lost.

Antonio had left his address at the Ellis Island barge office in case Ella's papa came for her. After Antonio had settled his family, he sent an urgent Western Union telegram to his friend Vincent in New York. Vincent Marcello always leapt up to help Antonio, just as he did when they traveled together to America.

The Buccis agreed Ella should enroll in school with Rosa and Raffaele in the fall if they did not hear from her papa, Donoto Tenaglia.

"Why has he not come for me?" Ella asked Francesca one morning at breakfast. "Antonio said he left this address."

"Ella, I don't have the answers for you. But we love you, and you may stay here with us as long as you like.

Antonio has friends in New York, and they are trying to locate your papa. Whatever the outcome, you are a part of this family forever." Francesca hugged Ella, and she realized she could not stand the thought of being separated from this girl—her accidental daughter. "If you want to write a letter home, Antonio will mail it for you," Francesca said. "Your family needs to know what has happened and that you are okay." Francesca had found an address in Silvia's pack and wrote it down for Ella.

With Easter a few days away, Antonio took his newly-arrived family to Wolf Wile & Co. to shop for Easter clothes. The girls chose white dresses with pinafores, and hats with large, silk pink and yellow ribbons. Francesca selected a light blue and white seersucker suit with buttoned knickers for Raffaele, though he protested that he looked like a clown. They planned to attend Easter Vigil and Mass at Saint Peter's Cathedral, and their next-door neighbors, Louis and Maria Ginocchio, invited them over to their house for Easter dinner.

On Good Friday, while they stared at their last plates of white fish, Francesca's thoughts took her back to her Castel Frentano home and family. "One of my favorite Easter trips was to Venice for *Carnevale*," she began. "My family tried to visit every year, but some years travel was too difficult if the weather was bad. By the time I had you, Rosa, it was just too hard to make the trip."

"My *nonno* called it the two days of the shepherds," Antonio chimed in.

"Yes, Venice came fully to life with revelers from all around the world," Francesca continued. "The town square was full of music, laughter, and a banquet for all. Lavish costumes, parades, and masquerades filled the streets at night. The masquerade masks were, I thought, more beautiful than anything I'd ever seen. They were embellished with beads, gems, and brightly colored feathers. The cloak mask covered the person from head to shoulder, which looked somewhat eerie. The domino mask was small and round, and only covered the eyes."

"Why did they wear such masks?" Rosa asked, eyes wide with curiosity.

"Masks help lighten the mood so everyone can be themselves for a short while. The status of people who attended did not matter at *Carnevale*, only fun and celebration."

Francesca's story faded away as she thought of the anonymous sexual interludes that were rumored to take place at *Carnevale*. While she knew of no one who had gone to such extremes, she guessed those who engaged in such activity figured they had forty days of repentance ahead. She thought it best to leave out this part of her story.

"Lent is kind of like a second baptism because we are able to start to live again the way God expects." Francesca rose from the table to refill Antonio's plate. "When we returned from Venice, the countryside burst with whitethorn, lilacs, and hyacinths. I can see and smell it all now—heaven!" She paused, thinking of home. "*Nonna* made yellow dough to create bunnies, dolls, and Easter baskets. She inserted a colored egg under the arms of the bunny or doll. She always made me a rabbit. For my sisters, she made Bianca a bird, and for Adriana, a doll. She often baked a large circle of bread and placed colored eggs around it for the centerpiece."

With excitement in her eyes, Francesca said, "Tomorrow I will try to make something special for each of you, just as *Nonna* did for me. I will cook Mamma's frittatas, made of hot sausage and cheese, and I will make Papa's favorite pears *al vino*! Bear with me—tomorrow I will try to make these special treats for Easter."

Francesca spent all day on Saturday preparing for Easter. She was proud of her efforts, and by the time she passed out on the bed that evening, she had made Raffaele a duck, Rosa a rabbit, and Ella her first Easter dough doll. Nonna would be proud!

Early Sunday morning, they walked to Saint Peter's for the Holy Mass, and they looked as glorious as the day in their new, crisp Easter clothes. Raffaele was reassured to see all the other boys dressed as clowns. The trees were in full bloom everywhere around them, and birds sang sweetly overhead. Antonio had joined Saint Peter's Cathedral when he first came to Lexington, and Francesca was pleased by his choice.

As she walked into the cathedral for the first time, she stood in mute awe at its sanctified beauty. The vaulted ceiling reached for the heavens, and the elaborate décor took her home to Castel Frentano. Mostly, though, Francesca was relieved that Mass in America was said in Latin.

The ambience of flickering candles gave her a familiar safe sense of worshipful peace, and the golden walls glowed with warmth.

Francesca was pleased to find the sacred rituals of the old country were practiced in America. As in Italy, the men removed their hats, while women wore the traditional head coverings. As they entered the cathedral, she dipped the fingers of her right hand into the Holy water and made the sign of the cross at her brow, and she blessed herself as well as her children. Francesca smiled to see that making the sign of the cross was a global gesture.

Although there seemed to be some variation to the ritual, Francesca preferred to dip three fingers. In her heart, this symbolized the Father, Son, and Holy Spirit. Her papa had only dipped two fingers—for the two natures of Christ, divine and human.

With the smell of rich incense around her, Francesca genuflected for adoration before the Holy One at the altar and entered a pew. With her left knee down, first to honor God the Father, then her right knee down to honor God the Son, and finally with both knees, honoring God the Holy Spirit. She prayed for a long while before she found the black leather-bound missal.

The body of Christ offered by Father DelCotto was very similar to the way Father Donatelli had performed the sacrament. After he broke the Eucharist, the American priest placed the thin wafer on her tongue, and, as the Host dissolved, she made the sign of the cross.

Confession, or the sacrament of penance, had always been difficult for Francesca. She felt better after she completed her Hail Mary and Our Father, and she vowed to live a life more in line with the Blessed Mary. She found that confession in America was easier for her, since she chose the American priest who only spoke English. She confessed that she was uncertain at times about being reunited with her husband, which must surely be a sin.

Before the Mass was over, the father walked the aisles and swung his urn as fragrant smoke billowed toward the parishioners. As in Italy, the Holy smoke carried their prayers to heaven.

When the Easter Mass ended, the Buccis walked straight to the Ginocchio's home. While the women prepared the food, the children participated in a street-wide Easter egg hunt.

To Francesca's delight, many Italian families lived on Lexington Avenue. After a few days of settling in, they had all come to greet her and the children, speaking to her in Italian. With the same easy warmth she remembered from Italy, she found them to be instant *paesanos* – friends – on foreign land.

On the Bucci side of the street were Louis and Maria Ginocchio and their two children, as well as Baldasarre and Greta Amato and their three teens. Philip and Lucia

Angelucci lived next door with their seven children. On the other side of the street, Stefano and Margarita Buchignani and their four children made their home. Next to them, Nicola and Carlotta Dacci were raising five boisterous, young children. Next to them, even more Ginocchios. And so it went on Lexington Avenue.

Italians loved to see more of their own in Lexington and remembered how they, too, had endured difficult passages and confusing months of adjustments. They brought Francesca traditional house-warming gifts, such as wine for happiness, olive oil for health, and honey for sweetness of life. With her family around her, and with the encouragement of new friends, Francesca slowly began to feel more at home.

The neighbors gathered like family for every possible occasion and created a new kinship among themselves. It felt very familiar to be greeted with the traditional kiss on both cheeks, a gesture that Francesca appreciated more than she could express. Only those practiced in this greeting knew to kiss the right cheek first to avoid awkward collision.

On weekdays, Antonio worked for the racetrack on the outskirts of town. His accounting job was beyond hectic because of the constant revenue the track generated, and paid out just as quickly. After his family arrived, Antonio also took a part-time job at Angelucci's, a fine clothing store downtown on Main St., owned by *Zio* Salvatore's good friend, Philip Angelucci. Antonio was already a friend to Philip and his wife, Lucia, both of whom had come to the new country around the same time as *Zio* Salvatore.

A wildly popular haberdashery, Angelucci's was in desperate need of Antonio's money skills. Antonio's job at the racetrack called for him to dress nicely, and Philip Angelucci was happy to oblige with gifted and discounted shoes and suits in the latest styles.

With five mouths to feed, the extra job was helpful. Francesca could see that during the past six years,

Antonio had made good friends and that he had been determined to provide a good and secure life for his family. Antonio often found himself in the company of Lexington's elite, from the wealthy clientele at the clothing store, to the powerful horsemen at the track.

Within a few months of her arrival, Antonio brought home several pairs of trousers for Francesca to hemstitch. Philip Angelucci loved her needlework, and asked if she could embroider some men's handkerchiefs. She gladly accepted and retrieved her embroidery tools from a bureau drawer. *Signore* Angelucci was more than fair with payment, and Francesca greatly enjoyed contributing to the family coffers, just as she had in Italy. Mostly though, she was thrilled to once again have an outlet for her boundless artistry. The colored floss and meticulously rendered designs were her morning companions. Her skill, and name, grew.

Chapter 5

Lexington, Ky—Spring 1917

On the first Sunday after Easter, Antonio and Louis took their families to the park. The Buccis and the Ginocchios ambled companionably down to Gratz Park on the corner of Market and Mill streets. While the children amused themselves with races and the men proved themselves at *bocce*, the women shared confidences.

"Did you hear how Mrs. Schmidt sang this morning?" Maria asked with a laugh.

"Well, that was not the *Ave Maria* I remember," Francesca allowed with a small smile.

Maria added, "Ha! Not unless you learned *Ave Maria* from howling dogs!"

Turning the subject, Francesca smoothed her blanket and confided, "I feel sorry for the German-Americans. Some libraries and politicians say they will burn books written by Germans, and people are calling them traitors!"

"I know! Louis came home the other day and told me the diner will no longer serve hamburg steaks or frankfurters!" Maria shared, as she unloaded fragrant Italian bread and fat grapes from her basket. "And how shameful it is to pick on poor animals, I heard they are now calling the dachshund the 'liberty dog'."

"Just imagine if Italy had sided with the Germans," Francesca lowered her voice to whisper, furrowing her brow and making the sign of the cross. "We'd be just as shunned! Antonio tried to keep us out of harm's way, but as soon as we came to America, American soldiers headed straight into Europe."

"Louis said the *Lexington Herald* and the *Lexington Leader* reported that over nine million men have registered for the draft," Maria said, shaking her head in disbelief. "The paper said that anyone eligible who failed to register could go to prison for one year!"

"Yes, war is changing everything. Antonio told me just this morning that President Wilson has called on Americans to conserve flour, butter, sugar, and eggs. He said the government needs these items to send to the troops and allies in the war. Did you know Americans use three times as much sugar as other countries? At least, I have a tasty eggless cookie recipe."

"That's better than a tasteless egg cookie," Maria laughed, popping a pink Good and Plenty into her mouth. "On such a beautiful day, I have suddenly spiraled into despair thinking about rationing and post-war food shortages! For now, we have good and plenty—let's talk about that!"

The children ran to the blanket to pick up a few pieces of cheese and crackers. Maria and Francesca then lapsed into easy silence. With the sun lulling her, Francesca's daydreams carried her, as they often did, back home to Castel Frentano...

"Come on, Francesca, let's watch the boys play!" Francesca's best friend, Sofia Filla, urged as they walked past the playground where Antonio and his friends, Sal and Marco, played *bocce*. Sofia was crazy for Marco, but he was promised to another girl. Sofia was to meet soon with a young man her parents had planned for her since she was born.

"Okay, we can stop, but just for a little while. I must get home to help Mamma," Francesca answered. As they stopped to watch the intense game, the boys immediately tried to impress them. Sal pressed a finger to his cheek and twisted it back and forth, his signal for pretty girls nearby.

Antonio had tossed Francesca the white *pallino* so she could start the next game. She threw the target ball as hard as she could, which made her slip on the damp grass and land in an embarrassing heap. All three boys collided as they rushed to her aid.

She blushed brighter than an August sunburn until Antonio's hand reached out for her. Without a second thought, she reached back to him. As they all laughed, Marco rolled his *bocce* ball, trying to knock the white ball that Francesca had comically thrown. Sal tossed his ball next and tried to knock Marco's ball out of contention. The competition went on and on, and eventually Antonio took nine out of the eleven games that day. He could see a look of pride flicker across Francesca's face, and he suddenly felt elated and inspired.

"*Mamma, Raffaele is not playing fair*," whined Rosa, dropping onto the blanket, snapping Francesca back into the present. A mother. In America. And no longer a silly girl pining for Antonio.

"Now, now, let's all get along," Francesca soothed, wiping the bangs out of Rosa's eyes. Francesca looked over at Antonio, now also grown to adulthood, and playing *bocce* with a new set of friends. She smiled at her fierce competitor clasping hands high over his head, signaling he was victor to the vanquished. Louis offered a 'well done' pat on the back, but the other men flicked fingertips across their chins, Italian for 'get lost,' and Antonio roared with laughter. Watching them, Maria commented with a smile, "Italians don't really need voices. As long as we have our hands, and arms, we can say anything! My *nonno* said that gesturing with hands might have originated in Rome, where a thumb up meant death for a defeated gladiator, and a thumb down meant he was spared to live until the next match."

Francesca thought of her own family—they spoke Italian and body language with equal fluency. She remembered how her *nonna* usually said more in one dramatic motion than most could say in a whole sentence.

She chuckled at the memory of *Nonna* slipping off her shoe to throw at anyone who provoked her ire.

Maria suddenly pointed toward a pair of elderly nuns walking through the park. She jumped up, and while she glanced back at Francesca and the children, she ran hollering, "Your nun!" Francesca and the children joined in the game, racing each other to reach something made of iron. With a strong lead, Maria sprinted toward an iron arbor just outside the public library. Maria gloated about her win, and the children ran off to play again. After the women had caught their breath on the steps of the library, they returned to their blankets under the fan-shaped leaves of a ginkgo tree.

"I had no idea it took this long to see two nuns," Maria laughed breathlessly. "Back home, we saw nuns out walking every day!"

"We did too! I learned how to play *Your Nun* the day Antonio and I became friends—not as children running through the village, but as teenagers, understanding that someday we would marry," Francesca recalled, smiling. "It was St. Joseph's Day, and I spotted him across a large buffet that stood in the middle of the town square across from Santa Maria della Selva Church, I was fourteen. I knew right then I wanted to marry him, and later, we married in that very church."

"How romantic!" Maria sighed, patting her friend's arm. The women called for the children. Louis and

Antonio returned to blankets, gathered the baskets, and the two families returned together to Lexington Avenue.

The next morning, Antonio had a coffee and biscotti with Francesca, and left for the track as usual. Louis left his eldest, Martino, to mind the market, so he could take Maria and all five children to pick strawberries at a farm on Bryan Station Road. The children piled into the back of his truck and bickered over the choice seats.

Alone in the sudden quiet, Francesca opened the back door and tried to recall the morning breezes in Castel Frentano. With eyes closed, she could see silvery olive groves and low leafy vineyards, bright sunlight splashing over all of it and coaxing familiar flavors to ripen and swell.

With a dreamy smile, Francesca remembered the night Antonio came to propose. He had taken both of her hands in his, and with his dark amber eyes suddenly very serious, he said, "*mi vuoi sposare,* will you marry me?"

Francesca glanced down at her modest diamond set in silver, and hummed to herself the soft ballad *Come Prima*, the lover's tune Antonio had whistled that night. Francesca thought the beautiful ring had sparkled like stars in the candlelight, but there were a thousand more facets to her own happiness that night, and she had sparkled even more.

They were married on the first traditional wedding day in June. Before Francesca had left for the church, *Nonna* gave her a *corno*, a gold horn charm, to wear around her neck to repel evil. Francesca giggled to herself when she recalled how *Nonna* had tested the Holy water in the font and sprinkled a few drops of olive oil into it. When *Nonna* nodded and smiled at her, she knew the drops had not joined to form an evil eye. Good fortune in marriage was theirs to claim.

Francesca recalled how handsome Antonio was in his black suit and tie that day. He made her laugh aloud when he rubbed the wool lapel with his fingertips. His 'look at me,' gesture was the prelude to Francesca kissing her fingers, admiring her soon to be husband. He lifted an irregular shaped piece of iron, for luck, from his suit pocket and winked at Francesca. After the ceremony, many families and friends joined together at the Viviano's home where a celebratory feast awaited.

Long wooden tables and benches lined the backyard under the trees near the olive terrace. Carafes of wine, antipasto platters, and a vast array of cheeses displayed on large wooden boards awaited the guests. At the center of the table, *Nonna* had arranged a dazzling bouquet from the wildflowers she had picked that morning. She must've filled three gathering baskets!

The aromas spilling from *la cucina* were tantalizing scents of wild boar, sea bass, eggplant, and sage roasted onions—and no one wasted any time filling plates.

At the end of the meal, Antonio and Francesca each ceremonially drank a glass of sparkling wine, and threw their glasses into a large round oak vat as family and friends cheered their union. Two had forever become one.

Francesca dreamily remembered the musicians in the orchard, playing *mazurkas* and *tarantellas* on mandolins for the dancers. With arms linked, the dancers shimmied as one, and then, each separated to perform flirty whirls, twirls, claps, and finger snaps. The dancers rotated away from the sea in a large circle. The tempo quickened to a boisterous frenzy, and the exhilarated dancers suddenly reversed direction, following the frenetic beat. Wine flowed and breathless laughter filled the air.

The last dance of the evening was for Francesca and her papa. The song was *Lauretta Mia*. Francesca remembered how she began to cry immediately, as did her papa. As they danced under the pergola, spent petals from the climbing bougainvillea fluttered down to color the dance floor every shade of pink. Francesca had never seen tears on her papa's face, but they shined with pride.

The thought of her papa's tenderness brought to mind the unsmiling *Signore* Bucci, and her good wedding memories faded fast.

Her father-in-law was a short, round man with thick brown, bushy eyebrows and very little hair. It was obvious that Antonio's mamma was a great cook and his parents ate well, perhaps too well. Antonio's mamma had beautiful long, black hair which she kept pulled up into a neat bun worn like a crown. It seemed Antonio had certainly benefited from his mamma's beauty, and had been spared his papa's temperament, as well. *Signore*

Bucci seemed to only care about moving numbers on a page, and he did it exactingly and well.

Immediately after the wedding celebration, Antonio had taken Francesca to his home, where she was expected to live with him and his family. The house was full of Antonio's younger siblings. Giggling, the children left the newlyweds alone in a room at the back of the house.

Antonio's parents approved of Francesca and seemed thrilled to have her under their roof. She knew that they had just acquired a strong, young bride with an even temperament to perform daily domestic duties.

Just then, as she was getting more lost in memories, the sun-kissed berry pickers arrived back on Lexington Avenue with stained fingers, pink cheeks, and full bellies. Francesca directed them to wash their hands and run off to their rooms for much needed rest. Francesca and Maria hugged as though they had been separated for weeks, and began sorting the berries for canning, always with so much to say.

That evening, as jars of strawberry jam cooled on the kitchen table, Francesca prepared the children for bed, and only after she had made Antonio another dry martini, did she take off up Lexington Avenue for an evening stroll. In the gleam of twilight, bright hydrangea blossoms carried her on their sweet perfume back to 1907 Italy when they were younger.

…the walkway to the remote mountaintop retreat near Pescara was crowded with luscious hydrangea blossoms vying for the sun. Bees drunk on nectar, seemed to dance the *tarantella* in the sweet air. The ages-old villa was situated in an enormous crevice on the hillside, revealing the most stunning views of the sea below. Olive farms and vineyards filled the ridges between sheltering mountains. Mostly destroyed by Lombards in 600 A.D., Amitemum still offered up its ancient secrets for lovers and adventurers.

Antonio held Francesca's hand as they traced a stone pathway winding down toward the sea. At the base, they crossed through a gated passage leading to a surprise of smooth, fine sand. Francesca couldn't help herself as she broke away and ran into the surf, up to her skirts, laughing like a schoolgirl.

Antonio followed, pointing down the coastline to the *trabocchi*. These piers constructed of wooden stilts and ladders were built along the cliffs and scattered along the beach. They stretched out into the turquoise water and offered fishermen a place to cast their line. Antonio took her hand once more and they strolled up the coastline and ventured out onto a *traboccho*.

As they sat quietly on the edge of the pier, they watched a school of iridescent fish darting like sleek rainbows below. Antonio ran his hand across her shoulders and down her spine. She felt like she had swallowed the school of fish and they flopped inside her.

Eventually, reluctantly, they left the beach hand in hand and headed back to the villa where they came upon a shade *allée* of cypress trees that led to a hidden garden flanked by low hedges of yew, laurel, and boxwoods. The shrubbery was manicured and sculpted as if made of clay. Antonio lay on the cool lawn while Francesca ran back to gather a *pasto leggero*.

Francesca found their soft-pink, weathered villa and opened the veranda doors to allow the *Adriatico* breeze to envelop her body. From the veranda, she could see terraced hillsides full of olive trees, and just off to the left was a parterre designed of boxwoods and santolina, each quadrant bursting with salvias and herbs. Ceramic urns spilled over with profuse blooms of hot-pink and fiery-red geraniums.

An elaborate stone fountain cascaded musically, glistening in the sun. From the veranda, Francesca could see the exuberant beauty of the gardens, the aqua sea moving endlessly below, and nearly more countryside than the imagination could hold.

Francesca prepared a basket of pears, bread, honey, and wine and rejoined Antonio just off the formal veranda. Under a stone pergola laden with trailing vines of red bougainvillea, they lounged, laughed, and toasted their luck in love.

Later in the day, they meandered upon a second secret garden designed as a sanctuary. In the quiet, Antonio stroked her face. He moved her hair away from her neck and kissed it gently. Francesca remembered how as soon as Antonio kissed her lips, she melted just like butter and honey on sun-warmed bread.

Antonio took her hand, and they ran back to the privacy of their villa. In one motion he closed the door and removed Francesca's hair ribbon which allowed her dark hair to fall to below her shoulders, exactly as he'd been longing to see her. As he removed her dress, the touch of his fingers on her skin weakened her knees, and he gently eased her back on the bed, layered in soft linens and down pillows.

Later that evening on their veranda, they could hear the rhythmic call of the fountains and could almost taste the scent of perfectly clipped rosemary below, wafting up to the balcony, as though for remembrance of this day.

As they relaxed with glasses of wine, an owl hooted just as it began to unexpectedly rain, and the dampening wind delivered up a licorice scent from a nearby field of fennel. The cloud burst seemingly had come from nowhere, and they were instantly soaked and laughing.

Antonio removed his clothes first. The steam from their bodies filled the air as they loved each other on the veranda while warm rain puddled unnoticed on the cool tile floor.

Chapter 6

Summer 1917

On Sundays after Mass, if weather permitted, Antonio would treat his family to long country drives in Donna Bella. Francesca and the children were captivated by the picturesque countryside that surrounded Fayette County, so different from home, yet uniquely beautiful in its own way.

Antonio explained how white paint was costly and the more elite horse farms could be easily identified by their miles and miles of white wooden split rail fences.

The fields of painterly wildflowers and gleaming horses soon captured Francesca's heart. As she exclaimed with delights at each new vista, Antonio teased her that she was Kentucky's new number one fan.

When they stopped, Antonio and Francesca let the children run through the fields, just as they had done when they were young. Raffaele kicked off his shoes, and waded into the rocky stream, looking for fish, turtles, snakes, and crawdads. Ella seemed most at peace in the fields and meadows; her sadness seemed to lift away in the sweet floral breezes. Rosa and Ella talked like sisters, sang, picked flowers, and created bouquets and hairpieces from white daisies and yellow black-eyed Susans.

Francesca always loaded up the picnic basket on these occasions with surprises like *ricciarelli* or *spumoni* cookies. The children ran as carefree and wild as young deer.

Lying on a quilt next to Antonio, Francesca found herself mesmerized by the intricate design of a moisture beaded spider web. As she so often did, Francesca memorized the pattern to recreate later in shimmering threads, and wished she had brought her needle and hoop. Just then, the thunder of six excited feet came upon her.

"Mamma! Tell Ella the story about the fairy!" Rosa begged, out of breath.

Sitting up and arranging her skirt, Francesca closed her eyes and could clearly hear her own *nonna's* voice, as though she was on the blanket with them, her braids glistening like silver in the sun, and her hands warm on Francesca's.

"Okay, okay! Sit down, and I will tell you *Nonna's* story," Francesca agreed. "There once was a beautiful Italian fairy named Folletti-Farfarelli. She was so tiny. She traveled through the wind on seeds and leaves." Francesca waved her arms theatrically in the air. "Folletti-Farfarelli joined her friends every day, and they played in the open fields. As they amused each other, they created swirls of dust." Francesca waved her arms in the air once more. "Fairies are quite sneaky and when they come in contact with people, they take on the form of butterflies!"

Raffaele said excitedly, "Tell me about Basadone!"

"Well, Basadone only rode on the breezes at noon. He stole kisses from the female fairies, and in the fields, he was known as the woman kisser." When Francesca reached over with lips pursed to kiss Raffaele, he got up and ran. Ella and Rosa also took off to find fairies disguised as butterflies. Antonio reached for her, "I'm Basadone. I'm here to steal a kiss."

The day grew warm quickly, shortening their outing. The ride home was unmercifully muggy. Francesca pulled her shirt sleeves free of her dampening skin. She looked out across the fields full of lacy white blossoms and tiny blue wildflowers, and wondered how much hotter her new home could become. As she wiped more moisture from her brow, she realized the heat of the summer had crept up on her. Francesca remembered the Castel Frentano heat and how important it was to ripening crops. "You need sun drops and raindrops to make an olive," Papa had said many times, his way of saying life is a balance.

"Antonio," Francesca suddenly asked. "Will you please bring home extra tomatoes this week?"

"I can do better than that! I will take you to the downtown market this Saturday and you can choose the best for yourself," he smiled and took her hand.

As promised, on Saturday, they set out to load up on tomatoes and green beans to preserve for the winter months. Antonio was very helpful as he negotiated the purchases. Since Francesca spoke very little English, she did not feel confident without him. If Antonio was not available, she sent Ella to the market with empty cans or labels to help restock. Her lack of English was, of course, a huge problem for Francesca, and Antonio saw how frustrated she had become with her limitations. She was determined to learn English so she could shop for herself.

At the market, they bumped into a very pretty young woman with her little girl. Antonio introduced Francesca to the woman. Violet Gallager was an Irish-American widow with her three-year-old daughter, Lauretta, at her side. Antonio explained that Violet worked at the track and also taught English at night. Francesca smiled pleasantly since Violet only spoke English.

"Hello," Violet smiled. Francesca noted her fair skin, waves of strawberry blonde hair, and warm hazel eyes. "It is nice to meet you. Antonio has spoken of you often," Violet added in her faint Irish accent. Antonio translated to Francesca. Suddenly, the young girl with Violet dropped her doll into a puddle and began to cry. Antonio plucked the doll from the water and picked up the beautiful child, whispering *ragazza dolce* into her ear. He pulled his handkerchief from his back trouser pocket and wiped the little girl's tears from her pretty brown eyes. "See? All is well. Shh."

Suddenly inspired, Francesca said to Antonio, "Please invite Violet and her daughter over tonight for dinner!"

"That sounds lovely!" Antonio smiled again at the brightening child.

Antonio invited Violet to join them at their home, and she accepted. Antonio handed Lauretta to her mother and Francesca loaded up on tomatoes and beans; she also found plump, glistening eggplant for the evening meal, one that even Papa's thumb would approve of.

"I will invite the Ginocchios over for dinner, as well," Antonio said and loaded his arms with their purchases. "Louis will be impressed with my new table wine."

On the way home, they excitedly made plans for company.

Violet arrived with Lauretta on one hip and on the other she carried a bottle of red wine, of which Antonio immediately relieved her. The Ginocchios arrived shortly afterward with children in tow, and offered up a fat jar of sun-dried tomatoes in olive oil to their hostess. With an aroma of fried prosciutto spicing the air, Antonio poured glasses of dry white wine, and the evening began.

Before Francesca came to America, Antonio had hired a lady to help him with tasks around the house. From time to time, Antonio called on Gracie Samuels to help Francesca, and the two women seemed to collaborate in a language of their own. Francesca loved Gracie's even manner, and Gracie felt just as at home with the easy-going Buccis.

Alongside Gracie, Francesca passed around warm *antipasti* of thinly sliced crostini layered with cheese, shaved ham, and capers. When her guests had devoured the first round, Gracie brought out a cold *antipasti* platter filled with stuffed olives, pickled peppers, fresh tomatoes, and prosciutto-wrapped cantaloupe.

"We are so pleased to meet you, Violet. How did you come to be an American?" Maria asked.

Violet took a slow sip of wine and haltingly began to tell the story of her family's difficult migration from Ireland, "My granda and grandma came from Ireland in 1847. They nearly died in the town of Skibbereen. They had to leave, they had no choice. It was either watch each other starve to death or find a way to get on the ships. Granda has told me the story over and over. Times were hard. My grandma said her mamma and dada did not eat anything, so the children could."

"That is awful!" Maria translated for Francesca and both women nodded sadly.

"When my granda went to the field to check on the potatoes, he prayed that all was okay. Instead, his potatoes were covered with a black, sooty film. He said when he touched the foliage, the greens just crumbled into slimy dust. Blight had taken Granda's fields and rotted every last potato." She squeezed her hands into fists, as though filled with worthless, inedible pulp. "Granda said the odor of the rotten foliage, the stench of death he called it—helped them lose their desire to eat."

Maria translated quickly for Francesca, and asked, "How did times get so bad?"

"My granda blamed the British. He said they hoarded all the food. Granda knew they were in trouble, and with the help of God, they came to America. Grandma still believes the famine was God's punishment for all the sins of the world."

Violet paused to take another sip of wine. "Here in America, they raised five children and ran O'Donnell's Tavern downtown on Mill Street for the remainder of their lives. Dada took over the tavern and married Ma." Violet raised her glass to toast and said, "Cheers to the land of opportunity, overcoming hardship, and to bountiful food shared with friends!"

They all raised their glasses and each one yelled, *"Salute!"*

"Buon appetito." Francesca raised her glass again and they all sat down to a beautiful table on which Francesca artfully displayed a potpourri of flavorful dishes from both land and sea.

Antonio started the sign of the cross by pointing to his brow. As his guests followed suit, Antonio prayed, "Bless us, O Lord, and these Thy gifts, which we are about to receive from Thy bounty. Through Christ, Our Lord."

Everyone said, "Amen," and each made the sign of the cross.

Antonio raised his glass again, as did the others. "It is a blessing and great gift to have good friends in our home. *Mangia!*"

They enjoyed savory minestrone soup, followed by Antonio's favorite: eggplant parmesan served on a huge platter painted with gold sunflowers. As everyone ate and drank in appreciative silence, the soft lights from the candles flickered. The ambiance of the evening suited Francesca, and for the first time she understood what *Nonna* meant when she had said that she felt proud to serve guests.

"How do you like Lexington, Francesca?" Violet asked.

After Antonio translated, Francesca, in broken English, replied, "I believe that it is the second most beautiful place in the world." The guests laughed appreciatively while they passed platters.

"Francesca, if you let me teach you English, we can speak more easily," Violet offered.

After Antonio translated, Francesca's eyes lit up as she nodded her head and smiled.

Francesca passed around a basket of bread, while Antonio refilled the glasses with dark, red wine.

"Well, I guess the draft is under way," Louis interrupted the quiet with a worried sigh. "I hope America knows what it has gotten into. I know I need my boy Martino at the market. He is not old enough now, but next year he will have to register." Louis glanced at Maria and took her hand.

"My cousin Patrick is old enough," Violet said, breaking off a piece of bread. "He has already registered and says he is ready to fight." She shook her head. "He says he does not want to be called a slacker."

"Maybe this isn't proper conversation for dinner, but the paper talked about the German soldiers who use chemicals to attack their enemies," Louis said. "The American soldiers reported greenish-yellow clouds that overcame them in the fields—poison."

After Antonio translated to Francesca, she frowned, and replied in disgust, "Well, that seems cowardly!" Gracie removed the breadbasket, and the guests enjoyed a *dolce* made of iced melon and whipped cream.

As the meal ended, Antonio invited the men to the *salotto* for an after-meal smoke, coffee, and liqueur. The evening was a success, and Francesca smiled warmly at everyone in her home, glad for their company.

As the evening wound down, Violet picked up Lauretta, who had fallen asleep on the couch, and said her goodbyes. She accepted Antonio's offer to drive her home since the evening had grown dark and Lauretta was fast asleep.

Violet lived with her parents on Willard Street, which was not far, about halfway to the racetrack from Lexington Avenue. She walked many days, but Antonio was too much of a gentleman for that. Gracie lived a few more blocks away from Violet in Speigle Heights, and he usually walked her home, or drove her if he had the company car.

Gracie had the kitchen in good order and went to Francesca to be excused. "Thank you, Gracie!" Francesca said in English and handed her bills from her apron pocket and a heaping plate of food for her nephew, Jacob.

"*Arrivederci!*" The Ginocchios waved goodbye, and the house fell into contented silence.

Francesca had the kitchen tidied when Antonio returned, and they went upstairs to tuck in the children. After quick goodnights they retired to their bedroom, and Francesca went to the bedroom window to cool off. As she closed her eyes, the wind blew at her face.

Antonio approached her and took her in his arms. "You are quite a cook and hostess, *Signora* Viviano," he whispered in her ear as he kissed her neck.

From the reflection in the large, oval mirror atop Francesca's dressing table, she watched as he slowly unfastened the buttons that lined the front of her dress. He slid one hand down and around to find her bare lower back and pulled her close. With the other hand, he brought her face to his and kissed her brow, then her cheeks, until he reached her lips.

"I have missed you. I have missed my family." Antonio led her to the bed. He removed his clothing, while he continued to gently kiss her. "Thank you for tonight, *Madre*."

She took him in her arms and kissed him with true desire. He touched her, as never before. They became one while the moon shone down onto their bed. In the dim light, she could see the love in his eyes, and she knew she was home.

Chapter 7

Summer 1917

After that evening together, Violet and Maria became regulars around Francesca's kitchen table, and she welcomed the company with endless pots of coffee and plates of biscotti. Violet loved the biscotti, but always watered down the thick brew.

To Francesca, the ladies were like surrogate sisters. Her only communication with her family in Italy had been the letters she'd sent each week, never knowing if they were received. Thanks to the war, after four months in America, she had not heard even one word of reply. No one on Lexington Avenue, it seemed, was receiving letters or telegrams from the old country.

Violet worked seasonally at the racetrack as a mutuel teller, and taught English in one of the storage rooms at the track to employees a few nights a week. She kept her promise to teach Francesca English, and with Maria's help, Francesca's English vocabulary quickly grew.

It wasn't long before vocabulary grew into sentences and sentences into conversations. How much are these tomatoes? Surely you can do better! Don't boil the pasta to death. Children, wash your hands for dinner! I miss my mamma and papa. I hope they are okay!

In the meantime, the three ladies spoke the international language of food. Francesca and Maria taught Violet a few favorite Italian dishes, and Violet taught Francesca and Maria how to prepare colcannon, a savory and filling Irish dish made of mashed potatoes and cabbage mixed with milk and butter.

Violet brought stacks of expired magazines from her hair salon: *Ladies' Home Journal*, *The Modern Priscilla*, and *Collier's*. Francesca and Maria practiced as they read unfamiliar words in the publications, many of which were actually French: *couture, en vogue, chic*. She couldn't wait to create dresses and accessories like the ones she saw on the glossy pages. So many ideas swirled in her imagination, making the beautiful designs even more splendid.

When Francesca was not tending to her children or needlework, she gathered with her friends for English lessons and conversation. As always, Maria dared to ask the awkward questions, "Violet, what can you tell us about your husband?"

After a few moments of silence, Violet lifted sad eyes and said, "We met in high school, me and my John Gallager. John was tall and blond, with broad shoulders, and the greenest, prettiest eyes I had ever seen. He was my first love, and I was his, and as soon as high school ended, we married. Nothing fancy, just a small ceremony in front of family down at Saint Paul's. We had a good marriage, we were happy..." Violet took a slow drink of her weakened coffee, lost in memories.

"John and I took jobs at the racetrack, and everything was peaches. We had our future all planned. Then he started to crave the pint, and stayed in the taverns after work. This created a fuss every blessed night, and he began to stay out later and later. Some nights, he didn't even come home! His friends said he was often drunk at the track and I fretted that he might lose his job due to the drinking. Sadly, it is true that an Irishman with a love of drink soon comes to love no others.

"One day while he was at morning workout, his boot got tangled in some loose reins, and a young stallion named Pale Hellion dragged my poor Johnny about two hundred yards. He was barely recognizable after the trampling." Violet looked down at her folded hands on the table, shaking despite clasping them tightly together.

"Oh, Violet, how horrible!" Maria put her hand on Violet's. "I guess the horse killed him?"

"Not immediately; he lived for about three weeks in the hospital. The doctors said it was the internal damage that couldn't be repaired." She pointed to her own abdomen and chest so Francesca could understand.

A few moments of silence followed this news.

At last, Maria consoled, "Such a tragedy my friend, but you are so blessed to have your angel, Lauretta."

"Yes! I found out I was pregnant several weeks after I buried John. He never even knew." Violet looked away and pressed her palms to her eyes, as though she had learned how to dam the tears.

Maria and Francesca hugged Violet, tears in both their eyes, and the three sat together in silence until the last light of day had faded away, and Violet's memories seemed to have eased back into the past, where she preferred to stow them.

"No one escapes sadness in this life," Francesca mused, as she cleared the dishes and tidied up the stacks of magazines they'd set aside.

The following day, Francesca assembled ingredients to cook a large pot of tomato sauce, following Mamma's recipe by memory. Maria stopped in to share a plate of cannoli she had just baked, and within minutes, Violet also came through the back door carrying a fresh stack of magazines and looking like she'd regained a bit of her pluck.

Violet and Maria helped themselves to coffee and sat down to hunt through the magazines for recipe and fashion ideas. They laughed at articles about keeping your husband satisfied with a tidy home, well behaved children, and tiny waistlines. "Who writes this stuff?" Maria laughed. "Men?"

From the bubbling sauce pot, Francesca dipped chunks of fresh bread, and handed them to her friends, a wordless invitation to taste.

"Fran!" Violet exclaimed. "This is wonderful!"

The endearment 'Fran' took Francesca by surprise. Feeling suddenly light-headed, she turned off the stove and hurried out of the room.

"Fran, what is wrong! What did I say?" Violet called out.

With her friends close behind, Francesca slumped down on her sofa, and leaned forward with her face in her hands. When the dizziness had passed, she haltingly began to look for the words to explain that her friend Silvia from the ship had called her "Fran." Silvia's tragic end haunted her, and Francesca knew she needed to finally share her story with trusted friends.

"I hold secrets deep inside me, they sometimes scream to get out," she said quietly. "I have not shared this with anyone since I got off the ship, and I think it is time."

Still reeling, Francesca stood up from the sofa and the three slowly walked back into the kitchen. Maria poured fresh cups of coffee, and Violet grabbed the plate of cannoli. They sat down at the kitchen table once more, waiting for Francesca to unburden herself of some horrible secret.

"While I feel my choices are regrettable," she began, "I believe what I did was the only choice I had." She looked at her friends and a tear ran down her cheek. "I haven't even shared this with Antonio, and I have only confessed to the English-speaking priest, I am so ashamed." Realizing this must be serious if she had not discussed it with Antonio or in confession, the friends pushed aside the coffee and cannoli, ready to absolve their friend.

Mixing English words with Italian, when necessary, Francesca told them she met Silvia and Ella on the ship, and how their friendship grew in just a few hours. She explained how wonderfully funny and bold Silvia was. "Silvia was so beautiful, and invaluable to me on the ship. We protected one another, and our children, like sisters. What I tell you must stay in this kitchen." Francesca made them swear to secrecy. "I must protect Ella."

After a deep sigh, she began again, "After we were at sea for about eight days, Silvia left one evening to find blankets because the nights were cool, and the children were shivering and complaining." Looking at hands folded on her apron, Francesca quietly continued, "She found the blankets – and a man, if you want to call him that – found her. He no doubt did horrible things to her, and no one was there to help." A sob caught in her throat and tears threatened to cover her face like storms over the *Verdi*.

She fought to compose herself and continued, "I went to find Silvia and heard her scream. I ran in the direction of her voice, but it was so dark! I could see, though, that a filthy man had bent my friend over a bench, her dress pushed up to her waist. She screamed, kicked, and bit him as he violated her. The grunts he made, the scratches and blood that ran down the sides of his face just fueled his violent need. Screams stuck in my throat and I ran as hard as I could, like through a nightmare to push him away. I might as well have run into a marble statue. He turned then, furious, and grabbed me. He held his filthy paw over my mouth so I couldn't scream and tormented me with the other. He reeked of cheap rum. We struggled, and I fought as hard as I could, but he was a brute. The stubble from his beard was thick and rough. I smelled his nasty breath on my face, as his hot sweat dripped on me.

"I thought I had passed out from exhaustion and fright, when out of nowhere, I felt his hands release, and he fell on top of me. The weight of his body threw us onto the deck. It was not until I saw slick blood spilling onto the deck did I realize what had happened." Francesca paused, sickened by the memory, and realized her hands were shaking. Finally, tears filled her eyes and she let them come.

"Jesus, Mary, and Joseph!" Violet sputtered, making the sign of the cross.

Francesca counted the stitches in her shirt sleeve until she could speak again, "Silvia stood over us. She held an iron belaying pin that she had pulled from the railing. The strike was hard, he never came to. We both shoved him off of me. He... the bastard... died right in front of us." Francesca looked down at her coffee cup, heat and shame rising in her cheeks. Violet and Maria stared in horror, both stunned into silence.

Francesca stammered as if to plead for their mercy and understanding, "He was so strong… and he almost raped me. I was not sure I wanted him dead… but he was." The women nodded wide-eyed at the evil their friend had endured.

"Silvia escaped into a trance. She just sat there on the deck staring out at the water. I composed myself, covered his body with the blankets she'd found, and helped her back to her berth.

"Rosa and Raffaele were sound asleep when we made it back, but Ella had waited up to see her mamma. I told Ella that her mamma had a touch of seasickness and that she had fallen on the steerage deck and cut her arm and leg. I convinced her to lie down and go to sleep, while I tended to her mamma.

"After I got Silvia's wounds bandaged as best I could, and changed her into a clean dress, she lay down. I gave her some water, and laid a cool wet rag on her forehead. I took her soiled dress and went back to the deck."

"There were only two or three lanterns lit, and it was very dark that night," Francesca continued. "Silvia should have never been out there alone. Even then, understanding the dangers of the night, I feared little, as if a stronger power possessed my mind and body. I had to take care of the problem for all of us," Francesca paused. "I went back to the deck and approached the heap of blankets slowly, as if he might come to life and grab me again. The blankets were soaked with blood, and I could tell in the faint light of the moon that no one was around. I threw Silvia's bloodied dress overboard, and went for his vile body.

"Before I knew it, I had help. Olga, a ship's maid who had befriended me and Silvia, appeared out of the darkness to help. We managed to roll the *mostro's* lifeless body onto a blanket, hammock style, and we tossed him overboard, blankets and all." Francesca took a deep breath, and Maria reached out to lay her hand over Francesca's trembling hand.

"I couldn't have lifted him without Olga," Francesca continued, "She was as strong as a man, and when he was gone, she said, 'Let the sharks and the devil take him.'

We cleaned up the area as best we could, and agreed never to revisit that spot again. I thanked Olga and cried. She hugged me and said, "Silvia was not his first, but he'll never hurt anyone ever again." Francesca picked up her coffee mug and the liquid sloshed onto the table, but she didn't seem to notice her shaking.

"I went back to the berths, and changed my dress. Olga took that dress, and tossed it, as well as her own. I checked on poor Silvia—she was just staring at the slats in the berth above her head. She seemed to have no more life in her than the *mostro* sinking into the black water," Francesca whispered sadly.

"The next morning, Silvia just lay there and continued to stare at nothing. I returned with food for her, but she didn't hear me. She withdrew from life, from me, even from her own child. I couldn't get her to eat, talk, or even look at me. Ella tried to get Silvia to snap out of her hypnotic state by comforting her mamma with memories of home. But Silvia couldn't pull herself back to us.

"I'm sure she was scared and unsure how her husband might handle this if he found out. He was sure to think she had prompted the incident. She had only defended her friend from violence and had killed a man. Though she certainly never intended to kill him, she saved me." Francesca looked up at her friends, eyes pleading for understanding or consoling words, but they were speechless.

Finally, ever so softly, Violet asked, "What happened to Silvia – to Ella's mamma – where is she?"

Francesca sighed, "I guess the rape and the fact that she killed a man was more than Silvia could bear? I blame myself, but I had no idea what she planned to do. After everyone was in bed sound asleep, I saw her leave her berth and stand as though in a trance for a moment beside Ella. She laid her crucifix on the straw mattress next to Ella's head, and walked away. I didn't dare leave her alone again, so I followed. The waning moon offered very little light, and the lanterns were so dim." Francesca put her face into her cupped hands, shuddering now.

Again, she looked up at her friends, beseeching them for understanding. "It all happened so fast! Silvia walked straight to the rail and jumped! I screamed out to her, but it was too late. She was determined to end her life..." Francesca ended her story and cried into her hands, wracked by revisiting the trauma and loss.

Violet whispered, "Oh, my God in heaven. How... awful."

"Francesca, I'm so sorry." Maria put her arm around Francesca and pulled her into a maternal embrace.

Haunted by the memories, Francesca sputtered various excuses for her friend. "I'm sure she was ashamed about what happened... She lost all hope to live... She was probably afraid of her husband or the *poliza*." Francesca eased away from Maria and put her face back into her cupped hands. She rubbed her temples slowly as though she hoped to erase the dark images flickering in her mind.

"I just stared over the railing into the black water as long as I dared and tried to come to terms with everything that happened... and what Olga and I had done. When I returned to our berths, Ella was awake, and she knew something was wrong. I had to tell her. I chose to make the story as painless as possible. I told her that Silvia slipped and fell through a broken stanchion. I couldn't tell Ella that Silvia was tortured by her bleak thoughts and ending her own life – and leaving her only child – seemed her only way out." Francesca nodded sadly to her friends and went to the backyard to steady her breath before the children returned home from school.

Violet and Maria tidied the kitchen in stunned silence—a promise of silence both would keep.

Chapter 8

Fall 1917

As the ginkgos on Lexington Avenue turned brilliant golden yellow, Antonio enrolled the children at Saints Peter and Paul School on West Short Street, about a twenty minute walk away. Rosa entered the second grade, Raffaele excitedly skipped into first grade, and Ella, thinking of her friends in Italy, hesitantly entered the eighth.

"Ella," Antonio assured. "This is Mrs. Taylor, and she will help you find your desk." Before leaving, he kissed Ella's forehead and whispered, "You are the smartest one under the Bucci roof—you will do well, dear."

Busying herself at home, Francesca counted the minutes until the children returned. *Will they make friends? Did she pack enough for them to eat? Are they okay?* With the children out of her hands, and Antonio at work, Francesca found she had many hours alone.

Antonio brought home more and more custom needlework requests from Angelucci's Clothing Store. Mr.

Angelucci was delighted with her work, and said everyone in town wanted their initials embroidered by her on everything possible. He opened the haberdashery for Francesca to select from many colors of floss, gilt bullion thread, needles, and various items for the embellishments. She imbued every assignment with all of her creativity, and her clever use of appliques, Jacobean designs, and spangles made her handiwork a coveted indulgence. The compliments from admiring strangers were nice, and she happily pocketed away some extra money for Mamma and Papa, if the mail should ever run again.

Within a few days, Francesca could tell that the children were learning English very quickly, and had fallen quite naturally into the American way of life. Antonio helped them with their homework each evening while Francesca prepared family meals.

Meanwhile, in Europe, war raged. It was difficult to breathe and not think of home and the friends Francesca had left behind. *Zio* Sal stopped by often with news. Uncle Salvatore Bucci was a short, stocky man with an aggressively receded hairline. Patience wasn't his forte, but he was generous with the family, and he had certainly helped Antonio get established in Lexington.

Zio Sal invited the family to join him for a ride in his bumble bee yellow and black roadster pickup, prompting a seating disagreement in the truck bed. After Ella, Rosa and Raffaele agreed to pick their seats and settle down, *Zio*

Sal said he knew a place just outside of town full of history, with open places for the children to run wild.

Zio Sal handed each child a handful of silver foil wrapped candies for the drive. "Try these, *piccoli*," he said in a baritone voice. "They call them 'kisses' because when the machine drops them onto the table, they make a kissing sound. And don't throw your wrappers down on the ground!"

After a scenic drive, *Zio* Sal parked the car, and theatrically pronounced, "Welcome to McConnell Springs, *famiglia*, a settlement founded by William McConnell at the start of the Revolutionary War! This is where Lexington gained its name, in honor of a great battle with the British." With the sweetness of chocolate melting on their tongues, the children whooped loud battle cries and ran off to win an imagined war.

The changing leaves overhead ranged from soft yellow to bright red and shimmering orange, as though a warm sunset had painted the trees. As they approached a stream, luxuriant purple blossoms and towering stems of unfamiliar gold caught Francesca's eye. Antonio, ever eager to teach, pointed to each, saying, "aster" and "goldenrod." He laughed and applauded when she repeated the words perfectly.

Finding the water's edge, Raffaele immediately removed his shoes and socks to splash around. He smiled, knowing he could advance to the knee before his knickers got wet. Just a bit farther, they came upon a gurgling natural spring that cooled the air.

"See the abandoned mill?" *Zio* asked. "The Trotter family used the mill to produce gunpowder," he said, pointing to a nearly hidden structure long since covered with lush vines.

"Gunpowder! Cool! I wonder if I can find some!" Raffaele shouted.

Ignoring Raffaele, Rosa asked, "What kind of bird is that, *Zio*?"

"I believe it is a yellow warbler in the bush, and that one over there on the fence is a chickadee, my little chick a dee."

Antonio gazed into the deep, blue spring. "Children! Be careful here. I cannot see the bottom!"

Francesca removed a quilt from the basket Antonio carried, and smoothed it on the ground away from the tempting stream. Under the canopy of a large bur oak that was probably just a sapling when Lexington was christened, they gazed across a pasture full of bluish-purple blossoms of mature bluegrass. Francesca took note of every color and filed them in her memory. It wasn't long before the children spotted two small, gray rabbits nibbling grass by the creek, and they ran off to chase them. They left the adults to soak in the cool autumn air and talk privately about the war, always on their minds.

"I read that all across America, farmers have lost their sons and workers to the draft. This will make it difficult for them to make harvest, so the price of produce is sure to increase. So many are affected by this war." Antonio shook his head then, as though loosening worries from a stubborn hook in his mind.

"Why do people have to fight?" Francesca lamented. "Why can't they just go about their ways peacefully?"

"One thing is for sure: the government has plans to arrest anyone who is disloyal to America, the military, or even the flag." *Zio* dropped his voice and with an index finger to his lips, warned, "So, be careful, watch every word you say!"

On the way home, *Zio* Sal stopped off at another favorite spot, the Lexington Cemetery. The burial ground was well tended and quiet. Warm fall colors enveloped mossy tombstones—and Francesca thought it a most beautiful place for the departed to rest.

They found two lakes filled with ducks and geese, and keeping Raffaele from chasing them was quite a challenge. The lake was surrounded by large willow trees, dripping and falling like shimmering tears. The Romanesque gatehouse reminded Francesca of Italy, and in the serenity, she found her thoughts leading to her mamma and papa— and home. For perhaps the thousandth or millionth time, she wondered when she would receive word.

Zio Sal interrupted her thoughts, pointing to another cemetery across the road, chuckling, "Now I will show you where souls lie that get to enter heaven." He drove them over to Calvary, a graveyard designated for Catholics.

Calvary was small, but just as lovely. Francesca saw names she recognized: Ginocchio, Dacci, Amato—people who had never had the desire or means to return to Italy.

On the drive home, they passed a crowd of women in white dresses downtown with signs that read *How long must women wait for liberty?* and *Women's suffrage now!* Hecklers called out, "Back to the kitchen!" and "Dangerous she-devils!" But the women just continued marching, determined to achieve the vote. Francesca secretly thought she would enjoy voting once she could finally read the newspapers herself, instead of waiting for Antonio to explain everything. With women voting, maybe there would be no more war. No mamma alive wanted to send her son into battle!

When they arrived back home at 246 Lexington Avenue, Francesca began to prepare chicken parmesan, penne pasta, and steamed brussels sprouts for the family. Ending such a lovely, contemplative day around the table felt nearly perfect to Francesca. She looked from one dear face to the next, and only wished that her mamma, papa, and sisters could join them. Castel Frentano was never far from her thoughts, and its food never far from her busy fingertips.

The next day, while the children were at school, Violet and then Maria stopped by to report the latest tittle-tattle. Violet brought some sugarless molasses cookies that she and Lauretta had baked the night before, and a tin of

Palmer's Biscuits she had bought down at Murphy's Grocery.

"Violet, these are *delizioso*," said Maria with a mouth full of molasses cookies. "I need the recipe. My Martino and Alessandra will love these!"

Violet had also brought a bottle of red wine for Francesca. "*Grazie*, my friend, you should not have done this," Francesca said to Violet. She smiled proudly because she now spoke most of her sentences in English.

Maria took the bottle and read the label. "Tuscan! I will never forget how in late September, our family traveled by train to Tuscany to visit family and help out in any way we could." Maria looked at Francesca for approval and uncorked the bottle. "It is never too early for wine!" she laughed.

"They called Tuscany the 'Garden of Italy,' and, to me, it is the most beautiful region. The air was always so pungent in Tuscany with the scent of *sangiovese* grapes ripening on the vine.''

Maria found glasses and poured wine for her friends and continued, "My cousins live in San Gimignano, and they make the most *magnifico* Chianti with bottles wrapped in straw baskets. Their village is full of farmhouses with rippled clay tile roofs, and walls washed in shades of peach and gold that shine just like seashells in the sun. Cypress trees circle the village and I always thought they looked like green soldiers standing guard. It's so inspiring, no wonder that so many literary geniuses such as Dante, Petrarch, and Boccaccio came from such an enchanted place! Bacchus truly blessed Tuscany with the best growing conditions and wine." Maria lifted her glass to her friends and took an approving sip.

"My sisters and I climbed into the large wooden vats and stomped grapes into sweet juice. We sang our favorite songs and laughed. I can still smell the fermenting grapes, so rich it nearly felt like color blooming in our noses, if you can imagine!"

"Once, my sister fell face first into the mashed grapes, and we laughed so hard that we were removed from the vat by Papa, who scolded us for being childish. He was such a serious man—he had very little patience for fun when it was time for work. He sent us inside to help with the more boring chores." Maria topped off her wine glass and sniffed it deeply, as though the familiar scent could bring Tuscany, and her family, to her.

"Oh, I remember the chores," Francesca chimed in. "My sisters and I had to harvest tomatoes in late summer. Mamma and her sisters set large iron pots outside between our homes. They built a fire under the pots and boiled tomatoes all day. They bottled enough thickened tomato paste to get us through the winter. Mamma and my aunts always sang *La Figlia Mia*, a song about daughters who cook pasta and count on the aroma of the sauce to lure hungry suitors. They were not the best singers, but they sure had fun. I will miss the harvest this year."

Refreshing their glasses, Maria said, "You know, Francesca, we can recreate the tomato paste party right here! I will have Louis bring home lots of tomatoes from the Farmers' Market Saturday and we can sing *La Figlia Mia* and have a lot of fun." Maria suddenly smiled brightly. "What do you think, Violet? Do you want to come learn a recipe that is better than anything in your fancy magazines?"

"That sounds fun, I'll be here!" Violet smiled in return.

Maria raised her wine glass and said with a little slur, "Find your biggest iron pot, Francesca! Here's to tomato paste!"

"And maybe I will lure a hungry suitor," Violet added, laughing.

Maria raised her glass again. "Yes! Here's to saucy suitors!"

"You know," Francesca wistfully recalled. "On those afternoons while Mamma boiled tomatoes, my sisters and I went out to pick berries. When we returned, we felt sick. We always ate too many, but berry season only came once a year, so we made the most of it."

"You are in luck, Francesca, because Kentucky overflows with berries of all sorts!" Violet said excitedly. "I even have a mulberry tree in my backyard, and, when ripe, its berries have the sweetest juice that leaves our fingers dark purple. We can pick those as well. The kids will love it!"

"I think I've had too much wine," Maria admitted. "It was good. *Grazie*, Viola."

"Is there anything such as too much? Wine is life to my family since Papa is a ninth-generation vintner." Francesca swirled her glass of wine to the light. "I was taught at an early age that color indicates quality. Papa, who had a passion for good wine, said that darker wine has a fuller body. He believes there are five steps to wine appreciation." She continued in her papa's deep, raspy voice, "The first is mental, second is pleasure to the eyes. Third is the scent after the wine has been exposed to air, and, of course, fourth is the pleasure that the mouth receives. Lastly, the appreciation from the brain after drinking. My brain is enjoying this one!" Francesca laughed and finished the wine that remained in her glass just as the screen door flew open and slammed shut.

"Mamma, we're home!" Three lively children entered.

"Oh, hello, Mrs. Gallager and Mrs. Ginocchio," Ella said.

"Where is Lauretta?" asked Rosa.

"She is at the house with her grandma. I should leave to pick her up." Violet smiled as she rose from the table and said, "I brought cookies."

"Yay!" screamed Raffaele.

After she slapped the back of his hand, Francesca said, "Only one cookie."

Maria carried their glasses to the sink and left to greet Martino and Alessandra at home. With a kiss to each of Francesca's cheeks, and an *arrivederci*, she left.

"I'm hungry, Mamma." Rosa reached for a second cookie, but Francesca waved her away with a gesture more persuasive than any spoken words.

"So you don't starve, tonight I will make your favorite ravioli. Get your lessons finished, wash up, and then come back and help me roll out the dough. We'll have Mrs. Gallager's cookies for dessert."

Chapter 9

Fall 1917

One warm Sunday after Mass, while Maria kept an eye on the children, Antonio took Francesca for a ride in the Model-T. He knew how much she enjoyed country drives through the rolling hills of central Kentucky, so full of barns, woodland pastures, and grazing horses. On such a lovely day, Antonio removed the top of the company roadster, handed Francesca her touring hat, and they took off.

"Don't make this thing fly. *caro!*" Fracesca laughed, as the blurred jumble of changing leaf colors raced past.

As a flock of migratory birds flew overhead, Francesca tightened the ribbon beneath her chin and leaned her head back, wide-eyed at the unfolding vistas of her new home.

She had learned that the roads were lined with serpentine, dry-stacked limestone fence rows. These structures had been painstakingly built more than a century ago by slaves, indentured servants, and Irish and Scottish immigrant stonemasons.

Over the years, ever-aggressive English ivy had disguised some of the complex architectural beauty of the walls, but still, they stood; gravity and meticulous placement of each stacked stone required no mortar. Out in the fields beyond, farmers and hired hands tended to crops while livestock grazed nearby behind wooden fences.

"The scenery is as lovely as Italy," Francesca admitted to Antonio. "Castel Frentano has more drama in the hills, but the palisades that line the rivers are so pretty and quite similar. I will embroider this scene for Mamma and perhaps you can mail it to her?"

As they drove, Antonio taught her the word 'limestone' for the ubiquitous rocks.

They sped on in silence through the lush countryside rich with dense foliage and hidden wildlife. The cool wind helped neutralize the sun that blazed down on Francesca, suddenly very glad she'd worn her hat.

Every now and then Antonio reached over to hold her hand, barely able to conceal his excitement at the surprise he had planned. Next to a wide pasture in an area she did not recognize, Antonio pulled unexpectedly off to the side of the road.

"Is something wrong?" Francesca asked, looking alarmed at the abrupt stop.

"No, nothing is wrong! I want *you* to drive!" Antonio opened the door to step out.

"You must be *pazzo*," Francesca laughed, tapping her forefinger against her temple.

"I am serious, you can do it! I'll be right here to help you!" Antonio got out of the car and smiled down on her.

"Get back in. I am not able to drive!" she declared, as her heart thumped heavily.

"Oh, *Madre*, you will do fine," he smiled. "Where is your *confidence*?"

He knew just how to get to her. Francesca threw him an evil eye and scooted across the bench seat to take the wheel. "Here, you will need these." Antonio handed her his driving goggles. "This thing only has two speeds, reverse and drive, so you only need to learn the pedals."

Francesca tightened the goggles, arranged her skirts, shot Antonio a 'watch this' look, and took the wheel. She lifted her foot off a pedal and, after a few hilarious lurches, they were on their way - Francesca was a driver! If Mamma and Papa could see her now! Focused intently on the narrow gravel roadway, Francesca whispered, "C'mon, Donna Bella, let's do this!" She bumped over railroad tracks, and soon passed fruit orchards and tobacco farms. She saw a hairpin curve ahead and reduced speed. Gulping back fear, she pulled out of the curve.

"How's that for *confidence*, Mr. Bucci?" she laughed, looking straight ahead like she had been driving her whole life.

A lovely covered bridge loomed ahead, spanning a steep ravine. The distant view was spectacular, even from the driver's seat, but Francesca poured every ounce of her attention into keeping the loud contraption out of the plunging ravine below. She did not glance at Antonio, who sat with his feet pressed to the floorboard and his knuckles white against the dash.

Leafy deciduous trees on each side hung low to create a shadowed tunnel—far different from the erect cypress trees and tall maritime pines back home. A tangle of spent honeysuckle grew wild along the dirt road, and the fields they soon passed were full of hemp, tobacco, and corn in rows nearly as neat and precise as Francesca's best stitchery. The meadows were thick with goldenrod, and creeks were lined with white-barked sycamores drinking their fill.

As they approached a hill, Antonio said, "Pull over here, *Madre*."

"What? Did I do something wrong?" Francesca questioned.

"Not a thing, your driving is *perfetto!*" said Antonio. "It's just that in order for you to make the incline of this hill, you need to drive backward."

"Now I know you're *pazzo!*" Francesca pulled off to the side of the road, eyes wide.

"I know you think it is silly, but it is the only way to get up the hill unless the tank is full of gasoline," Antonio explained.

"Don't joke with me!"

"Ah, one of the flaws of this automobile, I am afraid," he answered. "It has everything to do with gas and how it gets to the carburetor—and nothing to do with style."

Taking off her hat and craning to look over her shoulder, Francesca aced the difficult backwards maneuver, and then pulled over to get her bearings.

"Great job, *Madre!*" Antonio shouted, laughing. "You are a natural motorist! Now, let's see if you can start this thing!" And with that, they both got out and walked to the front of the complex machine. "Okay, you must crank it and be prepared for the hand crank to spin out of control," he said ominously. "It's worse than a horse bite!"

He had seen many who were not prepared for the kick suffer broken arms. Francesca heeded Antonio's instructions and successfully started the automobile with both arms intact. Antonio shouted, "*Donna potente!*"

As she triumphantly drove back towards the city, Francesca erupted in delighted laughter. Antonio sat beside her, also smiling despite his tense muscles.

Francesca pulled over to the side of the road and turned the wheel back over to Antonio. "I think that is enough for one day." Francesca smiled. "Thank you, *amore mio,* I loved it!"

He reached over and pulled her near him. He took her chin in his hand and kissed her lips sweetly. "You were *fantastico!* Next time you will drive in town and make all my friends jealous," he laughed.

As they approached town, Antonio stopped off at Bradley's Drugstore on the corner of Main and Walnut. "Bradley's has a soda fountain, and they serve the best chocolate ice cream. It's like gelato, just not as rich or silky. Would you like some?" Antonio knew he didn't have to pressure her.

"*Si*, that sounds wonderful. I just hope it is better than the American coffee," Francesca teased.

They sat side by side on high stools at the counter and Antonio ordered two chocolate ice cream cones.

The man at the counter handed Antonio the daily paper. On the cover was a beautiful woman dressed in a very provocative outfit. "They're gonna kill her," the man said. "You gotta watch them, the pretty girls. They are up to no damned good! Pardon me, ma'am." He shook his head.

Antonio read the article to Francesca, "The lady in the photo was convicted at trial because she worked with the Germans. They claim she is a spy. She is an exotic dancer in Europe and apparently made a high-ranked military officer her bed partner. She was arrested this past February in Paris and found guilty. They will execute her by firing squad in a few weeks." Antonio finished the article and laid the paper on the counter.

"Her name is Mata Hari," Francesca said. "Maria, Violet, and I have discussed the *sgualdrina* all summer. She calls herself 'The Eye of the Dawn.' Francesca picked up the paper. "You didn't know I kept up with the news, did you?" Francesca grinned.

"Is that right?" Antonio laughed. "What else do you girls talk about?"

"We just think it is funny that she stuffed her brassiere with stockings because she was flat-chested," Francesca whispered with a smile. "Violet, with her teaching, and Maria with her translations, are helpful to have around."

"I am proud of you and your English lessons, Francesca," Antonio said seriously. "Life will be a lot easier when you have two languages under your pretty hat."

"Speaking of America, I want to have a few friends over to celebrate this holiday that they call Thanksgiving, if that's okay?" Francesca queried hopefully, ever mindful of the war effort, and food rationing. "Maria and I have been saving ingredients for a special holiday meal."

"I think that sounds wonderful!" Antonio said.

"I thought we could invite the Ginocchios, of course, and the Buchignanis. What about Violet and Lauretta?" Francesca asked. "I will cook Italian food, of course, but I thought I might try to include a few American dishes, too."

"Whatever you fix will be wonderful!" Antonio patted her hand.

They arrived home to find the children playing in the front yard. They had raked small mountains of colorful leaves and were about to jump in.

"Mamma! Papa! Did you have a good time?" Rosa shouted, dropping the rake.

"I did. Your papa taught me how to drive!" Francesca said proudly.

"Your mamma could engineer a train if she wanted—she's a natural!" Antonio beamed at the children.

Raffaele ran up to Antonio. "I want to drive, Papa! Teach me to drive!"

"Soon, *bambino,* soon," Antonio laughed. "You have to grow to reach the pedals."

A Sunday drive with his love, ice cream, and now a holiday feast to anticipate with friends. If he could help it, Antonio knew he would never willingly be apart from his family again.

Thanksgiving arrived, and to Francesca's dismay, it rained all day. Carrying umbrellas and bottles of wine, the families soon arrived, eager to celebrate friendships they had formed. The Bucci house was full and echoed with laughter and mingled conversations. The rain trapped the children inside and this made for more noise and chaos—the kind of raucous atmosphere one expects at a holiday. But after a few stern looks from their papas, the children settled down to play snakes and ladders, jacks, and blow football.

After Antonio led a prayer for Thanksgiving, Francesca surprised her guests with a large, succulent turkey on her best ceramic platter. The bird was cooked to golden-brown perfection. Most of the dishes were traditionally Italian, but Francesca had also made a bread stuffing with celery and onions, mashed potatoes, buttered corn, and cranberry sauce. Maybe she was becoming an American, after all!

The best dish of the night was a shepherd's pie that Violet made from her grandma's recipe, along with a bacon and cabbage casserole, and warm soda bread. There was no lack of food, and no one hesitated to fill– and refill – their plates.

After the feast, Antonio tore the clavicles from the picked-over bird—another Italian custom brought to the new world. He offered one end of the bone to Rosa and they pulled together until it snapped in half. Rosa's face lit up. She knew that her larger piece brought her good luck since it carried the bird's divine power.

Maria had made pumpkin pies with real whipped cream to share—a new taste for Francesca, and a recipe she definitely would request.

The rain, at last, let up, allowing Violet and Lauretta a window to walk home. Full of delicious food and warm memories, the neighbors departed contentedly, offering many thanks to their hosts.

After the house calmed down, Antonio read *Mother McGrew, Daniel Donkey,* and *Hopalong Cassidy* to Raffaele, and the girls headed to the kitchen to help out.

As Ella passed through the *salotto*, she picked up a framed photograph of Francesca and Antonio, a gift from Francesca's parents to commemorate their wedding day.

They stood under a pergola that dripped pale violet wisteria in the garden at Santa Maria della Selva Church. Francesca, adorned head to toe in white lace and satin that revealed only her high cheekbones, full lips, and eyes just as dark as her hair. Antonio wore black on black with a bow tie. He had a classic angular face with dark, wide-set eyes and a much thinner mustache. They made a handsome couple. No wonder they were always reaching out to each other to touch, to pat, to say wordless things with their eyes.

"Francesca," Ella asked, "What was Castel Frentano like? How was your life before you came to America?" Francesca took a seat at the table, and patted the empty chair next to her.

"Come and sit," she smiled, sliding a plate of biscotti closer to the child, now more a young woman with each passing day. "Ella, we share a beautiful homeland, *Italia,* and I know you must miss it as much as I do…" Too full of emotion for words, Ella nodded her agreement.

"What was Castel Frentano like? Well… at the turn of the century, life had changed—not just in Italy, but all over the world. I feel very blessed to have lived there."

Rosa joined the two in the kitchen and Francesca wrapped her arms around both girls before continuing, "Unlike you, Ella, Rosa was raised in a remote village in the Apennine Mountain range, near the *Adriatico*. It was the most beautiful place on earth. I never wanted to leave."

"Mmm," Ella breathed, imagining.

Francesca closed her eyes and continued, "I still can picture my toes buried in the fine, golden sand of the *Adriatico*." Her mind drifted away to the beach. "I have accepted that I may never see Italy again, but I will never - ever - forget," Francesca said with a sad smile. "I'll keep it here," she said, tapping her breast. "As I know you will."

"Castel Frentano has tall snow-covered peaks." She continued, "As well as lowlands where the sheep and goats graze. Close to home, we have hot mineral springs, or fumaroles, as well as deep, crater lakes, and even a few active volcanoes. In the eye of my memory, I can still see the view from my family's front porch, vineyards and olive groves all around."

"It sounds like a beautiful mirage. Could you see the sea from your village?" Ella asked.

"No, but not far away is a fishing village, Francavilla al Mare. It has a long coastline with a small harbor. The beauty and serenity of Francavilla al Mare was so mesmerizing to me. Papa often took me and my sisters, Bianca and Adriana, there on his days off from the vineyard. We sat for hours on the docks, felt the sway of the sea, and gazed out at the multicolored boats that filled the harbor. The warm seawater misted our bodies and left us tasting salt."

"My papa's uncle, *Zio* Pasquale lived there, and he took us out on his boat to watch the dolphins. *Zio* Pasquale was a short man with very little hair, thick black, expressive brows, and a bulbous nose. We all loved him, for he was very funny.

"The dolphins enchanted us as they swam and played alongside our boat. *Aferre fa bene, o forrone fa male*, – 'the white dolphin does well, the black one bad,' *Zio* Pasquale told us. Apparently, the white dolphin protects the fishermen, but the black dolphin causes havoc.

"*Zio* Pasquale let us watch other fishermen set traps for octopus. The traps were baked clay pots where the octopus liked to hide. The fishermen used sardines or mullet as bait to lure the octopus. The fisherman collects the pots… gets his octopus! My papa said to avoid injury, the fisherman would bite the slimy creature between the eyes. This prevented the poor creature's ability to see, bite, or inject its dangerous venom. Whether he told the truth, I don't know, but I am very sure I would not have made a good fisherwoman if biting on the face of a wriggly octopus was a job requirement!"

Both girls giggled behind their hands and exclaimed, "Eww!"

One memory Francesca didn't share with the children remained all too vivid. As a nine-year-old girl, she had watched as a man leaned his rear-end off a boat not too far away, relieving himself in open water. Stunned, she watched the man pull up a rope that hung to the outside of the boat and floated in the water. After he cleansed himself with the wet, frayed rope, he threw it back into the water for the next sailor to use. Francesca shot a surprised look at her papa and he laughed, saying, 'This is just the way of life on the water.'

"My papa was so handsome; he had curly salt and pepper hair with wide-set blue eyes that brightened like lamps when he looked at Mamma, Adriana, Bianca, and me. I guess he forgave me for not being born a son. Instead of a source of labor in the vineyards, I was a burden – like all girls – that had to be supported until marriage," Francesca added with a wink, and the girls giggled again.

"You are not a burden, Mamma! You hardly ever sit down!" Rosa exclaimed.

"Our family, like yours, Ella, is Roman Catholic, and to have children is a blessing from the Holy Spirit. Mamma was never bothered that she only bore girls. She declared three girls were enough joy, and we gave her plenty of reasons why. Ella, your dear mamma told me many times that you were her greatest blessing." Ella suddenly disappeared behind that lost look that Francesca knew well, so she continued, more lightly, "And just like you, I was educated in the public school until I was fourteen years old. Even if I wanted to continue, that was it, *eccellente!* Children, you are so fortunate because you will get a better education here in America, so you must always diligently tend to your studies—a great gift!"

"What did you do after you finished school, Mamma?" Rosa asked.

"I mostly spent my days working in the family garden. I read, and cared for my parents and *Nonna*." Francesca walked to the kitchen window. "When money was tight, I learned to sew and do needlework in exchange for goods we needed.

"My entire family worked in the garden every day. The dark soil was like magic, and we easily grew carrots, zucchini, onions, string beans, peppers, and, of course, tomatoes and garlic," Francesca smiled. "We grew herbs in clay pots everywhere the sun could reach.

"*Nonna* Angelina – my papa's mamma – was an old-fashioned herbalist – a medicine woman. One easily became her patient at the hint of a sniffle or cough. She grew chamomile, parsley, rosemary, witch hazel, and several varieties of mint.

"Like her mamma, and her mamma's mamma, she constantly concocted remedies, tinctures, and poultices for every ailment. *Nonna* said, 'That which does not grow, dies,' and she applied this philosophy to her life and ours. I can see her now with her small frame, hands on hips, ready for whatever came her way. *Nonna* made it very clear that the fundamentals in life were nourishment, growth, and love. But her speciality, I believe, was love."

Francesca paused to see if the girls were still interested. They both sat wide-eyed and rapt, so she continued, "Along with strong religious beliefs, my family is chock-full of superstitions. Papa was always careful to exit from the door he entered. I am sure he got the habit from *Nonna*. As long as I can remember, *Nonna* lived with us, and she had many unusual ideas.

"She always got upset when a bird entered the house, for example. She hung thin, cotton scarves with silver threads over the windows to reflect the sunlight and to scare the birds away. If one came in, and they did quite often, she would run around the house screaming at the bird like it was the devil himself."

"Your *nonna* sounds funny like mine!" Ella said, laughing through a mouthful of biscotti.

"Our house where *Nonna* chased the birds was small, but very cozy. The mosaic tile floors were cool on my feet in the heat of the summers, and there was a wooden ladder that led to a loft where we slept. Mamma said we were closest to heaven there." Francesca recalled how the walls were textured with thick stucco the colors of autumn, squash, peaches, and the last glimpse of daylight. "As soon as you walked in the front door, you were greeted by a Madonna and Child portrait surrounded by golden wall sconces with taper candles."

"We had many of those paintings, too! And candles!" Ella exclaimed. "Everywhere in our house!"

"Maybe a great many things were true in every Italian home," Francesca mused, smiling at Ella. "From our front door, a short hallway led through a large open arched doorway into the *salotto*. Just off the great room is *la cucina*, with a great cooking hearth. I believe that hearth perhaps knew a good many of Castel Frentano's secrets," she said, smiling at the girls as her mind wandered once again home.

Francesca could see the homes in Castel Frentano with their tiled terracotta roofs, undulating warmth and color across the rolling countryside. She saw her friends' homes snuggled into the hillsides, covered with beautiful, tangled vines, echoing with the cheerful sounds of children at play. Everywhere around them, ancient cobblestone streets wound into town, sometimes requiring the balance of a goat—or the persistence of an Italian.

Francesca could almost smell the statuesque cypress providing windbreaks and shelter for the waving sunflower fields, vineyards, and neatly terraced hillsides.

"Almost as soon as we'd finished the grape harvest, it was time to gather olives. Just as we gathered grapes for good wine, my mamma believed one should harvest olives at the point when the moon fades from waning to new. She said this allows for the plumpest, most life-giving fruit. The mules, walking in endless circles, turned the stone cold press around and around to mash the grapes. The mules always made me sad. They are so smart and hard-working and truly unappreciated!"

"Just like women!" Rosa exclaimed, and the three burst into laughter.

Francesca composed herself and continued, "For extra money, my sisters and I tied large willow baskets around our waists and helped our neighbors handpick olives. The harvest left our hands stained with green, and it took days before the color – and scent – faded. Papa used to check the color of our hands to see who had worked the hardest.

After the harvest, the fruit was soaked in brine for several months before it was soaked in diluted lye, to remove the bitter taste." Francesca paused to take a bite of a biscotti, the snack her mamma always had waiting when they returned from olive picking.

"The groves were so beautiful with their silver-gray foliage and gnarled branches. It still amazes me how long it took for an olive tree to bear fruit. I believe it is about ten years! I guess when a tree can live up to one hundred years, it can take its own sweet time to produce fruit."

"Ten years? That's older than me!" Rosa exclaimed.

"Papa told us that Athena, the ancient Greek goddess of peace, war, and wisdom, had given the olive tree to humans as a symbol of peace. He always said, 'Olive trees give life to Italy, and man's wealth is measured by how many olive trees he owns.' Now girls, that's enough for now. Let's get these dishes dried and put away!"

As the three worked side by side, Rosa shyly requested, "Mamma, please tell Ella about your first *bacio!*" Rosa and Ella's cheeks reddened, but they both craned to hear.

"I remember one beautiful spring day, the kind of day that carried sweet jasmine on breezes, your papa picked me up on his bike for a ride through the village. Back then, it was a tradition to wear colored ribbons from the waist that were actually gifts from boyfriends or suitors. Your papa... Antonio... knew purple was my favorite color so he gave me deep lavender and pale violet silk ribbons.

When I wore this outfit on the handlebars of his bike, with his ribbons streaming behind me, it was obvious that I had eyes for only one boy.

"The first kiss happened close to our house under a large chestnut tree. We were both very nervous, but your papa later carved our initials in that tree, and we met there regularly to picnic and talk about our future. He carved, '*cresent illae, crescetis amores*' - as these little leaves grow, so may our love.' Such a poet! He was right, though. For our marriage to work, we had to grow together and grow our love. Your papa… Antonio…
and I hope you both will meet nice Italian boys to love and one day marry. Now, let's save more romance for another day and get this kitchen shining again."

Chapter 10

Winter 1917

The talk of Castel Frentano had only made Ella more curious about her family. After school one day, she went looking for answers. "Francesca, I need to know the truth. I am old enough, and I can handle it. You said we should talk someday. Now I am ready, so please tell me," Ella implored. "It has been nearly eight months since our arrival in America, but I still can't help but hope Papa will come for me."

Francesca looked up from the needlework Mr. Angelucci was expecting, and thought for a moment. Ella was a good child. After losing her mamma to the ocean, and after her papa had not surfaced to claim her, she was still such a brave and kind girl. It broke Francesca's heart every time Antonio reported that his contacts in Manhattan were unable to find Donato Tenaglia.

Reaching for Ella's hand she said, "I am afraid I know nothing about your papa. Antonio's friend, Vincent Marcello, who is well connected in New York, looked for your papa after we moved to Lexington." Francesca searched Ella's face for signs of understanding. "I am sure he had every intention to meet you and your mamma when you arrived in America. I am still hopeful we can reunite you." Francesca put her lips to Ella's trembling hand and kissed it gently.

"Antonio wrote a letter to your mamma's family, as well as to The Società Unione e Fratellanza Italiana when we arrived in Lexington. The war has complicated communication, and you know how big the water is that divides us. Maybe you should write another letter home and let them know how you are? We can try the mail again!" Francesca quickly retrieved a piece of stationery and pen from the hall secretary. "Of course, we want you to stay here in America with us, but if you want to return home to Sicily, we will understand. Whatever you wish to do, Antonio and I will help you. Every step of the way."

Ella went to her room and wrote a letter to her mamma's sister, *Zia* Sanella. She tried to find the words to describe what had happened and how she felt. She reassured her aunt that she was healthy and safe. She was getting the highest marks in school, and the Buccis treated her with kindness always. Rosa and Raffaele, she wrote, were like the younger siblings she had always wanted. Even so, by the end of her letter, she knew she wanted to return home to see her grandparents and aunt, her friends, and her dog Rocco—but she also knew she would never board another ship.

The Christmas holiday season arrived, and Francesca also longed more than ever to be reunited with her own parents and *sorellas* in Italy. But that winter, Kentucky delivered an unusual antidote for fierce homesickness in the form of record snowfall.

As the crystalline flakes covered the Bluegrass region in an icy enchantment, Francesca's spirits lifted and she happily told Antonio she would make their Kentucky Christmas just as magical as the mounds of glimmering snow now covering Lexington Avenue.

Even Antonio had never seen such a thick blanket of snow that lay across the front lawn, covering the bushes and reaching all the way up to the porch.

"Rosa, Ella, Raffaele! Wake up and look out the window!" Francesca ran into their rooms to wake them.

"Oh, my!" exclaimed Rosa, blinking as she pulled back the curtains.

"It's more beautiful than a snow globe! Because it's real!" Ella gazed at the swirls of white air.

"I want to go out there!" screamed Raffaele, already heading for the steps.

"After breakfast, young man." Francesca grabbed the collar of his pajamas and turned him around.

As promised, after breakfast, with three children layered in woolens, Raffaele was the first to jump in the snow. While the girls built a snow family, Raffaele threw snowballs at them and he wallowed in the cold, soft flakes, now two-feet deep and mounting.

Unable to get to work, and with the entire town at a standstill, Antonio puttered contentedly, happy to stay home with his family in the surprise wonderland.

He had hidden a wooden Flexible Flyer sled for the children for Christmas, but he simply couldn't resist this opportunity. He surprised them with the new toy, and you could hear them squealing, sliding up and down Lexington Avenue.

Francesca prepared a batch of *cioccolata calda,* and when Antonio finally brought the pink-cheeked children inside, they peeled off mittens and scarves and warmed themselves in front of the fireplace.

"Okay, family, I have a special treat for you tonight!" Francesca called, gathering them into the kitchen for an early meal. "Violet gave me a recipe perfect for a cold night."

"Oh yeah, did you finally decide that Americans can cook?" Antonio winked.

"Ha!" Francesca laughed as she gathered thick crockery bowls, spoons, and linen napkins she'd embroidered with blue, white, and silver snowflakes. "Violet said it is a German dish—she called it burga!"

Antonio's eyes lit up as he laughed, "It is called 'burgoo,' *Madre*, and I had it at the Derby last spring." As he peeked over her shoulder into the fragrant, simmering pot, he added, "If your burgoo is half as good, I will kiss your whole face!"

The family devoured the stew of beef, tomatoes, potatoes, corn, okra, and butter beans seasoned with sage and red peppers from the cellar. Francesca served it with homemade cornbread, and for dessert, pecan pie in a flaky, buttery crust, like *sfogliatella*. Antonio patted his stomach appreciatively after cleaning his bowl, and made good on his promise of kisses.

For her first Christmas in America, Francesca was determined to bring a bit of Italian merrymaking to America. On December sixth, they celebrated the Feast of Saint Nicholas of Myra. Francesca's mamma had always told her girls the legend of Saint Nicholas, the loving protector of children, and how he gave gifts each year to the good boys and girls. Francesca continued the storytelling tradition and the children listened raptly.

Rosa added excitedly, "If we leave our shoes by the door on the eve of Saint Nicholas Day, he will leave us a surprise!"

Raffaele's eyes lit up, "Even though we are in America, do you think we should put our shoes by the door, Mamma?"

As he walked in from the kitchen, Antonio said, "You never know, you may get a shiny new coin." The children ran to their rooms, and came back with shoes to place outside.

"Raffaele, you can place only *un* pair of shoes outside," Antonio laughed, seeing his son with several pairs.

"You never know, Papa. Saint Nicholas might not know how many children live here," Raffaele grinned.

Francesca took the extra pairs of shoes out of Antonio's hands and said, "Raffaele, Saint Nicholas is smarter than you think. Now, children run along to bed. I will be up to tuck you in soon."

After the children ran up the stairs, hollering their excitement, Francesca approached Antonio, wrapped her arms around him and whispered playfully into his ear. "You know, next year Raffaele will be able to put out an extra pair of shoes," Francesca smiled, stepping back and placing a hand on her slightly swelling abdomen.

"Oh, *Madre*! God has blessed us again?"

Francesca beamed up at him in reply. Antonio kissed her and tenderly placed his hands over hers, and the young, new life growing within.

A few days before Christmas, Antonio brought home a live Christmas tree and the children danced around it excitedly, intoxicated by the piney scent filling their home. Francesca tatted small, white snowflakes to hang all over the tree and the children strung a popcorn garland, and each made a few ornaments from paper and bits of ribbon. Francesca took just enough aluminum foil that she had saved and covered a wire-framed star for the treetop. By the time they each had finished their contributions, the tree was perfect and Francesca's spirits greatly buoyed.

She told the children about shepherds in Italy who came out of the mountains each Christmas, meandering door-to-door, playing pipes and flutes, filling the air with music and celebration. With excitement quickening her words, she explained how villagers gathered around a *presepe* – a wooden manger – that was carefully assembled every Christmas in the town square. Francesca's family had gathered with candles each night around the *presepe* and they said prayers of thanksgiving for the sweetness of life and the redeeming grace of the Christ Child.

After trimming the tree, Antonio had another surprise for his homesick wife: he brought in a lovely ceramic *presepe* that included Mary, Joseph, and baby Jesus. "*Grazie, amore mio!*" Holding a bit of Italy in her hands, Francesca began to softly cry. She took the baby Jesus and kissed its head, and handed him to Ella. "Please, gently place the baby Jesus in the drawer of the sideboard. You can bring him out on Christmas Eve." Francesca hugged the little Blessed Mary before arranging the *nativita* on a side table. Antonio had done everything in his power to bring an Italian Christmas to her.

"Antonio, I believe I would like to invite the Ginnochis over for Christmas," Francesca exclaimed suddenly. "Perhaps, we should invite Violet and Lauretta, as well?"

"I think that is a wonderful idea. I will ask them all today!" Antonio replied, smiling.

Antonio pulled Francesca close and kissed her forehead. "I knew your Christmas spirit would fly as high here as in Italy," Antonio said. He realized again how lonely and empty his six years had been without her, and he could not get enough of her melodic singing as she set about necessary preparations for the Christmas gathering.

Finally, Christmas came, and 246 Lexington Avenue was filled with excitement and enough food to strain every table. Francesca had worked tirelessly on the meal that she served after midnight Mass. Since it was a Holy night, no meat was served.

Instead, she had observed the long Catholic tradition of serving seven types of fish, representing the seven sacraments of the church. Antonio could find eel nowhere in the landlocked town, so he improvised with Francesca's shopping list. He did his best to enable her to make calamari, pasta with anchovies, baked shrimp, steak fish, and other traditional dishes.

With the fish dishes settled, Francesca also prepared a grand display of treats: *struffoli*, cream tarts, macaroons, and fresh-roasted chestnuts.

Scents of holiday traditions, both old and new, swirled around them.

Francesca wiped her hands on her apron and called out, "*Famiglia!* Before we leave for Mass, I need you to help me clean the house."

"Why, Mamma?" asked Raffaele, whose young nerves ran predictably high with Christmas anticipation.

"Because, Mary may come into our home to warm baby Jesus by the fire while we are gone. We can't have her come into a messy house now, can we?" Antonio explained, shooing the children to their chores.

When the sparkling house met Francesca's approval, the family put on coats, scarves, and mittens, and walked down to Saint Peter's for Christmas Eve Mass. The evening smelled of burnt firewood and crackling winter air. Illuminated by hundreds of wax candles, the church was filled to capacity and Francesca noticed that a few younger parishioners had to stand.

The service gave Francesca the same hope and serenity as it had each year of her life in Castel Frentano. She gave thanks to God for keeping hands on her family, no matter the ground beneath their feet.

When they returned home, they were greeted by tantalizing aromas of tomatoes, basil, olive oil, and garlic filling the air. The Buccis and their guests sat down for a celebratory meal that, of course, included the uncorking of several special bottles of wine. On this night, the children were allowed a few sips and happily stayed up well past their bedtimes.

Antonio snuck out of the house as quiet as Saint Nicholas himself, and returned with an enormous burlap feed sack full of presents. He gave a cuddly brown teddy bear with a red velvet bow to Lauretta. For Raffaele, he pulled out a bow and arrow like the one he had in Italy, and for Rosa, he presented a beautiful China doll dressed in pink lace with matching hair bows. Wonderfully-scented sachets and hairbrushes with brass hibiscus flowers were passed to the older girls, Ella and Alessandra. Martino, the eldest boy, received his very first Case pocketknife, that he snapped open and shut, open and shut, until his mamma gave him the look.

The children were thrilled with their gifts, but as early morning hours approached, they could hardly keep their eyes open. Little Lauretta was already asleep on the couch, and Louis ushered his sleepy brood home through the snow. While Francesca and Maria cleared the table, Violet led Rosa, Raffaele, and Ella to their rooms and sang the Irish lullaby her mamma had sung so many times to her:

On the wings of the wind
Over the dark rolling deep
Angels are coming
To watch over thy sleep

Angels are coming
To watch over thee
So list' to the wind
Coming over the sea

Hear the wind blow
Hear the wind blow
Lean your head over
Hear the wind blow

Downstairs, just as his papa had each Christmas season, Antonio lit a Yule log in the fireplace. The sizzles and pops of the fire reminded Francesca of home, and she glowed as warmly, remembering her papa gathering their logs.

After he had cut down an apple or oak tree, he said, "The Yule log must burn until New Year's Day, to burn away any evils of the past year." He spread the ashes on the fields in the spring, bringing good luck to the crops.

Violet returned downstairs and gathered her things to leave. Since it was dark and cold out, Antonio insisted on driving them home. He bent down to the couch and picked up Lauretta, cradling the young girl in his arms like a baby. After Violet hugged and thanked Francesca for a wonderful Christmas and got into the Model-T, Antonio handed Lauretta over to her. He saw them home to Willard Street and returned through the silver and diamond snow to his family.

On Christmas morning, the children woke to find Tinker toys, a few new outfits, Lincoln Log Timbers, Raggedy Ann and Andy, and colored Crayola crayons and paper. It was a wonderful, lazy day. Antonio rarely left his brown leather chair while the children played. Francesca spent long hours in the kitchen as usual, but this Holy day cast a sense of gentle peace throughout the entire house. Francesca hummed *Astro del Ciel* as she worked, and prayed her family in Italy was just as content and warm.

As 1918 soon approached, Francesca remained still as eager to practice the old country traditions. On New Year's Eve, Ella, Rosa, and Raffaele stayed up to place shiny coins on the windowsill just before midnight. *Nonna* had taught them this ritual to bring good luck. Ella said her family in Sicily had done the same thing.

Then the entire Bucci clan ran all through the house shouting, *"Buon Capo'd Anno!* Happy New Year!" New year, new land, new friends, and a new child on the way for Antonio. Francesca smiled to herself, grateful for everything new, and sure she would never get tired of the old.

On the fifth of January, while Antonio enjoyed a cigar on the front porch, Francesca called out to her children to come downstairs and hear the legend of *La Befana*.

"Tonight, is the Eve of the Epiphany," she said, handing each of them cups of fragrant *vin brulé* with cinnamon sticks to stir. "This is the day the Three Wise Men arrived to see the Child King. Befana was an elderly lady who was awakened in the night by a very bright star.

"She was so startled by the great, celestial light, she grabbed her shawl and made her way outside. There she found three men in silk robes. The men told her the bright star was leading them to the Child King and that they carried special gifts." Holding fast to rituals, Francesca passed a plate of *pizzelles* to the children and took one for herself. "Befana also wanted to send a gift with the men for the Child King, so she went inside to bake. She baked pizzelles like ours and other delicious treats until she grew very tired. She slept soundly, and when she awoke, the bright star was gone, as were the three men."

"I can't believe she fell asleep!" Ella snickered. "My *nonna* would have done the same!"

"Well, Befana was so disappointed that her gifts did not make it to the child that she committed every year, on January 5th, to pass out special gifts and treats to all the children. She always hoped that one of them was Christ the King." Francesca wiped up spilled confectioner's sugar from the table, and turned to the window only to see that it was lightly snowing again. Soon she would have more mittens and scarves to sort by the fire.

The next day, a whistling Antonio returned home from work, with exciting news for his wife. "Francesca, now that our family has grown with Ella, and especially with another *bambino* on the way, I will proceed with my plans to become an American citizen." He sat down at the kitchen table, smiling broadly. "Three years ago, I went to the courthouse and filed my Declaration of Intent papers. I have lived in America for more than five years; I am now eligible to petition the court for naturalization."

"That is wonderful, Antonio!" Francesca hugged her husband and handed him his afternoon cocktail of vodka with two olives. "Do you have everything you need?"

"I hope so, but they'll tell me what I lack. I have learned to read, write, and speak English pretty well, and except for my cigar habit, I believe I am of good moral character," he winked. "I will need to prove that I understand and am committed to the Constitution of the United States. There is a night class where I will study American history to prepare. I'll stop by the courthouse in the morning and pick up the required forms.

"You do know my naturalization automatically makes you and the children American citizens?" He looked at Francesca for approval. "If you wish to take on the Bucci name, this will be the time to change it. You will have dual citizenship and can return to Italy someday!"

"*Incredibile,*" Francesca clapped her hands. "Italian law cannot stop me now from taking your *cognome!*"

After Antonio's required paperwork had been filed and approved, he went nervously to City Hall to stand before a judge. With one hand on the Holy Bible, Antonio swore under oath to support the Constitution and to obey the laws of the United States. He looked across the room at his family all dressed in red, white, and blue, and his face flushed with pride. Francesca had stitched a special monogrammed handkerchief for this day, with his initials and the date in the same patriotic colors. Seated on oak benches, the children waved small American flags and smiled their biggest, proudest smiles at Papa.

Before God, family, and all in that room, Antonio renounced any foreign allegiance and said that, if required, he would bear arms for America. After they took his fingerprints, Antonio Bucci became a naturalized citizen of the United States of America. Like thousands of other immigrants pouring into this new land of promised opportunity, Antonio had weathered a long, difficult, and lonely journey—and all for the love of his family.

Chapter 11

Spring 1918

Winter eased, and the mountains of snow melted into brown running rivulets in the streets. An early spring coaxed forth brilliant yellow daffodils and dreamy purple hyacinths. As the days gradually lengthened, returning woodcock, geese, and sandhill cranes filled the air once more with lively honks and hollers.

Francesca had survived her first year in America and was very pregnant with another child. Finally, after many fretful months, a letter at last arrived from her sister Bianca. Since the war had begun and the postal service had slowed substantially, no one knew when correspondence would come, if at all. Francesca held the letter in trembling hands on the porch. She opened it eagerly and read every syllable aloud as she paced back and forth, awash in feeling.

Dearest Sorella,   January 25, 1918

You and the angels are missed terribly. We miss sharing our days with you, and we often wonder how you, Antonio, and the children are doing. How is America? Have you found gold yet? Sadly, war has destroyed much of Europe from what we have heard. It is getting harder to make do around here. Adriana and I have been sewing for extra money, and it seems to help. The winter has been slow for Papa at the vineyard, and Mamma rarely leaves the kitchen. Papa is upset today because wild boars destroyed one of his gardens. We are all, of course, always anxious for your letters.

I ran into Sofia at the piazza at Christmas. She says she thinks of you every day, and misses her dearest friend. She said her brother, Marco, was called to serve with the Italian militia at Isonzo. Luckily for him, he broke his leg in training, and was sent home. She said he is home now on crutches. Her mamma just had a stroke, and her papa is also very ill and might be called home to heaven very soon. Sofia worries about the bakery and who will tend to it.

These are trying, difficult days for all, sorella. May God be with us. Everyone sends their love!

I love you, Francesca, and we miss you very much. We keep the gravesite of your little one clean and well-tended, so please worry about nothing here.

Bacio, bacio, Bianca

Francesca steadied herself against the porch railing and held the letter to her bulging tummy, as though the growing baby might feel *Zia* Bianca's love and devotion, too.

Francesca read the letter a half a dozen times, savoring each word like tickets back to the home she remembered—and still longed for.

Bianca's words reminded Francesca of Antonio's long absence from Castel Frentano, and how she had suffered, missing him. With a young daughter and a second baby on the way, Francesca's days had careened wildly between resentment, longing, loneliness, resignation, and moments of sweet contentment in Italy with her family.

More than anything, though, the empty place in her heart gnawed, and she knew only Antonio could return her to wholeness.

Antonio must've been working day and night because over time, fewer and fewer letters arrived from America. When they did come, Francesca did not recognize her Antonio and his new life. He wrote that he had learned English and attended dazzling social events with his employers from the racetrack. He had become a patron of the theater and mingled with important people. He wrote about the horse industry and things Francesca knew nothing about. Was he becoming a stranger to her? Did he now desire a more sophisticated partner, perhaps with perfect English, horses, neat blonde hair, and elegant finery?

Looking down at her plain pinafore, Francesca's worries compounded, and she grew unsure of her desirability. What if Antonio never sent for her and the children? She wanted him home. She missed their day trips to the coast, and their romantic adventures. Francesca needed more than her children and housework in her life, and Antonio's overbearing parents were more than she could take on some days.

The Buccis always asked where she had been, and what chores she had or hadn't completed. A few months after Antonio had left for America, Francesca's mamma fell ill, and this gave her the excuse to move home to care for her. Francesca knew her sisters could take care of their mamma, but she had to leave the Bucci household—hopefully forever!

Francesca's mamma could read her daughter's deep loneliness. She was not naïve to love, and Mamma knew that when two have set their minds on each other, one hundred people could not keep them apart. An *oceano,* however, could.

Just before he was to leave for America, Antonio and Francesca traveled in a cart pulled by two black Murgese draft horses. The ride to the coast was bumpy, and the seat was rough on her backside. She did not care. The amazing view of the countryside and the nearness of Antonio always made the journey worthwhile. Wild horses ran along beside them, matted and dirt-clad, roaming freely on the Apennine Mountainside. Sheep and cows grazed lazily in the fields, and Francesca envied that they had no cares about tomorrow.

She could feel Antonio's dark eyes as he watched her take in the view. Just after the seaside village, the sea came into view, and it took her breath away, as always. On that day, she remembered how calm the water was—a sheet of endless glass, reflecting an equally magnificent sun.

After they tethered the horses under a shade tree and offered them water and a flake of hay, they walked past the tall maritime pines that opened to a sunny, deserted beach. They laid out a blanket on the golden sand and listened to the rhythms of the waves. They breathed in the heady breezes scented with myrtle, salt, and wild roses. They could have lounged there all day—or forever. Lost in time, the sun and surf lulled them to a place of secret reverie shared by only two.

Soon, they carried their shoes and strolled along the shore, hand in hand, and with the cooling breeze fresh upon their faces. They buried their toes in the fine sand of the *Adriatico* coastline and privately released small prayers and wishes for their future into the wind. *Bring him back to me, bring him back to me,* Francesca's beating heart and the rhythm of the waves echoed the thoughts looping in her mind.

As though sensing her anxieties, Antonio moved closer to Francesca, took her chin in his hand, and pulled her lips near his. She could feel his strong body next to hers. Her heart raced as his mouth broke into a smile just before he laid a quick but thrilling kiss upon her lips. Francesca pulled away and ran up the coastline, and Antonio raced after, laughing like the schoolboy she remembered.

After a short while, they came to a winding rock staircase mysteriously embedded into a hillside. The rugged path was covered with spongy moss that cushioned their bare feet. Lavender and wildflowers took purchase and bloomed in crags. Flanked by towering cedars, the path led to an abandoned monastery surrounded by an imposing medieval fortress. Large filigree cast-iron doors, gothic arched windows, and turrets at every corner long forgotten challenges of the past. The salted sea air, as yet, had been unable to claim it.

After slipping on their shoes, they stood at a large arched doorway recessed between impressive, fluted columns. They creaked it open on rusted hinges, and entered reverently, tiptoeing across a dirty but intricate mosaic tile floor full of indecipherable, sacred meaning. Broad and shallow stone steps just inside the door led somewhere, so they held hands and followed wordlessly.

As they ascended, up and up, their footsteps echoed down from the vaulted ceilings into a well of abandoned emptiness. No rugs or tapestries remained to absorb the sounds of human life. At the top of the curved stairway, they discovered a bare parapet that overlooked the cliff they had just climbed. They tested the sturdiness before venturing out, and protected by an elaborately filigreed wrought iron fence, they were rewarded when an extraordinary panoramic view opened just below.

On one side, a steep, jagged coastline rose and plunged straight into the sapphire sea. The waves crashed against the rocks as rhythmically as a clock, and Francesca thought the ocean was counting down their remaining time together. Antonio took Francesca's hand to explore further.

The emerging view held miles of stately trees that blended into the hillside, encircling the monastery like silent sentries. Neither could inhale enough of the tranquil pine-washed air. As they luxuriated in the sea breeze and spectacular view of the *Adriatico*, they pointed in delight at the bright painted farmhouses and barns nestled in zigging pleats of the surrounding hillsides.

They soon passed through an abandoned courtyard, appreciating its timeless, enchanted beauty, and quiet solitude. The garden was overgrown and neglected, but still lovely, and ivy clung to almost every surface. Fat clusters of white lilies in bloom perfumed the entire courtyard, adding to its seductive magic.

Just below the monastery, they loped down a gentle, grassy slope, and passed through an *allée* lined with hawthorn trees. They happened upon a decaying but still beautiful grotto that had been cleverly wrought in earlier centuries.

The shell-speckled grotto proved to be a cool and shadowy retreat away from the intensifying Mediterranean sun. The splashing of a natural waterfall surprised them both, cascading down the side of the hill over a slab of dolomite and finally spilling into a pool of blue water.

Before Francesca knew it, Antonio had stripped off his clothes and dived into the cool water. He motioned for her to do the same. She could tell from echoes that the place was abandoned, so she followed suit.

"*Bellissima!*" Antonio exclaimed as he kissed his fingertips in frank approval. Is there anything more full of promise than two lovers alone in sparkling water, kissed and teased by piney air, and enticed by their own nearness?

They splashed lazily for what seemed hours. They watched as the sun emerged from the clouds, generating still more heat. Antonio climbed out of the water and lay on a large, flat rock to dry his body. Francesca tried not to gape, but he was so beautiful. His broad shoulders and lean torso were hard to ignore. His dark brown hair was slicked back away from his smokey amber eyes, and his brown skin glistened in the sun. He had full lips she desperately wanted to kiss. Francesca kept her distance, however, and acted as if she did not care that he was a magnet pulling her always toward him.

She clambered suddenly out of the pool behind a tangled green shrub. She dried her body in the sun, and as she slipped into her dress, from across the cove, Antonio said, "You are beautiful, Francesca. I just want to look at you." Blushing to her hairline, she could feel him as he admired her.

Just beyond the grotto stretched a field of sea swept red poppies. They removed their shoes once more and raced barefoot toward the field filled with a thousand vermillion blooms, flaming brightly on tall stalks in the sunshine.

Antonio smoothed out the blanket for them among the poppies and Francesca mused, "*Nonna* sometimes makes tea from poppy petals to ease the broken-hearted."

"Francesca, you will never need such a cure. I love you; I have always loved you," Antonio whispered. He brushed back her hair and kissed the nape of her neck, and she weakened. After a long kiss, Antonio wiped her wisps of loose hair away from her eyes, and said, "*Amore mia, vivo per te,* my love, I live for you." His hands trickled through her hair as he softly kissed her brow, then once more lightly on her neck. Francesca could feel the pound of her heart and the engulfing desire to touch and to be touched.

Her fingers traced his angular face while her eyes locked on his. He slowly caressed her neck with the tips of his fingers and ran them over her shoulders with a light tickle. His warm touch excited every part of her as his strong arms pulled her closer.

The evening air descended like a sigh as they kissed, touched, and became as close as two lovers could be.

The sudden peal of clanging church bells from the First United Methodist Church snapped Francesca back into the present, where she found herself leaning breathlessly against the front porch rail. She was in Kentucky. In her new life. With Antonio. They had found their way back to one another, just as he had promised.

Weep no more, my lady
No, weep no more, today
We sing one song
For my old Kentucky home
For my old Kentucky home
Far away.

— Steven Foster
My Old Kentucky Home, Goodnight

Chapter 12

Spring 1918

One morning in May, Francesca found a hatbox on her front porch, decorated in a splendid pastel floral print. An oversized violet silk bow draped around the box.

"Mamma, what is that?" Rosa exclaimed, reaching out to touch the fanciest package she had ever seen, and instantly hoping she might have it for her doll clothes.

"Well, it appears to be a hat box?" Francesca wondered aloud, retrieving an embossed Wolf, Wile & Co. card tucked under the ribbon.

Ella could wait no longer, "Open it! Please!"

After Francesca had confirmed her name on the card, she gently untied the silk bow and pulled off the lid. Inside was a lovely, shell-pink hat adorned with cream silk peonies, and a delicate spray of lavender lilacs.

"Ohh, it's so pretty!" sighed Rosa as Francesca breathlessly picked the hat up out of the box. It was the most elegant item she had ever seen outside of *Colliers*.

Ella pulled out a small note from the bottom of the box and yelled, "Guess who is taking you to the Kentucky Derby tomorrow?"

"Papa!" yelled Rosa.

Francesca ran inside, and the girls followed. Standing in front of the mirror in the foyer, she eased the hat over her hair and sighed, "Well? What do you think?"

"I think you are *bellissima!*" hollered Ella.

"Thank you, Ella. I feel beautiful. This is by far the prettiest item I've ever owned," Francesca smiled, admiring herself in the mirror. "But it might just need a few teeny embellishments."

"Can I try it on, Mamma?" asked Rosa.

"Of course, you can!" Francesca placed the hat on Rosa's soft brown curls, and then on Ella. "You girls are beautiful. Yesterday, Maria gave me a box of dress up clothes for you to play with. Now might be the perfect time if you want to see them?"

"Yes!" they both chimed. Francesca left the room and returned with a large fabric box full of vintage ladies' clothes.

"Thanks to the war, dresses today are not as beautiful as these!" Francesca enthused, opening the lidded box. She pulled out a long, burgundy velvet dress and handed it to Rosa, who nearly swooned with happiness.

"My sisters, Bianca and Adriana, and I took scrap material and tried to recreate the fashions of the day, but they were much too fancy for our little hillside far away from the cities." Francesca held up another full-length, golden silk dress for Ella and said, "See how the dresses had bodices that were heavy and worn over corsets? Jackets were worn with draped bustle skirts and blouses with high-laced collars that just reached under the chin." Francesca found a string of silver beads she was sure would look lovely on her new hat and dropped them into her apron pocket.

Leaving the girls to play, Francesca smiled at the thought of attending her first Kentucky Derby. She had heard a lot about it from Antonio, *Zio* Sal, and Violet. In the kitchen, she brought out a large pot from the cupboard, spread flour out across the counter, and began to knead dough for one of Antonio's favorites, *zuppa di tortellini.*

As she cooked, she mentally designed more flowers for her hat envisioning beads, velvet scraps, and sequins. Not that it wasn't lovely already, but Francesca felt she might need a bit more garnish on top to redirect eyes from her growing waistline.

When Antonio arrived home from work, he was greeted with a fashion show that rivaled *Carnevale*. Francesca hugged him and whispered many thanks in his ear. The girls screamed with excitement until he sat down with a martini to watch their show. While the girls giggled and changed into their next outfits, Antonio told Francesca that he had received the Derby tickets from his boss at the track, and had wanted to surprise her.

"I am just glad you got me a pretty hat and not a horse's feed sack," Francesca laughed, rubbing her midriff. She was nearly seven months into her pregnancy and felt more each day like a shapeless lump of pasta dough.

"You will be the prettiest lady there," Antonio reassured. "And I will be the proudest husband."

The next morning, they left the children with the Ginocchios and boarded a train at Lexington's Union Station, disembarking a few hours later in Louisville. A gray Pierce-Arrow touring car waited on the corner of Broadway and Tenth Street to take them to famed thoroughbred racetrack, Churchill Downs.

A soft drizzling rain didn't deter the day. "The rain is good, *Madre*! It means the race may go to any horse, not just the favorite," Antonio explained excitedly.

Although this outing was sure to be tiring, Francesca thought of home and her three busy children; being alone with Antonio was a rare treat. When they arrived at the racetrack, Francesca noticed two twin hexagonal spires that rose from the top of the roof. Trying to match the refined elegance of her hat, Francesca resisted the urge to point and exclaim in Italian at every passing marvel.

The rain began to lighten, and the Kentucky sun finally emerged through towering white clouds after the first race, wiping away the earlier gloom of the day. The sea of rain-slicked black umbrellas that had once surrounded them vanished. And the real show began.

For the Kentucky Derby, ladies wore bold, eye-catching spring hats and fancy dresses in so many colors, Francesca thought the crowd resembled a meadow of wildflowers moving in the wind. Due to the damp, many of the women sensibly wore silken wraps. On her own wrap, Francesca had stitched a family of chestnut thoroughbreds in rolling green pastures. A few older ladies wore furs with muffs that matched. The shoes, Francesca noticed, had high, slightly curved heels. A few women dressed *en vogue*, copying the sassy style of a famous dancer, even lopping their hair, like her, into blunt bobs. This freeing hairstyle looked chic with a small, brimmed hat trimmed in lace. Antonio had commented to Francesca that the bobbed hair looked like the horses' tails, which made her laugh. Francesca privately longed for Bianca and Adriana to see this spectacular fashion parade.

Not to be outdone, the men sported vested wool suits, some striped and some checked. Ties were narrow and tied discreetly with the Four-in-Hand Knot. Even in the damp, cuffs of trousers were pressed to perfection. Smart fedoras or white bahamas with wide, thick bands topped the men's ensembles.

Several women stopped to admire Francesca's hat with its artful additions of shiny sequined beads. She was glad she had stayed up late to design a windswept horse running across the wide velvet ribbon. In the glinting light of the afternoon sun, the horse appeared to gallop animatedly, catching everyone's eyes.

Antonio laughed, "I knew you would find a way to make it even prettier!"

After finding their box seats, Francesca took her first sip of the traditional mint julep, a sweet concoction of ice, Kentucky bourbon, water, sugar, and, of course, muddled sweet mint. "Mamma Mia!" Francesca cried. "I will need another julep, Antonio!"

Antonio seemed to prefer the local Falls City Beer, of which there was also plenty. It seemed Kentucky knew how to throw a fine party. Francesca noticed the center field was already full of people. Antonio explained to her that the infield was free and open to the public, allowing everyone a chance to witness the great race. As the crowd grew ever more massive, the energy was positively magnetic. Devoted racing fans had arrived in Louisville from all over the country. Out of sixty-nine possible horses, Antonio explained that only ten horses would make it to post. The races started promptly at two-thirty p.m.

With his keen head for numbers, Antonio handicapped and wagered every race, and tried to explain all his computations to Francesca.

Horses at home in Castel Frentano had labored in fields or delivered goods in town, she thought. The sleek thoroughbreds in Kentucky, however, were well muscled like premier athletes and groomed to glistening perfection.

Before the seventh and featured race, Antonio took Francesca down to the paddock to view the horses. She wanted to see them up close before she chose her favorite.

Right away, she noticed a lanky chestnut at the back of the paddock. "There is my pick; he has the look of a clumsy youngster. He must have lots of energy," Francesca said to Antonio. "I want to wager this time!" she said with confidence.

Antonio opened the Daily Racing Form, and read it to Francesca. Antonio just laughed and said, "Says that he is a three-year-old gelding, and he is seventeen hands high. You picked a tall one, *Madre*. He is a long shot, and he will go off at thirty to one odds on a muddy track. Two and half inches of mud."

Antonio read aloud more of the program, "His name is Exterminator, trained by J. Cal Milam, and owned by Willis Sharpe Kilmer. He was foaled at Almahurst Farm in Lexington and trained at Merrick Place, not too far from our house! Francesca, you never know, you may be Lady Luck today."

As the horses clip-clopped to the large oval track, Francesca couldn't keep her eyes off of the tall, thin chestnut with a distinctive white mark on his face. Antonio told her the white spot on his face was called a star. His jockey, Willie Knapp, weighed in at 114 pounds, and wore the Kilmers' brown, green, and orange racing silks.

While Francesca watched the other horses prepare for the race, Antonio made his way to the mutuel window to place their bets. He put two dollars to win on Exterminator and a bit more across the board on the favorite: War Cloud. The thought of money just thrown away on horses seemed completely ludicrous to Francesca, but she could sense that Antonio was confident in his choices. *Zio* Sal often said Antonio knew how to pick a winner, and had won him enough to buy his yellow truck—and then some.

They heard the bugle blow—the traditional call to post.

"Let's get to our seats—we don't want to miss this race!" Antonio said over the noise of the crowd. They watched as two soldiers from the Fort Campbell Army Base lifted the Stars and Stripes to the wind from a flag pole situated in the center field. The 149th Infantry Band played *The Star-Spangled Banner* as Old Glory blew in the breeze. As the horses lined up one by one at the post, Francesca felt a fluttering in her tummy; whether it was excitement or the baby, she couldn't be sure.

After the last horse had lined up behind a starting barrier, the assistant starters slashed long whips through the air. The woven barrier dropped away as thousands of spectators screamed in unison. The warriors took off! With Exterminator slotted in the fifth position, and War Cloud in fourth, the horses immediately cut toward the rail and accelerated down the track. Exterminator bolted out onto the thick, muddy track, along with the other horses. He trailed at first, but picked up the pace. Then, in the back stretch, he passed one horse after another and stayed in fifth place for the first three quarters. Antonio yelled right along in the frenzy of voices hoping their horses would come in, bringing big payouts and bigger bragging rights.

When the horses rounded the final bend, Exterminator slipped through to the rail at the head of the stretch. War Cloud tired in the heavy mud and dropped back. Exterminator flew by Escoba, and took the lead, never losing pace. Exterminator won the sloppy mile and one quarter race by a length. War Cloud finished fourth and out of the money.

The crowd cheered and the roar could be heard across the river in Indiana. Exterminator had won the forty-fourth Kentucky Derby, the richest event of the year.

Another man in the crowd threw his ticket to the ground and groaned, "I can't believe a long shot won the Derby!"

Antonio hugged Francesca and kissed her on the lips. How wonderful! She had really picked the winner—the 'toddler' with lots of energy had come through!

They hurried to the rail to watch the triumphant horse in the winner's circle. Tiny beside the towering chestnut, the mud-splattered jockey accepted a large bouquet of red victory roses and held them aloft to the cheering crowd.

Francesca watched as the race officials draped a garland of red roses over the horse's withers. "*Magnifico fiori!*" Francesca exclaimed. Exploding camera flashes lit the day, and many in the circle waved their hats and cheered, later to appear on the front page of the *Louisville Courier-Journal*.

A jubilant Antonio cashed the ticket and gave Francesca her prize money. "You deserve this—

Exterminator was your pick!" Antonio handed her nearly sixty-two dollars.

Francesca's large smile broadened when she saw the money. She quickly put it in her purse, and then she turned to Antonio and hugged him. "You're quite the teacher. Please allow Lady Luck to treat you to dinner tonight," she laughed.

Antonio and Francesca checked into The Seelbach Hotel at the corner of Fourth and Walnut for the evening. When they entered the grand lobby of the hotel, Francesca noticed huge murals of pioneers painted in vivid detail overhead. Just like the Derby, the hotel boasted fantastic opulence and style. From marvelous hardwood floors to fine forged metals and shiny marble surfaces imported from all around the world, the hotel was conceived to provide its guests a luxurious escape from reality. Francesca caught her breath and was, indeed, transported.

Just twenty years earlier, women had not been allowed to enter the establishment, but times were changing... Antonio left Francesca to rest her swollen ankles before dinner and departed to find the billiard hall.

Antonio located the bar, and the tuxedoed bartender served him a signature cocktail made of Old Forester, a Kentucky-made bourbon, spumante, triple sec, a splash of bitters, and topped off with a twist of orange peel. After a few drinks and one exceptional cigar, Antonio returned to the room with lots to tell. He tried to describe the décor of the billiard hall with its hand-carved oak walls. "Men gathered there to play poker and blackjack and smoke," he shared. He did not tell her the jokes he had overheard, nor the notorious gangster he had spotted, surrounded by his lieutenants, presumably in town for the Derby.

After Antonio had (mostly) filled her in on his outing, they set out to dine at the famed Rathskeller. This Bavarian-style dining hall was covered in medieval pottery. The red terra-cotta ceiling added warmth, while ornate pottery pelicans circled each square column. The waiter told them the pelicans were a symbol of good luck, and Francesca laughed as she thought about the racehorse she had picked. More hand-painted murals portrayed in elaborate detail a German city, home to the hotel owners.

It isn't the Sistine Chapel, but it is breathtaking, Francesca thought.

Although she could only manage a few bites of each, Francesca sampled the sauerbraten, rouladen, red cabbage and sauerkraut. She loved the dumplings the best, and they comforted her like nothing else could at this last trimester. They tried to figure out ingredients in the unfamiliar dishes as they recalled the exciting day and Exterminator's unlikely triumph.

Lifting his glass, Antonio proposed a toast, "To Lady Luck, her perfect hat, and one very feisty toddler!"

"And to mud!" Francesca laughed, clinking her glass to Antonio's.

A rich dessert of Black Forest cake studded with dark cherries sweetly capped Francesca's first Derby experience.

Satisfied as never before, they left the dining hall, and exited the main entrance of The Seelbach. Francesca spotted two bay draft horses harnessed to a shiny, cream surrey with a fringed top. Antonio saw the longing in her eyes, and waved his arm to summon the carriage. Francesca's feet were swollen and her back arched, and she would've gladly ridden on the curve of a mule if offered.

"Good evening," said the coachman, who was tall and dressed in a brown frock coat. The driver tipped his black top hat toward them before he climbed down off his perch. "My name is David Dominé. Please allow me to help you, *Signora*." The driver offered his hand to Francesca. With the assistance of the driver, Antonio eased Francesca into the carriage. In Italian, the driver noted the cool evening air, and offered a bison fur throw to cover their laps. "What do the love birds and *bambino* desire to see tonight?"

"How about a nice ride, good sir, and then back to The Seelbach!" Antonio answered.

The driver took the reins in his gloved hands, and with barely a touch of urging, the horse gently pulled the carriage to the Southern Extension. Antonio helped Francesca with her shawl as she leaned back onto the tufted, leather bench. He took her feet into his lap and loosened her lace-up boots. Under the bison throw, he rubbed her swollen ankles tenderly as they traveled down Fourth Street.

"Society Louisvillians live in this neighborhood," the driver offered. "Some of the most beautiful homes in all of America line these streets. It is a very coveted address."

Francesca, who had loved design her entire life, nearly strained her neck as she tried to take in the overwhelming artistry of this posh neighborhood. On one side of the street, large modern mansions intermingled with antique Romanesque dwellings. On the other side, a massive Italianate home sat snuggly beside a Chateauesque residence. All striking, they were *palazzos* to Francesca, who could not fathom life here, where homes radiated power and prestige beyond anything she knew. Had she met any of these American royals at the Derby?

Even in the darkness, she could see that many of the homes were bejeweled with elaborate stained glass windows. Francesca wished it were daylight, so she could see the ornamentation on the large dormers, steep-pitched gables, and turrets that towered overhead. Stone gargoyles seemed to play peekaboo from behind tall trees. A vast wraparound portico flanked a lovely Queen Anne, and she could only imagine the exotic gardens that lay beyond the imposing wrought-iron gates.

The carriage continued on to Saint James Court, a grassy boulevard near Central Park. As they circled an iron fountain, the soft lights from gas lanterns reflected on the swirling water. The evening had turned crisp. The sky was starless and hazy; only the waxing, gibbous moon shone through. Francesca snuggled up to Antonio for warmth, and he held her tightly.

In Central Park, they thought they spotted a man dressed in a dark cloak and wide brimmed hat. Francesca had an uneasy feeling and snuggled up closer to Antonio.

"That's Mr. Dupont," the driver said as he pointed in the direction of the shadowy figure. "He's been known to roam about since he died in 1893," he added.

"What did you say?" Francesca recoiled, alarmed.

"I did not say he was alive," the driver replied. "He means no harm. He only comes back from time to time to check on his land, you see." The driver looked back at Francesca and smiled. "I see him quite often."

Francesca and Antonio exchanged a nervous glance and huddled more closely together—perhaps Francesca was more exhausted than she realized? Antonio silently wondered if perhaps the second bottle of wine with dinner had been unnecessary.

The carriage continued down Ormsby Avenue, and over the sound of the horses' hooves, Francesca was enchanted by tinkling music dancing over to them across the cool evening air.

"Do you hear a piano?" she asked.

"Yes, that is Mrs. Hattie," the driver pointed to an exquisitely manicured Gothic mansion that sprawled before them. "Mrs. Hattie likes to play Chopin, mostly nocturnes. Even after her husband, Mr. James Speed, passed away, Mrs. Hattie played for guests and neighbors in her front parlor," the driver paused as he lit his pipe. "Late at night, she often plays sad classical music. Sometimes she even plays until daybreak."

"How lucky for the neighbors, to receive such beauty in the night," Antonio mused, adjusting the throw across their laps.

"Chopin does soothe a lonely heart." Francesca laid her head on Antonio's shoulder. "Nearly as well as *Nonna's* poppy petal tea." The music faded as the carriage turned onto Third Avenue. The driver informed Francesca that the more lavish homes were yet to come.

When they returned at last to their elegant room, Francesca's swollen body ached to be horizontal. Antonio pulled back the covers and helped his wife get into the bed. He opened a bottle of red wine and poured them each a glass. As she tasted her wine, Antonio again rubbed her swollen feet and ankles. He undressed her as he always had, and kissed her neck before he took her glass away. He made gentle, sweet love to his wife, and they fell asleep in each other's arms. *So, this is the Derby,* she smiled to herself, drifting away into dreams.

The next morning, they gathered their bags, and boarded the train back to Lexington. The sun shone brightly in the clear sky, and the landscape exploded with the profuse blooms of dogwood and redbud trees. Like the colorful Derby goers, Francesca thought Kentucky also wore its best springtime finery.

After settling in on the train, Antonio handed Francesca a surprise gift wrapped in dark green paper with a shiny gold ribbon. Inside, a pendant of a mare and foal hanging from a gold chain, brought a smile and many happy tears to Francesca's face. "To remember your first Derby with your handsome husband and *neonato.*"

Francesca reclined in her seat with her arms extended over her swollen abdomen. "I adore it. Thank you, *amore!*" Turning the pendant in her hands, she asked mischievously, "And what will we name our filly?"

"His name will be Matteo, after your papa," Antonio laughed.

"But what if it's a girl? Maybe Angelina after *Nonna?*" Francesca looked out the window across the fields that passed, dreaming of the baby that would come soon.

"I don't care, *Madre*. You can pick. All I care is that he – or she – is healthy," Antonio smiled as he reached for Francesca's hand and lifted it to his lips.

Chapter 13

Summer 1918

Over the next few weeks, Francesca noticed that her usually high levels of energy began to wane. Although her doctor said she was healthy and foresaw no problems, he advised her to rest in bed until it was time to deliver.

"Bed rest!" she moaned, throwing her hands in the air. "Who will cook and clean?"

"Shh, now don't worry about a thing," Maria said consolingly. "Violet and I will take care of everything. And we can call on Gracie, if need be. The children are out of school, so they can do chores, as well."

"How can I ever thank you, Maria?" Francesca held her friend's hand and kissed it.

"You can tell me how to make your *nonna's* sauce," Maria said with a smile.

"Think of something else!" Francesca laughed despite herself.

Just as Antonio left for work the next day, Violet arrived, along with Maria. Violet had left Lauretta with her grandma, and walked the few blocks to Lexington Ave. She brought Francesca a bright bouquet of pink-and-blue hydrangeas in a large glass vase. "I thought these might brighten your day," Violet beamed. "Pink for a girl, blue for a boy!"

Francesca had never felt so useless and loved at the same time. She knew her friends would take shifts cooking, cleaning, and keeping an eye on the children. *Some things were exactly the same in any land,* Francesca mused—like friends who become sisters.

"All will be well," Violet consoled. "Soon there will be another Bucci to love! You will see."

At such tender words, Francesca rolled onto her side and salty memories began pouring out, as though from an opened wound. "When Antonio and I first married, we lost our first child," she wept. "I was about four months along when I miscarried. Our excitement turned just as quickly to grief."

"Oh, I am so sorry," Maria whispered, patting Francesca's hand.

"Not to worry, my friend, it was God's will. The doctor had to remove my baby. I gasped for air over and over, shaking with delirium until unconsciousness set in. I awoke time and time again to Mamma's voice. She called me back. The medication, if you can call it that, was not enough." Francesca paused and looked down at her swollen belly.

"We buried our child in the garden at Santa Maria della Selva Church. I often took flowers to the small marker. I went into the church and kneeled before the large wooden statue of *The Lady with Child.* The loss and failure haunted me. I will never forget the child I lost." Francesca rubbed her swollen midriff, pushed back hot tears, and shut her eyes.

She continued quietly, "I felt useless as a wife… and although Antonio understood, I knew he was disappointed. He always said, 'You should have taken it easy. Next time, you will do less work around this house.' That is why I gave into this bed rest. The procedure to remove the baby kept me in bed for weeks after. I felt like a worthless lump in my new family's life. I could do nothing to contribute. They never said a word to me, but I could see the disapproval in their eyes." Francesca sat up to adjust her white cotton gown and robe, gifts from Antonio.

"I'm sure they did not really feel that way," Maria soothed. "You just had guilt in your heart, but none of it could be helped." Maria thought quietly of her own miscarried child, but now was not the time to burden her worried friend. "I believe God wants you to have this child, and we are here to help you."

"Thank you. I wish I had known you then… Shortly after my miscarriage, I learned that my *nonna* had died. *Nonna* had been such a huge part of my life, and now she was gone. I didn't even get to say goodbye." Francesca looked away from Maria and out the window at a dark, passing cloud.

"They told me she just did not wake up one morning, and that she had passed in her sleep. Full of life and so headstrong, it seemed impossible that she was gone."

With Violet's help, Francesca tried to relieve her discomfort by rolling onto her other side. "At *Nonna's* funeral, she lay in an open casket for all to see. White votive candles burned throughout the church. As she lay there in her finest dress looking so at peace, I kissed her cheek and placed her favorite locket in her hand—because she once told me that ghosts return to retrieve the items they loved the most."

"Holy Mary and Joseph!" Violet cried, pointing her index finger to her temple. "Ghosts? Your dear *nonna* was crazy!"

Francesca smiled and shook her head, "I was horrified to find out later that Mamma had removed the locket from the casket. She said, 'You must not leave anything of value in a casket because someone will come and steal it.' Papa comforted me and said that I could place the locket in another coffin, to send to heaven for *Nonna.* Her death was very difficult for Papa, who adored his mamma with all his heart. We all did."

"It is very hard to lose a loved one." Maria shook her head sadly and walked to peer out the window. "No matter how long gone, they never really leave us."

"So True! *Nonna* had lived with us my entire life. Things were just not the same without her. Papa quoted Leonardo the Florentine, who said, 'As a well-spent day brings happy sleep, so life well-used brings happy death.' I think he was looking for a way to banish his own sadness."

Her friends murmured understanding and Francesca continued, "It seems that the entire year was just lost to me. Antonio and I really needed something good to happen. It wasn't too long before I found out that I was pregnant again. My pregnancy blessed my entire family; we needed life. I skipped like a girl the day I found out. It was an easy pregnancy – too easy – and that concerned me. I thought one had to lose one's meal to signify a healthy baby! Of course, I was wrong."

Francesca reached to pull out a pink hydrangea from the vase on her bedside table. After she inhaled its light fragrance, she continued, "On a beautiful spring morning in 1909, Rosalinda Carmela Bucci was born. I named her after Mamma and chose to use Carmela as a middle name. Carmela means garden, and, in my eyes, she was as beautiful as a rose garden. I was twenty years old, and Antonio brought in a wonderful midwife to help with the delivery."

Francesca laughed, "Mamma made me a medicinal tea from the inner bark of the alder tree to ease my pain during childbirth. I think it worked because it tasted so awful, and I forgot how bad the pain was!" Francesca wrinkled her nose in disgust. "I later found out this wood was also used by the Dutch to make shoes." Francesca laughed weakly and took a drink of her water. "Mamma must've learned that concoction from *Nonna,* God rest her soul." Violet and Maria laughed, imagining the brew of shoes.

"Maria, you're Italian—so you understand that sons are desired for labor and strength. I was secretly worried that Antonio might be disappointed that I had produced a daughter. When I saw his eyes light up with joy as he held our Rosa, I knew he did not care. Mamma said to me, '*Tempo, marito e figli vengono come li pigli*: Weather, husbands, and sons come as you take them.'"

Maria stood up to adjust Francesca's pillow. "Yes, I understand very well! After the birth of Martino, our house was full of friends and family who stopped by and brought food for us and presents for our newborn. Martino was so beautiful that my mamma filled us with her superstitious traditions. She said, 'You must immediately make a 'horn' with your pinkie and index fingers to ward off evil spirits around the baby.'" Maria demonstrated with her right hand.

Francesca chuckled. "My mamma also placed her thumb between her forefinger and middle finger and made a fist to defend Rosa from dirty looks from people who might have wished to toss an evil spell her way."

Violet said, "Dear Lord in heaven! Italians sure have crazy superstitions!"

After adjusting her body once more, Francesca reminisced, "After I had Rosa, I was happy, and my life was full again. Just when I thought life had turned to sorrow, change came, like spring following winter. You could say my little rose bloomed exactly when I needed her the most!"

"Why didn't you come to America with Antonio?" Violet asked.

"Well, everyone in the village was saying that the only way to avoid hardship or an early grave was to move to the Americas. We knew the streets were not paved with gold here, as reported earlier, but it was still a dream for many.

"'Francesca, this is what smart men are doing,' Antonio had said to me so often then. 'When I have saved enough money, I will return, or I will send for you.' Antonio was fortunate because his papa had trained him to be a *ragionere,* an accountant, like himself. '*Tale padre, tale figlio:* Like father, like son.' Men who are good with money are needed wherever there is money. And compared to Castel Frentano, America seems to be made of it." Francesca's eyelids began to grow heavy, so her company gathered their shawls and quietly left her side. Bleary from pregnancy and tedious bed rest, her eyes fluttered closed, and her thoughts drifted as though on an unstoppable tide back to the old country.

"Francesca." Antonio had cajoled, "It is becoming harder for me to pay the taxes. Even though we have work now, all the recent disasters have weakened Italian soil, making it difficult to grow grapes and olives. There are too many mouths to feed here, and not enough for all. Our townspeople, as well as all of Italy, have fallen on hard times. The banks will soon have no use for me." Antonio had turned Francesca's face to look at his. "Americans make eight to nine times as much as we do. We have to be practical. We have a family to raise. I must leave for America." He stroked her hair away from her neck and kissed her tenderly.

Antonio's favorite uncle, Salvatore Bucci, had often written to encourage Antonio to join him in America. Letter after letter arrived, and Antonio could no longer turn the temptation away. He wanted a better life for his family, and understood the odds were against them in Italy. *Zio's* glowing letters described an exciting place called Lexington, a land that was lush and green—a paradise people called the 'Athens of the West.' Antonio was convinced that he had to travel first, as most men did, to secure a safe place for his family to later follow.

Antonio figured that even if he did not find a permanent career in America, he would still return home with fat wads of cash, more than he would ever see in Italy. Francesca knew better than to express how opposed she felt. As a dutiful wife, she did what was expected and appeased his decision. Inside, however, she keened and grieved as though widowed.

Ever confident, Antonio seemed assured that Lexington was to be their home. Although many before him had failed and returned to Italy in shame and defeat, Antonio knew he was a skilled and determined worker, and this adventure called out for him. America offered a life free of crushing worry, and he had every intention to pursue the dream. Antonio's absence was to be just long enough to get a job, a home, and enough money to send for *la famiglia.* Who could have known that it would take six long years?

Reluctantly, Francesca swallowed every one of her scalding misgivings, and it was settled. Antonio left Castel Frentano and boarded a tall ship to America. Francesca did not have the heart to tell him she was pregnant again. She knew he'd postpone his trip, and she knew he was more than ready to seek their fortune. After a few more months, she mailed a letter with the news. This for sure would encourage him in the new land, especially if he had a son.

Antonio had every detail arranged in America, and *Zio* Salvatore was prepared for his arrival. A sharp accountant with a good head for numbers was very much needed where he worked at a horse racetrack.

The evening before Antonio left, Francesca gave him a silver Saint Christopher's medal on a chain to protect him as he traveled. They made love, and both knew it would be a long time before they would touch each other again. He held her in his arms while Francesca cried herself to sleep.

Antonio traveled lightly, as most did. After three hours by train to the Port of Naples, there was no turning back; he boarded the *S.S. Liguria* to America in the fall of 1909. Antonio's pack contained a few cotton shirts, one neckerchief, three pairs of underwear, one pint of olive oil, a dozen biscuits, and a few pears. He carried a small wad of bills buttoned inside his shirt.

Francesca fought tears when she saw off her love and the father of her child. All she could say was, "*Arrivederci, amore mio,*" before he held her face with both hands and kissed her over and over. Francesca had cried then. He picked up Rosa, who was just a toddler, took a long look at her, held her close for a minute, memorizing her scent before handing her back. Before Francesca could touch his face one last time, he was swept into a noisy river of migrants carrying an assortment of knapsacks, each filled with the same small necessities and hopeful dreams as Antonio. The New World awaited.

*There is no room in this country
for hyphenated Americanism.
There is no such thing
as a hyphenated American
who is a good American."*

— Theodore Roosevelt, 1915

Chapter 14

Castel Frentano, Italy 1909

While Antonio was on the other side of the ocean, Francesca filled many mornings at the market after walking with Rosa to her *nonna's* house, where Rosa played happily until Francesca returned. Rosa adored her *nonna* and asked to see her every day. If Francesca's papa was not at the vineyard, he usually joined her on visits to the market.

Francesca's calico cat, Sugo, followed her to market every day, and when they got close to the fish market, Sugo vanished. He'd rejoin her for the walk home with wet whiskers and a little swagger.

Just past a colorful banner of laundry drying in the earthy breeze, Francesca first visited the bakery where her friend Sofia Filla worked alongside her family. The warm smell of fresh *focaccia* and *grissini* drew Francesca in for a sample. Sofia always waited on her and the two exchanged a little news and jokes only they understood, just as they had as girls.

Her next stop was the small delicatessen owned by Luca Fusco, whose son, Vito, was a friend of Antonio's. After she made the difficult selection from the assortment of cured *bresaola, pancetta, mortadella, prosciutto,* and *salami* that hung from the ceiling, Mr. Fusco kindly inquired about Antonio and his journey. After a few months, the inquiries became fewer and fewer. Since many men in the village had also left for America and personal fortune, Antonio's absence was soon accepted by all—except Francesca.

The life of the *villagio* pulsed in the open-air market. With thoughts of meals to come, shoppers squeezed through the crowd with baskets and jugs. *Buon giorno, ciao, and grazie* echoed through the air. Francesca's papa sometimes yelled at people to get out of his way. Most of the villagers knew his impatience and some stood in his path just to hear him swear.

Soon they came to the Vaccaro Brothers' produce market. Woven baskets bulged with mounds of bright green peas, yellow and red peppers, dimpled oranges, prickly green and purple artichokes, bundles of freshly picked asparagus spears, and Francesca's favorite—juicy, red strawberries.

The Vaccaro brothers dreaded *Signore* Viviano's visits because not only was he impatient, he was quite particular. He examined each and every fruit and vegetable. He poked and smelled. He selected the glossiest eggplants, the ones that had tight, firm purple skin plumped with water. He pressed his thumb into the skin to see if it rebounded quickly. If the imprint lingered, he moved on to the next eggplant. The Vaccaros practically knew *Signore* Viviano's thumbprint.

Next, he inspected the red *pomodori* for the daily sauce, then the onions, peppers, and finally, the herbs. Like everyone, the Vivianos grew most of their herbs in a kitchen garden, but Francesca's papa had to have fresh basil, because most of the time his homegrown basil was ravaged by red squirrels—who tormented Papa surely as much as Papa tormented the Vaccaro brothers.

"You know, garlic is sweeter in the spring," he instructed each time, as if Francesca did not remember. "See how it shrivels? This one is too old!" he said it so loudly, everyone could hear his complaint. "*Porcini* mushrooms are *magnifico* in spring and fall, Francesca," he counseled for the hundredth time.

The final stop of the morning was the fish market. *Signore* Viviano usually bought the special catch of the day, not only because it was the cheapest, but because it was also the freshest. Other choices were: clams, tuna, calamari, lobster, eel, crabs, and shrimp—bounty netted and delivered to Castel Frentano straight from the sea.

The older men in the village lined up in chairs outside the shops, and smoked. They talked about politics, sports, and always, America. Some played card games such as *Scopa* and *Scartino*. Francesca usually lost her papa there in the chatter, and she walked home with Sugo winding satisfied circles around her ankles.

Some days the children stayed with *Zia* Bianca or *Zia* Adriana, and Francesca's mamma joined them on walks to the market. They visited the *piazza* in the center of the town where deals of all kinds were made—barter, buy, or sell. A canvas awning protected the vendors' stands from sun and rain. Baskets, spices, truffle oil, cheeses, and handicrafts of all kinds were available on the streets. Some lined up under shade trees to peddle their wares, noisily calling out to passersby.

Regular trips to the village helped keep Francesca's mind off Antonio. Most days, she also stopped at Santa Maria della Selva Church, so reassuring with its familiar cathedral ceilings, ornate fixtures, and a chiseled limestone façade perfectly recreating the angels in heaven.

In this most holy place, Francesca had taken her first Communion, married Antonio, and christened Rosa. Never to be forgotten, their stillborn child was buried there in the small cemetery shaded by white blooming dogwoods. Francesca often stopped by to say a prayer and place a sprig of rosemary for remembrance across the marker. She saw small bundles of herbs and flowers, and knew that her mamma and *nonna* had also visited.

Thinking of the unfamiliar new world troubled Francesca. She loved Castel Frentano, with its small, sweet, sun-baked moments, its warm familiarity, and the many reassuring traditions they all shared. She didn't need more than this. Each passing season has its own beauty, whether it was the fuchsia azaleas in the spring and blazing pink bougainvillea climbing every trellis and wall, or the snow-capped mountains glinting with a million stacked crystals in the winter. Francesca hoped that this place called Kentucky was half as beautiful, although she doubted anything could possibly be as lovely as this place, home.

Francesca often finished her mornings around the kitchen table with her mamma, sisters, and a cup of chamomile tea. Her mamma prepared the calming elixir for Francesca every morning. She knew well her daughter's wordless worries. Francesca took her time to drink her tea, chatting with her sisters. She dreaded returning to the solemn life with the Buccis, where she was now expected to live and labor.

The Bucci garden, in contrast, was unexpectedly exuberant and always brought a smile to her face. She knew it by heart: pale pink rugosas with a background of pear tree *espaliers*, arranged in perfect even columns and rows, like one of *Signore* Bucci's balance sheets filled with obsessively considered figures. The terrace was lined with pale terra cotta pots filled with sweet, fragrant jasmine alongside trimmed boxwood and s*antolina* in neat quadrants. Each square was full of parsley, basil, and oregano. Antonio's mamma separated the herbs and reminded Francesca to deadhead them. "If left to bloom, the flavor loses its *potenza,*" she instructed. "I only need the fresh foliage."

Besides tending to her children, Francesca's daily chores included hanging clean laundry to bake in the hot sun. She also cooked, cleaned, and tended to the many chickens that ran freely around the yard. Every morning after market and tea, she gathered eggs in her apron from the hen house and cautiously sneaked past the rust-colored rooster whom she called *il demone.* The day that the rooster came after her threatening murder was the last time Francesca gathered eggs.

"You dropped them all!" *Signore* Bucci grumbled and re-assigned the task to Antonio's younger brother.

With Antonio so far away, Rosa provided Francesca's greatest comfort and joy. Like Papa, Rosa was born under the sign of twin peacocks—smart, very well behaved, some days quiet, some days animated. In the evening, after Rosa had fallen asleep, Francesca stayed up to read books by Dante Alighieri, Leopardi, and Manzoni. These books, borrowed from the small library in the village and read by candlelight, captivated Francesca, and gave her needed hours of escape into other realities where she enjoyed varied company and suffered no pangs of loneliness.

Some evenings she just walked, serenaded by a chorus of crickets and perfumed by night-blooming jasmine. She looked up at the stars and asked God if she would ever see Antonio again. She often wondered if Antonio watched the stars, thinking of her. The celestial show overhead might be the same, but her love was half a world away. He might as well be on the moon.

Francesca's first letter from Antonio arrived months after his departure, and she could only stare in stupefaction at his careful handwriting on the envelope. She tore off her apron and raced with the letter out to a bench under the pergola. She started to rip it open, then hesitated, willing her breath to calm, and her heart to stop trying to pound its way out of her chest.

Dearest Francesca,   November 15, 1909

I hope this letter finds you and little Rosa well, amore mia. I think of you every day, especially as the holidays near. I know how much you love Christmas, and I wish we could be together.

My seventeen-dollar ticket to America was supposed to include a cot. However, there were only a few hundred cots for over 1,000 passengers! I found a spot on the iron floor between a few barrels of mackerel near the kitchen, and I made a friend. His name is Vincent Marcello. We shared the floor between the barrels. Vincent is a quiet but direct man who has taken to my humor. Vincent is from San Marino just north of us on the coast. He has family in New York City. He said he knows a man in New York who will help me find a job until I head to Kentucky.

I told him I am an accountant, and that I was headed to Lexington to work with Zio Salvatore as a bookkeeper at the harness racetrack. He said he had heard that

Kentucky was the hot spot for horse racing. He agreed there had to be a huge demand for money management since the 'Sport of Kings' brought in lots of cash, rapidly exchanged by many hands.

We discussed how people wager on standardbred horses who race along a red clay track, pulling two-wheeled sulkies.

Vincent said it all sounded very exciting, and promised he would come to Lexington someday and look me up. It has been helpful to have a friend on the ship to watch out for each other. Those who travel alone must sleep with one eye open to safeguard their belongings. Si salvi chi puo: Every man for himself. In exchange for my loyalty, Vincent shared with me his bologna sausage that he stored in the top of his socks, and I shared the pears you packed for me. Being a determined, confident man from the same region, he also knew the saying... 'There is no way to change the mind of a man from Abruzzo.' I will mail this from dry land, and write again very soon.

I will make sure your voyage is more favorable than this!

Take care, dearest Francesca, and kiss our Rosa for me.

Con amore,
Antonio

While she breathed with relief to hear from Antonio, the conditions he described sounded like any young mother's idea of hell. How could she endure that with two small children?

But still, she wondered: Where was Antonio on any given day? Was he okay? Was he thinking of her? Five long months passed before the next letter arrived. Once again, she carried the letter out to the garden and sat on a secluded bench, sniffing the envelope and hoping for any trace of his scent.

Dearest Francesca,   *April 23, 1910*

I hope you and Rosa are well, amore mia. Please give her many hugs from Papa and let her know how much I miss her. I often try to imagine your beautiful face, and hers, so much like your own. How quickly she must be growing!

Processing at Ellis Island is an experience I wish to prepare you for. Three hours! Luckily, Vincent had a sponsor, an apparently powerful man. I did not ask any questions, and gratefully accepted their help.

In New York, there is an Italian club called The Société Unione e Fratellanza Italiana already in place. Thank God, Italians are loyal to their own.

We headed to the society first to eat and meet Vincent's connection. Until the job in Kentucky is ready, I will stay in New York. Vincent says if I don't let his sponsor help us find decent work, I may have to be a sewer cleaner, shoe shiner, or any number of equally dirty jobs.

To save on money, I have rented a cheap apartment for ten dollars a month. It is more like a dark, windowless room. The buildings are so tall here that the sun cannot reach me. I think my neighbors are running small factories in their living rooms just to make ends meet. The children are barely old enough to sew on buttons, but they all seem to work. I see many items, such as hats, corsets, and shoes, emerging from these secret shops. Some apartments have as many as a dozen family members living in them. I worry that the crowded conditions are unhealthy. But I won't be here long.

I must also warn you of the bigotry in America. Vincent says it is because they think I am Spanish, with my dark skin.

Name-calling does not bother me, Francesca, and you will have to ignore it, as well. Communication is very difficult. I will soon learn to speak English. Vincent's sponsor, Riccardo D'Angelo, found a part-time job for me where I keep books for Il Progresso Italo-Americano newspaper. I will write again soon, amore mia, all my love to you and our Rosa, and warm regards to Mamma and Papa, Bianca and Adriana. I miss you all, but especially the lovely light of my life.

Con amore,
Antonio

This letter was special because it came with a return address. Francesca could finally mail the stack of letters she had written. Antonio had also sent a small amount of money, and asked for her to share it with her mamma and papa. Francesca secured the letters and the money in a glazed earthenware majolica container that they had received as a wedding present. The design was gallo, with a strutting rooster on the side, known to be a symbol of good luck. Hand painted by an uncle on Francesca's mamma's side, the container was painted in brilliant colors of cobalt, sunflower, forest green, and fiery orange. This beautiful piece of enameled pottery would be the only treasure Francesca carried with her to America—and likewise the only rooster she ever wanted anywhere near her.

It was May 1, 1910, when Francesca gave birth to Raffaele. He was born six months after Antonio left for America. She named him after Antonio's papa, as was expected for the firstborn male. By tradition, the first son would follow in his father's footsteps and learn his trade. She and her love were now blessed with a son to carry the family name and heritage.

Word from Antonio could never come soon enough. Francesca lived for the reassurance of his existence—and his love. Anniversaries and holidays passed without his smile, and Francesca began to surrender to the dark feeling of abandonment. One afternoon in the winter of 1911, the third letter arrived.

Dearest Francesca, *January 3, 1911*

Cara, sorry it has been so long. A son! How magnifico, Madre! Please know how happy this makes me, and I will work harder than ever to bring my famiglia here. Life has been a true struggle for me in New York. I hope the little bit of money enclosed will help the burden at home. I miss everyone terribly. Sometimes I wonder why I am here, so far away from my family and everything I cherish. But I am determined to press on and capture the dream of a good life for us. I can't wait to buy you and Rosa pretty dresses, and hold our son.

I heard from Zio Salvatore. My job is finally ready in Lexington, Kentucky. I will leave New York in two weeks. By the time you get this letter, I plan to be at work for the famed racetrack. Zio says the horse industry is booming. He is confident that I will settle in and be able to send for you and the children right away. Here is a poem written by Josiah Espy in 1806 that I hope encourages you.

But Lexington will ever be,
The loveliest and the Best;
A paradise thou'rt still to me,
Sweet Athens of the West.

Zio Salvatore says Lexington is at the heart of the Bluegrass state. Many well-to-do families have settled in the small, picturesque city surrounded, he says, by rolling hills of horse country. He says the city is full of tall, elegant buildings that reveal the wealth of the city. Besides the horses and manufacturing, they grow corn, rye, and hemp—and they have the largest tobacco market in the world!

Kentucky is also known for producing fine corn whiskey—not the whiskey from barley or rye that your papa drinks. I heard that some Kentuckians make their own brew late at night by the light of the moon. Vincent says this activity is illegal. They say if you get a toxic batch you could find yourself blind, which explains why they call it white lightning. Remember Papa's batch of grappa that could curl the toes?

I have learned a lot of English so far, and when I settle in Lexington, I plan to enroll in night school. The more English I learn, the better. I will try to write again soon. I miss you and Rosa, and I can't wait to hold our son. If he is as beautiful as his mamma and sister, then we are very blessed. Please hug the children for their ever-loving papa. I hold you every night in my dreams, Francesca.

Con amore,
Antonio

What is this war?
It is mud, trenches, blood, rats, lice, bombs, pain,
barbed wire, decaying flesh, gas, death, rain, cats,
tears, bullets, fear
and a loss of faith in all that we once believed in.

— Otto Dix
Corpse caught up in barbed wire (Flanders)

Chapter 15

Italy, 1914

1914 was a difficult year for all of Europe. Antonio had been gone for four years, and Francesca still yearned for him to return to Italy, or send for her and the children. The letters came farther and farther apart, and, when they did arrive, her urgency to open them was gone.

On August fourth, war broke out.

"What has happened, Papa?" Francesca asked.

"An Austrian archduke and his wife who were about to take the throne were assassinated in Sarajevo, and many are calling for retribution," *Signore* Viviano answered.

"Witnesses claim his last words to his wife were, 'Sophie, Sophie, do not die. Stay alive for the children,'" Francesca's mamma added sadly. Her parents exchanged a worried look.

As things unfolded, Austria-Hungary blamed Serbia and declared war. Russia joined Serbia, and the other Central Powers declared war on Russia. The Germans also went after France. The British, who vowed to help the

French, declared war on Germany. It was a continental melee.

Within sixteen days of the start of the war, Pope Pius X died. Even while war waged in countries that surrounded them, the curious and the faithful – including Francesca and her sisters – made the pilgrimage to Rome to pay their final respects to the pope. *Signore* Viviano's brother, *Zio* Armando, lived in Rome, and they had an open invitation to stay there. They couldn't afford a hotel, and, in any event, the mass of journeying mourners had taken all the rooms.

Zio Armando was a wonderful chaperone and enjoyed seeing his brother's daughters. Francesca's mamma sent money with the girls she had saved from selling *Nonna's* herbal ointments, elixirs and rubs. She said she would join them on the journey if she was younger and in better health.

For a total of nine days of *novendial*, before the announcement of the new pope, the faithful prayed for the soul of the pope and mourned. Although the pilgrimage was a time of mourning and reflection, the sisters could not help but enjoy the beauty of Rome.

They spent the days walking the ancient cobblestoned alleys, pointing to the Romanesque and Baroque carvings on the building façades, as well as admiring the large, marble fluted pillars topped with Corinthian trim. The Eternal City was an endlessly unfolding fossil of civilization, revealed layer by layer. Rome told its long story in fountains, monuments, and even mosaic floors. The Romans don't destroy, it is said, they bury.

Along with throngs of mourners pouring into the city, the three sisters and *Zio* Armando converged on the Piazza Navona to look up at the four tritons blowing into shells, spewing endless streams of water. The girls hooked arms as they walked as one, so as to not get separated. They admired the cool green-and-white marble monuments, alabaster statues, and the details of every tiled mosaic. They drank rich *caffe con panna* with their *zio,* and marveled at Neptune, god of the sea, as he stood watch over the thousands of reverent sojourners.

Bianca ventured, "See how the horse to Neptune's right is placid and the horse to his left is raging and wild? I read that this symbolizes the unpredictable moods of the sea—how true!"

They walked farther along the narrow streets and peered up at the elliptical amphitheater, a centuries-old relic still standing four stories high. They imagined echoes of the screaming crowds in the Colosseum, long gone now, throbbing with blood lust to witness fight-to-the-death duels between exotic animals or warring gladiators.

In the center of the Flavian Amphitheater, Bianca recited a scene from *Romeo and Juliet.* In her best dramatic voice, Bianca spoke up to an imaginary balcony:

"O Romeo, Romeo! Wherefore art thou Romeo?
Deny thy father and refuse thy name;

> *Or, if thou wilt not, be but sworn my love,*
> *And I'll no longer be a Capulet."*

As Bianca took her bows, her sisters applauded and fell to the ground laughing on the cool, pale stones.

"Oh, how I will miss you two when I leave for America," Francesca said with a sigh.

"Nonsense, you will never leave. Antonio has been gone too long!" Bianca protested.

"I agree, *sorella*," Adriana added. "We will never be apart."

"Well, until that day comes, let's have fun!" Francesca sat up, hoping to lighten the mood.

The sisters checked on *Zio,* who had found a bench for napping, and then continued their ambling. Soon, they approached the Arch of Constantine and stopped to soak in its ornate glory, a triumph of engineering and art. As the crowd began to thin and the air cooled, they worried they had perhaps ventured too far. Turning around, they found *Zio* smoking a cigar, and took his hand to head back.

As they walked toward the Vatican, *Zio* Armando pointed toward a small group of people peeking through a keyhole. Out of curiosity, they hung back, waiting for an opportunity to approach the mysterious metal doorway. In turn, each of them peered through the small hole. One by one, they looked, and then, in astonishment, looked again.

Through the keyhole, as if by magic, they saw a tunnel made of immaculately pruned evergreen shrubs. Just beyond the natural arch was the gleaming dome of Saint Peter's Basilica in the distance, framed by the secret view of absolute perfection. Francesca, her sisters, and *Zio* Armando murmured their amazement and wished for just a moment to venture through this portal of wonder. They reluctantly left Aventine Hill and crossed the Tiber River by way of a lovely stone bridge leading them back into Vatican City.

"Remember the story Papa told us about the ritual for the pope?" asked Adriana. "He said that many years ago, the cardinal actually struck the head of the dead pope lightly three times with a silver mallet. Each time the cardinal struck the pope, he called out to the pope by his birth name. After no response, the death was announced, and the Fisherman's Ring and Papal Seals were broken." After a short pause Adriana asked, "Do you think they bonked Pope Pius X with a mallet?"

"I don't know," answered Bianca, somewhat hesitantly. "Much of papal life is mysterious, just as God is mysterious."

Arm in arm, with *Zio* trailing protectively behind, they made their way to Saint Peter's Basilica, where the pope was laid out in a crimson vestment to receive public mourners. The basilica, guarded by Swiss security at all entrances, featured an impressive dome—designed by the maestro, Michelangelo. When their time came to view the pope, they noticed his face was covered with a white silk veil. At his feet, they saw a silk bag that was said to hold medals of silver and bronze that the pope had earned during his papal term.

"Papa says since this pope was on the plump side, we must hope for a thin pope to be elected," Bianca whispered to her sisters.

"Hush! That is ridiculous. Weight has nothing to do with how a pope runs the Church!" replied Adriana, glancing around to see if any of the devout nearby had heard and took offense. After they had genuflected before Pope Pius X, they left the basilica and returned outside to join the mass of mourners.

The Sistine Chapel was open to visitors until election day, so they all agreed they must see more of the works of Michelangelo. As a matter of respect, no sounds were permitted in the Sistine Chapel, where many were inspired by the great religious frescoes painted by the Italian master. In the worshipful quiet, Francesca believed God could hear her prayers for her family to be reunited.

The beautiful marble floors and mosaics beneath their feet had been removed from pagan shrines by order of the pope, and reconfigured for this place of proper worship.

The Creation of Adam fresco in the center of the ceiling depicts God's introduction of man to woman to create life. Francesca found it quite extraordinary how God held tight to a woman before he offered her as a gift to man. Did Antonio still believe their union was a sacrament, ordained by the Creator? She offered up another prayer that this was so.

Further along, a different scene revealed Michelangelo's insistence that he no longer wished to paint. The pope had said to him, "Paint or I will destroy all of Florence!" In defiance, Michelangelo painted himself exposing his backside to God. Generations of young girls could be forgiven for their surprised giggles on the way out of the Chapel.

The day before the sisters were to leave for home, the cardinals voted on the successor pope. During the papal election in the Sistine Chapel, the waiting crowd looked anxiously toward the Vatican chimney. After the votes were cast, the ballot slips were burned and smoke rose from the chimney. If the smoke was black, no pope had yet been selected. When the white smoke at last appeared, the crowd reverently yelled, "*Bianca! Bianca!*" and a new pontiff took the reins.

Church bells rang across Rome and across the world to signal to all that the Catholic Church had a divine, new pontiff, Giacomo della Chiesa, Pope Benedict XV.

To Francesca's relief, Italy had stayed neutral in the war, allied with both Germany and Austria–Hungary. The Italians could not agree where to put their loyalties nor their trust. But in his letters, Antonio worriedly described how Italians began to face more and more discrimination in America.

Just a short year later, Victor Emmanuel III, King of Italy, had no choice but to intervene. The Italians had joined the only side that mattered, the Americans.

Italian General Luigi Cadorna advanced his army and said, "Remember that here we defend the soil of our country and the honour of our army. These positions are to be defended to the death!" Italian soldiers invaded Austria-Hungary and fought on two fronts. They fought at the Isonzo River to the east, and invaded Austria to the north, with significant casualties on both sides.

Although Italy was ill-equipped for war, they fought anyway. Italy feared that if it did not enter the war, the war would inevitably come to them. Even though the fight was at the northern border, it was much too close to home for Francesca. Even in the remote hillsides, news of tragedies and death came often. Across Italy, mothers mourned.

Chapter 16

America, June 18, 1918

On a humid afternoon in June, with much needed help from Antonio and Maria, a very pregnant Francesca struggled up the street to deliver their child. Most of the mothers on Lexington Avenue had *Nonna* Izolla to thank as she had served as midwife for them, as well. Francesca thought *Nonna* Izolla surely lived much closer as she waddled toward her house at the end of Lexington Avenue.

Izolla greeted them at the door warmly, saying, "This way, *Madre*, I am ready to meet that *bambino*." Antonio nodded to Izolla, kissed his wife and took off up the street with Louis Ginocchio, who had a cache of cigars.

In a back spare bedroom, Izolla and Maria did what was necessary to deliver the child. "You did well, *Madre!*" Izolla soothed, presenting a wet and wailing bundle to the new mother. Francesca cried tears of joy and exhaustion as she counted baby Matteo's ten little toes and ten little fingers. He was perfect. Mother and child remained at *Nonna* Izolla's that night, and overjoyed neighbors brought food and gifts to 246 Lexington Avenue and watched over Francesca's children, who were more than eager for news of the baby.

One week later, Antonio and Francesca asked their closest friends, Louis and Maria, to be Matteo's godparents, and they were proud to consent. Maria offered an embroidered linen gown they had brought with them from Italy, and little Matteo looked exactly like a little cherub, dressed in white. Of course, he cried through the entire service, which all believed to be predestined for good luck and a happy life.

After the Christening, their friends came to the house for a celebration. Francesca served Veal Marsala with extra wide noodles and roasted garlic fingerling potatoes, and a buffet table stood laden with other steaming dishes brought by friends.

Matteo was a good-natured and content baby, and like every home with a new little one, life at the Buccis became much fuller.

A fourth child was comparatively easy, Francesca thought as three siblings hovered over the baby, rotating who fed, bathed, and rocked Matteo.

"Lordy, Francesca, Matteo won't hit the floor till he is ten years old," Gracie had observed as she cleaned. "This child will be so spoiled, he won't be good for nothing!"

Smiling, Francesca said in English, "Gracie, love is good for the soul and there is never too much!"

Maria stopped by to invite Antonio and Francesca out to a new restaurant, Giovanni's, which had just opened on the corner of Maxwell and Mill Street, only a short walk from Lexington Avenue.

"Francesca, you go ahead, and I'll stay with the children," Gracie offered. "You need a night out, and my babies are all grown. Maybe these young people will finally even let me hold baby Matteo. Now, run along and get ready. Antonio will be home directly."

When Antonio arrived home from work, he was delighted by the invitation to dine out at Giovanni's. He and Francesca had not been out since their trip to the Derby, and he was sure she needed a break. Louis and Maria showed up right on schedule, and the foursome strolled down to the *ristorante*. It had been a hot, humid day, but in the late afternoon, the air had cooled and fragrant scents of the old country reached them from a block away.

"Mmm. Smells delicious! Giovanni Bertolini just opened last night and this is his first Friday night. I am sure he will be quite busy," Louis said.

"It is so nice to have a restaurant so close to home!" Maria added. "This may become a habit," she added with a smile, hooking her arm through Francesca's.

Inside Giovanni's, the tables were covered with red-checked tablecloths, and the walls were slathered with pale ochre stucco. Framed black-and-white family photos adorned the walls along with large decorative platters and oil paintings of vineyards and olive groves. Sconces with lit candles and clay pots of fresh herbs filling every nook completed the homey ambiance.

A young Italian man approached them. *"Ciao, welcome to Giovanni's. Right this way, per favore*—I have a table for four next to the window."

Empty Chianti bottles had been placed on the tables, and each held green, white, and red carnations symbolizing the colors of Italy. With so many familiar sights and scents filling the cozy cafe, Francesca suddenly felt as if Italy was not an ocean away.

Louis ordered a bottle of red wine, and after the waiter offered a taste to him for approval, he poured three more glasses. "*Salute*! Giovanni Bertolini!" they toasted.

"This is a very good wine," Louis began. "I hear a vintner has created a vineyard just south of town, growing over thirty varieties of grapes. Your papa would approve, Francesca!"

"Speaking of wine, our own vines are thriving this year!" Maria said. "Should have several bottles of table wine first of September. I hope you will come over and help us enjoy them!"

Just then, Giovanni came over to introduce himself. *"Ciao, paesanos,"* he said in perfect Italian, "I am honored to have your company tonight! Please let me know if you need anything."

The couples introduced themselves, and Antonio inquired, "May I ask what you know about the vineyard here in Fayette County?"

"You mean, *used* to be here. A Swiss man, John James Dufour, was unsuccessful here for various reasons, and sadly, he moved his operation north to Indiana." Giovanni shook his head. "I, as well as many others, were disappointed it did not work out. Maybe someone else will take up the task."

The young waiter brought over a basket of fragrant, crusty bread and refilled wine and water glasses. He took their order and left them to chat.

Francesca spotted an American woman who swirled her pasta with a fork and a large spoon. "Antonio, does she know something I don't?" Francesca whispered. "I have never eaten pasta with a spoon!"

They watched in awe and wonder. Maybe this was the American way?

"She does not know that the Romans invented the fork in the fourth century," Maria laughed as she patted Louis's paunch. "Italians are the masters of the fork."

After a while, Louis asked Antonio, "Have you heard about this 'three-day flu'?"

Antonio nodded grimly as he swallowed a mouthful of bread.

"It sounds dreadful," Maria said, dipping a pinch of bread into a shallow bowl of olive oil and fresh Italian herbs.

The waiter returned with another bottle of wine that Giovanni had generously offered as a thank-you for the support of his new *ristorante*.

"Please tell Giovanni *grazie mille* from the Bucci and Ginocchio table," Antonio said to the waiter.

They returned to conversation while Louis topped off the wine glasses and said, "I read that over one hundred cases of the flu were reported at a military base in Kansas. They fear that the soldiers brought it home with them from Europe."

As plates of food arrived, the friends forgot all about war and illness. They indulged in caprese salads and scrumptious arancini balls filled with meat sauce and peas. They ordered Giovanni's specials of *saltimbocca alla Romana* and gnocchi with tomatoes, melted mozzarella and aromatic basil. They drank more wine and passed around the bread, which everyone agreed tasted like home.

After they had traded and tasted each other's dishes, they were all enthused that this was their new spot. "And no dishes to clean!" laughed Maria, clapping her hands.

Giovanni returned to the table and offered each of his new patrons one of his *nonna's* chocolate drizzled cannoli. Francesca smiled warmly. "You have given us a night in Venice, *Signore* Bertolini, *grazie*."

Loosened by the wine, and buoyed by sweetly refreshed memories of *Italia*, the couples walked home in companionable silence to Lexington Avenue.

Chapter 17

Summer 1918

The following day, Maria invited the children over to play with Alessandra. Francesca joined them, and they picnicked in Ginocchio's backyard. Orange trumpet vines crept along the side yard fence, as white and yellow butterflies drifted like fairies around the upturned flowers. Maria's grape vines were coming along; the clusters of small, green fruit would soon be ripening to plump aromatic purple.

Ella, Rosa, and Alessandra played with baby Matteo on a quilt, while Raffaele gathered specimens for a very important bug collection. Maria's oldest son, Martino, admired Raffaele's newest acquisitions, and then took off down the street to do chores for a few of the neighbors.

Soon after Matteo fell asleep in Ella's arms, she laid him down beside Francesca on the quilt. The children heard a game of kick the can beginning in the street and ran off to play. Francesca reclined in the sunshine with a small, private smile, remembering when she and Antonio had run off to Venice, for their belated *luna di miele,* as carefree as children themselves.

Antonio's *Zia* Florella, his mamma's youngest sister, had sent them train tickets to Venice as a belated wedding present. *Zia* had written to say the newlyweds could have her apartment to themselves, as she was traveling to Milan to care for her cousin who was in poor health. "Now will be a perfect time to visit Venice," she wrote. "It is the city made for love. I have filled the kitchen with goodies."

Antonio and Francesca, just as love drunk as they had been on their wedding day, traveled by train to Venezia Santa Lucia train station, and stayed for three rapturous days.

Zia's apartment was on the fourth floor of a lovely pale, yellow and white washed stone building overlooking the Grand Canal just across from the Rialto Bridge that connects San Marco and San Polo. It was more serene and romantic than anything that Francesca had ever seen.

It was the first weekend in September, Francesca recalled dreamily, just in time for the great regatta that took place in the canal, a waterborne flotilla celebrating the proud history of the Republic of Venice. A cortege of historical vessels preceded the Regata Storica, and everyone in attendance wore grand costumes. From any angle, the internationally renowned event was a sensory spectacle of whirling, thrilling sounds, scents, and colors. Francesca, of course, noted every stitch and embellishment on the lavish finery. Antonio teased her for her wide eyes.

Hand in hand, they toured a new modern art gallery called Ca'Pesaro and another museum called the Ca'd'Oro, full of works by the Old Masters as well as modern-day creators. Francesca loved Titian and Bellini's use of deep, rich colors and nuanced plays on light. She wondered if she could create them with layered velvet and silk.

The honeymooners had few extra liras, but they did stop to gaze at luxurious wares in a few tantalizing shops. They ate and drank away the waning moments of the day beneath a bright umbrella at the Piazza San Marco.

As evening began to set in, they headed back to the apartment, which had an unobstructed view of the stunning Saint Mark's 15th century clocktower. Venice's watery maze of navigable canals left them speechless—so different from the furrowed face of Castel Frentano. Francesca moved closer to Antonio. Each night on the balcony they stood, fused as one, marveling at the lights and sounds of the enchanted city below. The nearness was not enough; they anxiously went to the bed and made love.

The newlyweds slept little and awoke to the sunlight that skimmed across the canal. They took espresso and biscotti out to the balcony and, with their bare feet touching, planned their day. *Zia* had left generous picnic provisions, so with a basket stuffed with cheeses, grapes, bread, wine, and glossy chocolate truffles, the two set out to explore Venice, hand in hand.

Antonio pulled Francesca into the first *gelateria* they passed. "We are honeymooners," he said laughing. "We can have gelato for breakfast if we'd like. Francesca ordered a single scoop of peach, and he ordered a double scoop of chocolate. After they shared licks of each other's favorite picks, they strolled through the gardens at Giardini Reali, just off Piazza San Marco.

They came upon a hedge of surgically precise clipped yew at least ten-feet tall—a cleverly designed labyrinth to test and delight all the senses.

Hoping to master its riddles, they meandered through the maze, only to hit wall after wall. Francesca laughed so hard that she cried when she saw the determination flaring in Antonio's eyes. He hated to lose at anything, she knew, and he would be damned before the dead ends of greenery would defeat him.

As they inched steadily closer to the center, they discovered elaborate niches carved out of the hedge, each one containing a surprise statue, or perfectly manicured topiary in the shape of balls, cones, obelisks, or elegant spirals.

After Antonio muttered a few words Francesca had only heard before on the fishing boats, they finally arrived at the core, and the labyrinth held one last surprise for them. Their footsteps triggered a hidden lever that sprang suddenly loose, spraying spring water into all directions, drenching their hair and clothes. The designer had won, after all. They stared at each other, wringing wet, and could only laugh.

Antonio removed his shirt, and laid it over the head of a concrete lion to dry. Francesca appreciated the details of his body glistening in the sun. Francesca followed suit, and removed her outer smock to dry. Only their covered picnic basket had remained dry in the surprise deluge.

In her soft pink slip, Francesca spread a quilt across a sunny square of lawn while Antonio retrieved a bottle of wine they had left to chill in a cool fountain. Full of bread, chocolates, and wine, and surrounded by fragrant foliage, they were happily lost in the best labyrinth - love.

The summer breeze soon dried their clothes and hair. They retraced their footsteps out of the ingenious maze, and reluctantly found their way back to *il mondo reale*—the real world.

After a bit more meandering and sightseeing, hunger overtook them and they decided on a *ristorante* called Sole e Luna.

"*Ciao*," said a handsome waiter. "Good evening! I'm Luzio, and I will take care of you tonight. What may I get for you to drink, *Signora*?"

"I think I'll have the peach Bellini, *per favore*," Francesca answered.

"Make two of those!" Antonio chimed before lifting Francesca's hand to his lips to kiss.

They sat on the spacious terracotta terrace overlooking the renowned Giudecca Canal, a magnificent feat of ancient engineering. A sun-bronzed man strummed an acoustic mandolin and the classic tunes of love resonated through the air. As the sun began its descent over the canal, they watched gondolas glide past, escorted by soaring and dipping seagulls, and Francesca laughingly indulged tiny sparrows begging for tossed morsels of bread.

The waiter presented a bottle of wine to Antonio for inspection. After a quick nod, Luzio poured just an inch into a glass for Antonio to test. After he nodded his approval, Luzio poured two glasses and suggested an array of his favorite dishes of wild game, seafood, local cheeses, and fresh fruit.

They dined under the velvety Venetian sky with the blended sounds of the city falling like music all around them. For dessert, Luzio suggested a Venetian delicacy – cornettos – a crisp-layered cream-filled pastry. Francesca ordered a *specialita* beverage called a cappuccino, a frothy layer of steamed milk foam poured over a strong espresso.

When Antonio spotted white foam on Francesca's nose, he discreetly leaned over and kissed it off. "You are my dessert," he whispered, causing her to shiver.

Luzio reappeared to refill their wine glasses and asked if they had conquered the labyrinth. A native to Venice, Luzio had many tips and stories to share. He asked them if they wished to experience a unique Venetian festival.

As dusk gave way into night, Luzio explained that they could be his guests at a Bacchanalia, a traditional festival to celebrate the Roman god Bacchus.

"Of course!" Francesca cried. "My papa in Castel Frentano is a vintner, and Bacchus is the god of wine! Perhaps we will bring him home a souvenir of good luck!"

The three left *Sole e Luna* and stepped into a gondola that took them to the steps of what appeared to be an enormous Gothic mansion. In the dim glow of gaslit lanterns, the towering clay façade radiated a warm hue of washed rose. After the gondola was moored, they stepped out onto the wharf and walked up several dozen stairs to a massive bronze door, as exquisitely detailed as any sculpture Francesca had seen at the *museo*.

They entered a vast marbled foyer only to find two naked women in silk masks tangled on a large red velvet settee, seemingly oblivious to all around them. A small crowd of spectators turned participants looked on. Francesca, mortified, averted her eyes and held Antonio's arm tighter. In the front hallway, there were more women who indulged in the sensual pleasure of touch.

As they nervously entered the main parlor, discarded items of clothing and undergarments lay in haphazard heaps, and almost everyone was without clothing, save for a few masks. Men with men, women with women, women with men, people in writhing piles. The party goers drank, mingled, and gleefully debauched. Francesca studied her skirts, afraid to catch anyone's eyes, and gripped Antonio's arm like *Nonna* gripping a chicken for dinner.

Without a stitch of clothing or shame, a tall, masked man approached them and Antonio instinctively recoiled, pulling Francesca closer. They were as stunned as animals of the night caught in the blinding glare of sudden lamplight. Suddenly, Luzio began to undress, looking suggestively at Francesca. "Are you ready for your souvenir?" he asked. Francesca looked in alarm at Antonio, and they sprinted as one for the door.

As they quickly fled the grand mansion, full of answered carnal desires, they did not stop laughing until they stepped out of the gondola that took them back to their nest high above the city. The experience had deeply shocked Francesca, but a part of her was glad to have had her eyes opened to such affairs. This was a world unlike any she had known—or even suspected. She was glad, too, that they had taken their leave; they did not even say *arrivederci* to Luzio or thank him for his offered... memento. The grape harvest in Castel Frentano would have to do without this particular blessing of Bacchus.

Before retiring for the night, they strolled past the Palazzo del Doge Falier. They thought it must've been past midnight because the stars shone brightly. Gazing up at the waning moon, they talked of their devotion only to one another, and that's when the tricky subject of leaving Italy for America was first introduced.

"Antonio, please! Quit dreaming! I'm sure we will never leave for America! You don't even speak English!" Francesca protested, tossing her best evil eye. She was silenced by his kisses.

"Remember, we are in Venice. The language of our eyes and hands is all we need," he whispered in her ear. "Tonight, it is just us." He grabbed her hand and they hurried back to the apartment.

In the darkness of their room, she gave in to his soft whispers. He cupped her face with his hands and pulled her gently to him. Antonio picked up his love, now molten with desire, and carried her to the bed. No one at Bacchanalia, she was sure, had such an exquisite night.

The train for home left the next afternoon, and they were prepared to spend one night in a too small sleeping compartment. By day, the beds made a bench, and by night the bench turned into a makeshift bed. It was not the most comfortable night's sleep, but the adventurers – now a bit more worldly – made the best of it.

The next morning, as sunlight spread across the horizon, the train made a stop at a natural fumarole, said to be curative for a variety of maladies. Neither had ever been to a hot spring, so with two hours to fill until the next departure, they decided to indulge.

They changed quickly into swim attire, grabbed their day packs, and disembarked.

"Saturn created this hot spring with a single bolt of lightning," Antonio advised. "Myths say the water is meant to calm us."

As Francesca stepped into the warm pool, she tingled over every bit of her skin. She could feel her stress lift in the sulfurous mist that now engulfed and lulled her. Each of them floated in a reverie as though entranced.

"Francesca, are you asleep?" Maria stood over her, breaking the dream.

"What?" In confusion, Francesca covered her eyes in the sunlight.

"Try this bread," Maria said as she placed a piece of bread into Francesca's mouth. "It is so good, it should be a sin."

Chapter 18

Fall 1918

As Matteo grew and the family settled into new routines, a surprise arrived on the Bucci's front porch. When Francesca answered the door, her brow furrowed with worry that the stranger before her bore bad news. Instead, the capped courier handed a package to Francesca, saying with a pleasant smile, "Enjoy, *Signora* Bucci!"

Francesca stood wordlessly in the foyer, turning the box in her hands for long moments before she slid the soft green ribbon from the box.

Ella appeared and read over her shoulder, exclaiming, "Two tickets to the Lexington Opera House! For tonight!"

Francesca waved the tickets in the air like small flags. "What! Who are they from?" Francesca asked, looking more closely for clues.

"There's no note," replied Ella, turning over the box.

"Opera! How exciting!" Rosa sang out, hitting her highest note.

"I've never even been to an opera! What should I wear?" Francesca picked up Matteo, and the three ran to her bedroom to pick out a dress. She had only simple frocks made of inexpensive spun cotton, but she had adorned one with elaborate embroidered peacocks, and dazzling sunsets at the collars and cuffs.

"Oh, this is *so* beautiful," Ella sighed.

"Then I will make one just like it for you so we can be twins," Francesca smiled.

When Antonio arrived home, he was slightly puzzled by the generous gift and felt sure it came from his very loyal friend Vincent Marcello in New York. "He is a fine man, I tell you," Antonio said to Francesca. "No greater man exists in America!"

"Please invite him to Lexington! We must meet and repay him for his generosity." Francesca brushed her hair smooth before she braided it into a chic up-do. She chose to wear one of her beaded headbands that she had recreated from a magazine, with a fashionable swirl landing just at her left cheek.

Antonio and Francesca left the children at home with Ella and set out on the town. Maria promised to stop over and check on them from time to time. A horse-drawn carriage took the couple for a ride to the Lexington Opera House on North Broadway. Francesca loved the sound of the hooves on the brick pavement. Since she had come to America, she had ridden in a horse-drawn buggy only twice. She missed the feel of the cobblestones and the rhythmic to-and-fro motion that reminded her of home.

The coachman, wearing a smart silk top hat, took them on an extended ride through downtown past the grand homes on Ashland Avenue, and then wound back toward the Lexington Opera House.

At the front door, Antonio stepped out of the buggy and held out a hand for Francesca.

The Lexington Opera House, a newly erected three-story structure, and crown jewel in Lexington's growing downtown cultural milieu, delighted Francesca with its familiar Italian Renaissance design. The interior décor was equally ornate, with rich burgundy velvet curtains adorning a gilded stage.

Excited patrons bustled inside the opera house, dressed in their finest. Francesca had never seen so many fur stoles and exotic jewels.

Antonio seemed to know almost everyone who passed, and he proudly introduced Francesca to all. Antonio discussed everything from the trots to gentlemen's clothing with men they encountered. Their wives gasped with pleasure, and more than a bit of envy, at Francesca's chic artisanal headband.

On their way to find their seats, Francesca and Antonio ascended the staircase to a gilded balcony framed by a gleaming brass railing. Their anonymous benefactor had given them front row balcony seats, and for a few enthralled hours, Francesca sat transfixed by the lavish production.

Though written by Italian composer Giacomo Puccini, *Madame Butterfly* was performed this day in English. Francesca understood little of the words, but she nevertheless absorbed all of the haunting emotion played before her on the stage. With the help of Antonio's whispered interpretation, she followed the story.

Two acts, set in Japan, told the story of a Japanese woman named Cio-Cio-San who renounced her faith for the love of an American naval lieutenant. Francesca leaned forward into the railing, longing to be closer to the stage. The artistry of the colorful costumes, swirling with color, called out to her artist's soul. She gazed down at the audience below and could tell most men and women alike swept away tears, profoundly moved by the beauty and tragedy of Butterfly's story.

After the first act, an usher delivered a card with a chilled bottle of spumante and two crystal glasses on an etched silver tray.

To: Antonio and Francesca
I trust this note finds you well,
and I wish you both a delightful evening.
From: Vincent Marcello

After the performance, Antonio took Francesca backstage to meet the performers and mingle with his associates. On the ride home, they sipped the remainder of the sparkling wine straight from the bottle, laughing like teenagers, not at all like the decorous arts patrons of just moments ago.

The coachman, paid handsomely by Vincent, took them for an even longer ride through the city before they headed back to Lexington Avenue. The warm night air did not stop Francesca from snuggling against her husband, who looked more than handsome in his waistcoat.

"Antonio, *amore mio,* tonight was wonderful!" she said. "When will I get to meet Vincent and thank him for his generous gift?"

"I hope soon, *Cara,*" Antonio answered. "He is a great friend."

"I will send him a thank-you note and extend an invitation to come to Kentucky," Francesca smiled. "I will send his wife one of the scarves I've made with rhinestones and faux fur."

"That sounds *perfetto,*" Antonio gestured with his left hand. His right arm was clasped firmly around Francesca's shoulder.

Chapter 19

Fall 1918

A few days later, Antonio brought home a copy of the *Lexington Herald* to read to Francesca. As he sat down at the kitchen table, she handed him a cup of strong coffee, and asked, "What troubles you so?"

Carefully, Antonio chose his words, "They have warned of an epidemic that has crippled Philadelphia and Chicago. The paper says the virus has spread very rapidly.

"Now that it has hit the east coast, La Grippe is spreading everywhere. Listen to me carefully. I want you and the children to stay home. I will pick up enough supplies this week to get us through," Antonio reassured Francesca with a grim smile, and got up to put his jacket back on.

"Antonio! If it's dangerous, you should stay home, too!" Francesca cried.

"Don't worry, love. I will protect myself. The fall meet is about over, and *Signore* Angelucci plans to close down his clothing store for a few weeks. I will be back with everything we need in just a few hours."

While Antonio was gone, Francesca's mind clouded with troubled thoughts of the virus. She prepared a simple lentil soup and garlic bread, using only enough ham to flavor the soup. Who knew when food might be plentiful again in the scare?

Antonio returned with as many groceries and necessities as he could carry. "I will pick up more tomorrow. The shelves looked bare at the grocery. I guess the paper has spread a touch of panic.

"When the children come home from school, tell them they are to stay home for a few weeks. We will not concern them with the details, but you and the children *must* stay at home." Antonio, seeing the fear blooming on her face, put his arms around Francesca and held her tight. "Don't worry, *Madre*, everything will be fine."

The children were excited about their time off school. They did not quite understand the enormity of the problem that lay ahead, and this was probably for the best. Only Ella passed a flicker of concern across her face before smiling at the younger children.

They certainly did not understand why they had to bathe in the middle of the week. "The air is dirtier than usual, and Mamma just wants you to stay well," Francesca said as she filled the tub with hot water.

"Raffaele, it won't hurt you to stay a little cleaner," Ella added with a teasing smile.

Francesca was glad the children were to stay home. The days alone with Matteo were not enough, and Maria could only come over so many hours in one day. She and Maria spoke anxiously about the spread of the so-called "Spanish Lady," and agreed they could keep in touch if they spoke through their kitchen windows or across the fence in the backyard.

Antonio returned from work each day only to report increasingly worse news, "The flu is on the front page again today. There have been sixty-two cases reported in Lexington. The paper says that some people who have contracted this virus die very quickly. This is serious, Francesca. Allow no one in this house, not even our neighbors. I spoke to Louis earlier, and the news is now everywhere. No one really wants to commune with anyone for fear they will get sick."

"I am scared, Antonio! How will we protect ourselves? Do you think our family is safe in Italy?"

"Stay at home. The Department of Health has handed out masks to wear in public. I left a few at the front door and I wear mine every moment I am away. Please put one on if anyone comes to the door," Antonio said, pouring himself a cup of coffee.

Francesca picked up a mask that had a limerick attached written in both English and Italian:

> Obey the laws
> And wear the gauze
> Protect your jaws
> From septic paws

Speaking more seriously than she had ever heard, Antonio continued, "The city has already closed down the picture show, churches, schools, pool halls, and all places people gather. The saloons are open, but on a 'buy your drink and run' policy. Here is a pamphlet I picked up at work." Antonio handed Francesca a single sheet of paper with bold print and read it to her.

> **The Spanish Flu**
> **Ill? Call a doctor**
> **Go to bed. Avoid constipation.**
> **Eat plenty of healthy foods and liquids.**
> **Nature is the only cure.**
> **Do not panic.**

"The track will close in a few days, and then I will stay home, and we will ride this out together," he reassured, unloading a paper sack. "I will wear my mask and wash my hands often. Remind the children to wash their hands every hour or so."

Home became a comfy prison for the children and Francesca. No one requested embroidered goods for fear of La Grippe. Her only outlet was in the backyard and her kitchen window. She and Maria began to communicate through the window on an hourly basis. "Maria, Maria," Francesca yelled out the window.

"Ciao, Francesca," Maria called back, wiping a spider web from the windowsill.

"Antonio told me that Mr. Sartini over on Maxwell Street died yesterday," Francesca reported sadly.

"*Si*, Louis told me, too. Poor Felicia! With all those *bambini*! May God rest his soul. Louis's last day at work is today, and I am relieved. I am afraid he will get sick down at the market. He says that the few items left on the shelves have not sold, because everyone is too fearful to venture out, and there are rumors of citywide quarantine. How many more days will Antonio work at the track?"

"I am not sure, but I hope not too many more. As soon as he comes home every day, I wash his clothes with extra Persil, and fix him a hot bath with vinegar, rubbing alcohol, drops of lemon, and tea tree oils. He says he has worn his mask at all times. I scrub it to death!"

"Louis said that a man got kicked off the trolley yesterday because he did not wear a mask." Maria shook her head. "I guess he was not afraid to get sick. Foolish man!"

Francesca shared *Nonna's* remedies that were believed to repel ill spirits, including goose grease poultices covering the crucifixes worn around their necks. Francesca made a syrupy tincture from onions, garlic, and honey, and prayed over the liquid before and after giving the children daily spoonfuls.

On what was supposed to be Antonio's last day at the racetrack, a messenger came to the door. He wore a mask, and, after he knocked on the door, he stepped back off the porch.

Francesca opened the door and held the mask over her mouth. *"Ciao,"* Francesca said to the stranger. To her surprise, he spoke Italian.

"Ciao, Signora Bucci?" he spoke in a somber voice.

"Si," Francesca responded, now anxious.

In Italian, the man told Francesca that when Antonio arrived for work at the racetrack, he looked unwell. After a few miserable hours, he was taken to the Old Industrial School at Fourth and Upper Street. The city had turned the building into a provisional flu hospital, hoping to contain the deadly sickness.

"I must see him!" Francesca cried out, turning to grab her coat.

"No! He said to tell you not to leave the house!" the stranger said. "I am so sorry."

Francesca slammed the door and ran to the kitchen window. "Maria! Maria!" she cried.

"Francesca, what is wrong?" she answered.

"It's Antonio. He is sick! He is at a building on Upper Street," Francesca wept.

"La Grippe?" Maria asked quietly.

"I don't know. I must see him! I will be careful. I will have Ella call for you if she needs anything before I return. She is a very capable young woman, the children will be fine." With that, she left the window and went to speak in hushed tones with the girl who had grown to be a daughter to her.

"Ella, I must check on Antonio. Please take care of Rosa, Raffaele, and Matteo. Do not leave this house. Call for Maria only if you must," she warned before she left the house. Ella nodded grimly and hugged Francesca for a long *momento*.

A few blocks away, Francesca heard a child on a neighboring porch, skipping rope and singing out. Francesca understood enough for the words to haunt her.

> *I had a little bird,*
> *Its name was Enza.*
> *I opened the window,*
> *And in-flu-enza.*

Francesca hurried to Fourth and Upper streets. She wore her mask as well as gloves for warmth and added protection. The streets were nearly empty and those who braved the outdoors donned masks and looked quickly away. Neighbors had become strangers, and even threats.

When she arrived at the makeshift flu ward, people were slumped everywhere, ravaged by various stages of the dreaded illness. Among them, Francesca only spotted a few Red Cross nurses and doctors. She felt at a great disadvantage because her English was still halting and unsure. She combed the halls of the ward, frantically looking for Antonio, careful not to touch anything. Groaning and coughing patients of all ages were on cots in the hallways for lack of rooms.

"*Signora!*" A man called out to her from behind.

"Giovanni!" Francesca said with great relief. "Have you seen Antonio?"

After he sobbed to Francesca that his wife, Sonja, had just passed, he pointed to Antonio on the far side of the auditorium.

"Oh, Giovanni, I'm so sorry. May her soul rest in peace. We will check on you as soon as we can!" Francesca longed to hug him, but didn't dare. Instead, she made the sign of the cross as she bent her head to the floor.

She picked her way carefully through the surreal madness of the room. A masked Protestant minister read from his green pocket Bible and stopped to ask her if she requested a Protestant pastor or Catholic priest to offer a prayer or deliver last rites.

"Miss, are you ok?" the preacher asked. "You look faint."

Unable to focus on his words, Francesca pushed forward toward Antonio. She at last reached him, slumped over in a chair, among dozens of sufferers. She went as near as she dared and saw sickness in his eyes. He shook with fevers and looked like nausea might overtake him. He gripped a tin bucket between his legs like it took the last of his remaining strength. Francesca grabbed a blanket from a bench and covered him.

Wearily, he raised his head to find Francesca over him. "*Madre*, you shouldn't be here," he said through his mask in a weak whisper.

"Shh, I will be fine. What can I do for you?" she asked.

"Water, water please, my throat is on fire," he confessed with a cough.

Francesca hurried through the misery to find water. She weaved through the unwell bodies that littered both beds and floor. At the edge of the room, a volunteer for The Salvation Army poured water into small cups. Francesca could see the despair and exhaustion in her eyes. "*Grazie,* thank you," Francesca murmured, and picked up two cups of water and returned quickly to Antonio.

"The children need you, Francesca. Please, I beg you to leave, *Madre*." He drank from the cup of water she held to his dry lips.

"Antonio, the children are fine. You must get better. You must come home!" she said with tears in her eyes.

"You don't understand," he whispered. "People die very fast from La Grippe, us immigrants even more so than Americans. I will not survive, Francesca. You must leave me."

"I will not!" she shouted.

"Francesca, please—the children need you."

"How long have you been sick?" she asked, while she ignored his pleas. She wiped her handkerchief across his forehead and tucked the blanket back around his slumped and shivering body. She noticed he looked smaller than he had just days before.

"Not long ago, I felt tired and weak. Today was to be my last day of work," he said in a low whisper.

"I should have known!" she punished herself. "You ate very little last night. I should have kept you safe at home!"

Moans of anguish and pleas for help went on unceasingly around them. Francesca sat with him through the night and tried to ease his pain. By morning, she worried about the children, and prayed that they were well and safe within their home. She was confident that Ella and Maria had the ability to watch over Raffaele, Rosa, and Matteo.

At first light, those who had perished in the night were removed, only to be replaced by others. Francesca noticed the shadows had become darker under Antonio's eyes, and she could feel the heat that rose from his body. She held a small cup of water to his lips, and as he began to cough, she pulled the cup away.

Soon, he began to cough uncontrollably, and she saw blood pooling in his handkerchief. She tried to calm him, but his cough grew harsher and more violent. Antonio gasped for air in between cries of pain. Francesca could do nothing. She aligned with their faith and went to find a priest.

Father DelCotto soon arrived and did not step too close, but cleansed Antonio of all sins through prayers, so he would shine bright before the glory of God. Francesca knew the afterlife was protected by last rites and Antonio was now safely in the hands of the Lord.

The remainder of that day she comforted him when his spasms momentarily eased. She told stories of home and talked about the children. He sometimes seemed to understand with sad eyes, but he declined quickly, as the virus took greater hold. It was not long before he began to choke on sputum and blood. La Grippe was taking him from her. She listened in horror as his throat rattled, one last time, and life passed out of him.

"Help! Help!" she screamed. But there was no one to help.

The few doctors and nurses in the makeshift ward were too busy to come. Others were either too sick or too afraid to help. "Antonio, don't leave me! Do not leave the children!" she cried. His beautiful dark skin had become grey and dull, and she laid her head in his lap and cried, her sobs blending in with the other sounds of heartache and agony that surrounded her. Francesca removed Antonio's crucifix and his *nonno's* watch, and covered his body with the blanket, not daring to kiss his dear face. She left the hospital, feeling as though she, too, had left behind her own life in that miserable inferno of suffering.

She returned to Lexington Avenue in a mournful stupor. Arriving on the porch of her house, she stripped off as much clothing as possible, laid Antonio's items underneath, and ran to the bathroom. She drew a bath and added as many salts as she could stand.

Crying uncontrollably, she soaped her skin and hair, and scrubbed every inch of her body three times, then four, then another. She knew she had to gather her broken self back together, but she must be thoroughly sanitized first. Holding her breath, she washed out her nose and mouth with oregano oil.

When she emerged from the bathroom she found Ella, Rosa, and Raffaele waiting nervously in the hall.

"Where is Matteo?" Francesca asked in an expressionless trance.

"He is down for a nap. Are you okay?" Ella asked.

"I will be, I just need to lie down for a while. Can you please take care of the children?" Francesca asked, as she headed to her bed and shut the door.

Matteo woke up hungry, and Ella brought him to Francesca. "Ella," Francesca said, with tears in her eyes, "Antonio is gone. This flu has taken him from us, and I don't know how to tell the children. I am too weak now."

Ella began to cry. "I am sorry, Mamma," she said. As she turned to leave the room, she added, "I will cook something tonight and feed Rosa and Raffaele. You take the time you need." She paused and looked back at Francesca with tears in her eyes. "I loved him like he was my own papa. Never was there such a good man. We will find a way forward. You are my family now."

The thought of Antonio alone in the hellish gym, with no light in his eyes or teasing on his lips, made Francesca cry harder. How would she survive without him? How was she to live? Her sorrow turned to anger and then sorrow again. She was in a delirium of emotions when she passed out.

The next morning, Francesca awoke and told Rosa and Raffaele about their papa. They were distraught and retreated to their rooms to mourn.

A knock came at the front door. It was Maria. "Francesca, darling, I am sorry," she cried. "I want to come in and help you. Louis thought it should be fine, since I have not been anywhere to pick up the germ.

"But I have," Francesca cried.

Maria entered anyway and took her in her arms. "I am sorry. What can I do?"

"I don't know," Francesca cried. "I just left him there. I covered him with a blanket just like the man on the ship and just…" Francesca cried.

"That's all right, you had no choice then, and you had no choice now." Maria held Francesca close like her mother had, always patting her back and stroking her hair.

"I don't think he will even get a proper burial," Francesca cried, pulling away from Maria, stricken anew.

"This flu has devastated the country. Coffins can't be made quickly enough. Louis saw bodies on a few porches.

No one knows what to do," Maria stroked Francesca's face with the palm of her hand. "Louis said a wagon in town will pick up the dead. This epidemic has gone much too far. It took a fine man in your Antonio." Freighted with heavy sorrow, Maria lowered her head, and then continued, "The city has disinfected the streets, maybe to slow this terrible curse down. Louis read a sign that said if you even spit in public you will be fined."

"Antonio just told me a few days ago that an infected man in Chicago killed his entire family to eliminate the pain!" Francesca heard her own voice, but it seemed very far away.

"The stores are bare Francesca, and we will have to make do with the supplies we have. I made a pot of minestrone and brought some over." Maria hugged her friend. "We will make it. Don't lose hope, *sorella.*"

Father DelCotto stopped by three days later to pay his respects. It was a colorful October day and the cloudless blue sky, shining on just as before, cruelly mocked the bleakness and sorrow continuing to take shape below. The father's knock on the door took the household by surprise. He knocked four times, and stepped back off the porch. Francesca opened the door slowly, and peered outside, only to find the priest on the bottom step with the familiar white mask on his face.

"Ciao, Father, thank you for coming," Francesca said sorrowfully.

"Francesca, I wanted to stop by and tell you how sorry I am. The Lord will watch over Antonio, as well as you and your children." He paused and looked away. "We all have to believe that this dreadful outbreak will leave us, and life will return to normal."

"I want to let you in and offer you something to eat, but…" she cried behind her mask.

"It's all right, I understand, I just came to speak with you and tell you that Antonio's body has been taken to the armory. The city will arrange a burial at Calvary Cemetery as soon as possible. I wish it did not have to be this way." He paused and looked down to the ground to hold back his emotion. "I had hoped I could come back tomorrow to say a few words of hope. While his body is not here, his spirit will be." He bowed his head.

"That sounds fine, Father. *Grazie,*" Francesca managed.

"I will be back around eleven a.m. tomorrow."

"*Si, Padre.*" Francesca went inside and shut the door on a world she no longer recognized or understood.

The curious children had heard every word from the hall, where they stood tearfully listening. Francesca had learned early in life that the church is not a building, it is the people gathered together, bonded in faith and affection, even if that gathering meant on a front porch, keeping careful distance in a plague. Dully, she knew she was blessed to have made good friends-even family-here in Kentucky, so far from her own. But Francesca missed her mamma and papa as never before. She wished to go into her room and stay there forever, letting her parents raise the children. What good could she be to them with this shattered heart?

The children gathered a few items they knew were important to Antonio and created a small shrine in his honor on a table on the front porch. Raffaele placed a baseball and glove that Antonio had bought him in the first week of his arrival. Rosa added her papa's favorite fedora hat and his Saint Christopher medal to the shrine. Ella contributed his dress gloves that she remembered from the train ride to Kentucky when he had spoken to her so quietly and tenderly.

When Francesca saw what the children had done, she cried anew. They loved him so much—he was a wonderful papa and husband. She went to her room and put on a simple black dress and returned to the porch with one of Antonio's freshly pressed handkerchiefs. She had embroidered a B on the edge with her best needlework, along with a wild horse running free. She held the linen square to her face and caught the falling tears.

Shortly before eleven a.m., Father DelCotto arrived, wearing the traditional vestments over a large sleeved tunic and black stole. The children soon gathered, dressed in their nicest clothes, and held onto Francesca like a buoy in an ocean storm. Ella held Matteo in her arms, while Francesca stood on the top step of the porch. Francesca thought of how Antonio would never dance to *Lauretta*

Mia with Ella or Rosa on their wedding days, or coach Raffaele's baseball team, or even see Matteo take his first steps. The loss she felt for children overwhelmed her.

As soon as the priest arrived, neighbors also emerged from their homes, some with masks, and some without. Francesca and her children chose not to wear masks, they had no intention to leave the safety of their porch.

To gather strength, Francesca looked out across her yard and down the street to see friends and neighbors lined up on porches and on both sides of the sidewalk. Everyone was dressed in black; they mourned for their lost friend, for Francesca, and her children.

Francesca noticed that loved ones had also walked up the street. She began to cry when she saw Violet and Lauretta.

Violet cried and mouthed the words, "I'm so sorry," to Francesca and hugged her daughter tightly and kissed her repeatedly.

Francesca bowed her head and grieved. As Father DelCotto spoke, she heard him say, "Come to his assistance, ye saints of God, come to meet him, ye angels of the Lord." Francesca's thoughts faded away to Italy where she and Antonio had sat amid a field of wildflowers and dreamed of their life together.

She remembered the day he had proposed, and the day he had taught her how to drive his automobile.

When Francesca came back to reality, where the world seemed suddenly without color or promise, she heard the father intoning, "May Antonio Bucci's soul and the souls of all the faithful departed, through the mercy of God, rest in peace." He blessed the small shrine surrounded by small votive candles with Holy water, and they all bowed to pray.

In a high, clear soprano, Maria sang at the edge of the property. A few of the neighbors joined in. In the familiar Italian dialect, *Ave Maria* resounded over all of Lexington Avenue.

Ave Maria! Maiden mild!
Oh, listen to a maiden's prayer!
Thou canst hear amid the wild,
Thou canst save amid despair,
We slumber safely till the morrow
Though we've by man outcast reviled-
Oh, maiden, see a maiden's sorrow
Oh, mother, hear a suppliant child!
Ave Maria!
Ave Maria! Maiden mild!

After the song, the neighbors nodded sadly and dispersed to the confines of their own homes. They wanted to carry platters of comfort food to Francesca, but didn't dare. Violet, Lauretta, Maria, and Louis lingered in Francesca's peripheral view. Violet cried on her knees, still hugging Lauretta. Antonio had been a steadfast friend to Violet, always there for her when her husband passed, and she felt indebted to him. Now Antonio had been taken, too.

Father DelCotto, from a safe distance, reassured Francesca that, as soon as safely possible, he would place a memorial in Antonio's name at Calvary Cemetery. Francesca wondered how many other bereaved widows would join her there. Francesca was just over twenty-five, alone in a strange land with four children looking up at her for guidance about what would come next. Francesca honestly had no idea.

Chapter 20

Winter 1918

As the last brown oak leaf fell to the ground, the Spanish Flu continued its wrath, taking more and more lives, but the deadly war in Europe had finally begun to turn. Dispatchers from the front reported that Austria-Hungary had surrendered to Italy, and letters from home began to arrive again, confirming the hopeful news.

At least her family was safe from war now, Francesca thought.

Many had perished in Castel Frentano from the deadly flu, but her closest friends and family had survived. *Grazie a Dio!* Italians, like the rest of the world, had greatly feared the deadly, unpredictable plague. When would it be okay to drop the masks and resume greeting friends with warm embraces? No one knew.

Maybe the raging flu had at least helped dampen the enthusiasm for war? On November 11, 1918, a truce was declared. Germany, the last of the Central Powers, had accepted defeat and surrendered before facing total annihilation. Francesca remembered the date when peace came because of the unforgettable quote: 'Eleventh hour of the Eleventh day of the Eleventh month.' Eleven proved to be a lucky number for the exhausted world.

Christmas of 1918 – the first without Antonio – came and went like a ghost. Since it was still not safe to shop, much less leave the house, the season passed without friends, family, or brightly wrapped gifts. The children busied themselves with old toys, books, puzzles, and tried to comfort their mamma that nothing else was needed. But what each of them secretly wanted was to see the light return to her eyes, and for her laughter to ring forth easily, as it had before Papa had to leave.

Two days after Christmas, a brown package, postmarked New York City, arrived on the porch. The children didn't want to touch it, so it lay on the front porch all morning.

"Poke it with this, Ella," Raffaele handed her his arrow.

"What do you think it is?" asked Ella.

"Maybe it is a present," Rosa's eyes shined with hope.

"Step out of the way, children," said Francesca, unafraid. "I will open it."

With gloves on, she carefully opened it and found a box of children's books. Not able to read the titles completely, she carefully studied the covers before handing them out. She passed *Alice's Adventures in Wonderland* to Rosa. *The Tale of Johnny Town-Mouse* she gave to Raffaele. The last book was *Pride and Prejudice*, and she handed it to Ella. As the children ran off to read their new books, Francesca removed an envelope from the base of the box. Inside the envelope was a card and a smaller envelope that held a generous amount of cash.

Dearest Francesca,   Christmas 1918

I hope the children are well and will enjoy the books.
Please accept my gifts as I am deeply wounded by Antonio's passing; he became a brother to me. I hope this small token will make you feel better, and know that you are not alone.
My Anna loves the scarf you made for her, and she would like to commission five more as gifts for her friends. The scarf took on a life of its own at a recent dinner party. It is quite lovely! If you need anything at all, please let me know.
Next Christmas will be better, with God's will.
Your Friend Always,
Vincent Marcello

In the days that followed, Louis was the only one to leave Lexington Avenue, so he was the sole source of news for several neighbors. Those who were not sick shouted the news to each other from porch to porch.

Francesca lived her days as they came, and the children did their best to keep her spirits up. They kept their small quarrels to themselves and hugged her often. As mysteriously as the flu had come, it went away as abruptly, leaving the world to heal.

Maria came to visit almost every day, as did Violet and Lauretta. Though it took some getting used to after the long period of guardedness and paranoia, it was nice to once again have company and conversation with her friends. It helped take her mind off life without Antonio.

"I can't believe that the city will have a parade tomorrow!" Violet complained. "Even though the flu has subsided, I don't think a group gathering is wise."

"I know! Alessandra and Martino are begging to attend," Maria added. "Martino says the parade will focus on the war fund campaign, and there will be a large bonfire on Cheapside Drive afterwards."

"Well, I think it is too early for anyone to be out in public!" Francesca worried, as she wiped crumbs from the kitchen counter. "Are they not afraid to get sick? Don't they realize how many have died?"

"I told my two that there is no way they will attend the parade or the bonfire," Maria said sternly. "But they seemed to understand. They are just tired of home confinement!" She sipped her coffee and thought of her own bored children and of Francesca's grieving children, stuck in the house with no distractions, no school, and no games in the street. "I know! Bring the children, and come to our house tonight!" she said suddenly, eyes flashing with excitement. "I will make sauce and cheese balls, and the children can play. Louis and Martino can build our own bonfire in the backyard!" She got up from the kitchen table to make preparations. "I'll see you at around five o'clock!" Maria happily hurried off to tell her children.

"I'll bring the wine," Violet smiled, and held her hand out for Lauretta.

The slowing of the flu epidemic wasn't the only cause for celebration. America rejoiced, as though thoroughly mad, at the end of the long war. Those who were not sickened by the flu celebrated the returning of the troops – husbands, lovers, sons – with raucous parades and patriotic decorations in every window.

The three friends were perhaps wise to be wary of the gatherings. Not only had they lost Antonio, but forty million others in America had died from the flu, four times as many soldiers lost to the Great War. In Kentucky alone, 7,000 flu victims perished; it would take a long time to recover and heal.

Although Francesca and the children looked forward to Vincent's monthly packages of cash and small gifts, the days moved ever so slowly, and with school starting back, Francesca found herself often home alone with Matteo. By busying her hands with colorful handiworks and stitchery, Francesca could disappear into wild landscapes filled with peacocks, waterfalls, meadows, and olive groves, places where there was no heartache, and no flu, just the comfort of simple beauty.

With spring around the corner, Francesca decided it was time to part with a few things that had belonged to Antonio. Maria offered to take them to church on Sunday for the needy. As each piece of clothing passed through her hands, Francesca wept. She saved Antonio's Saint Christopher medal for Rosa, his crucifix for Ella, and his pocket watch for Raffaele. She found a few mementos for Matteo for when he was older. Antonio, other than the fine suits gifted by Mr. Angelucci had very few possessions; family had been precious to him above all.

Francesca set aside a few of the nicer suits for Louis and Martino, and then pulled a brown tweed jacket off its hanger, lifting it to her nose. She smelled Antonio's familiar warm scent and stifled a sob. Sadly, she slipped her hand into the inside pocket, and to her surprise, found a letter. It was written in English. She read a few words and got frustrated. She put it in the top drawer of her nightstand.

When Maria walked over for a cup of coffee later that day, Francesca hesitantly asked, "I found a letter, and I would like for you to read it to me."

"Where did you find it?" Maria asked.

"In one of Antonio's coat pockets," Francesca replied. She went to her bedroom and retrieved the letter. When she returned to the kitchen, she handed it to Maria.

Maria took the letter from Francesca and unfolded it. She noticed that the date at the top was October 11, 1914. The letter was over four years old. Maria's English had improved, and only a few words gave her trouble. First, she read it quietly to herself.

"What does it say?" Francesca pressured.

"Oh, you know, I am not very good with English. I can barely make it out." Maria had a troubled look on her face.

"Well, try! I want to know what it says!" Francesca urged.

"No, you don't, friend." Maria folded it up and stuck it in her skirt pocket.

"Maria Ginocchio, tell me!" Francesca reached for the letter.

"Francesca, this letter is from the past, and you are wise to throw it away."

"Maria, you tell me now what's in that letter or I will ask Violet!" Francesca demanded again.

"No, don't ask Violet!" Maria let out a huge sigh. "Sit down."

Dearest Antonio,   *October 11, 1914*

I am sorry about the other night. I know you long for your family to arrive someday. I want to tell you that you have helped me cope with the loss of my John, and I am forever grateful. You are the kindest man I've ever known, and I am sorry for loving you.

I am having your child. This child will bring life back to me. I have so much love to share, and since John died,

I need this light in my life. Soon it will be clear, and I will not subject you to the rumors. Please know how special you are to me, and I will honor your wishes to let go of us.
With great love, and regret,
Violet

Francesca sat there, as the heat rose in her stomach, her heart, and then her throat. After she took it all in, she got up and walked to the kitchen window. "Lauretta is Antonio's child." She looked out at the bright sunshine. "How did I not know? Her brown eyes look just like my Rosa's!" Her mug hit the wall as she fought tears.

"Francesca, I am sorry. Violet got so close to you. She acted like your friend just to stay close to Antonio? She is a *strega,* and that is all!" Maria picked up pieces of the mug from the floor.

"No wonder it took him six years to send for me! He did not need me here, he had his own lover!" Francesca did not recognize her own voice—she sounded like a wounded animal howling. "I loved him! He belonged to me. I came to America for us!" She threw her hands in the air wildly. "I risked the lives of our children for him!"

"Shh, Francesca, I am sure Antonio did not want to hurt you. He was alone. He loved only you," Maria tried to calm her.

"I was alone, too! For six years!" She turned to Maria, "Thank you so much, Maria, I think I need to be alone and lie down."

"I will be back to check on you later," Maria whispered sadly, not knowing what to do.

In her bedroom, Francesca couldn't control her tears. She wanted to scream, she wanted to rip out Violet's eyes with the tips of her fingers, and she wanted to die. Her friendship with Violet had been a lie from the start. Francesca had invited her into their home and spilled her secrets to her. Violet had betrayed her, from the first friendly hello at the market. The lies detonated like bomb after bomb in her heart, destroying everything Francesca once thought she knew and counted on.

Trying to make sense of madness, she sought to see Antonio's side. She had been an ocean away and he desired someone to fill the void in his life. Yet she had been lonely, too, and remained loyal. Deception scalded, and for now, the silver and diamond ring on her hand for the first time looked like a glittering lie. Where it once shone with love, it now reflected betrayal and her own brokenness.

She also cried for Lauretta. She was fatherless, as were the rest of the children. She cried for Ella who had lost two fathers in a short period of time—the first of whom had seemingly vanished, leaving a wound that could never entirely heal.

How can life be so unfair? How could God be so cruel? Francesca grabbed her rosary and began to pray, until she fell into an exhausted sleep.

Francesca woke to the sound of Matteo, standing in his crib, mumbling and playing. He was beautiful—a wonderful baby. She pulled herself together and picked him up out of the crib and changed him. She sat down in the rocking chair to nurse. Her life was not over, by any means, but it was certainly forever changed. With four children to raise, she could not afford to provide a home for this compounding grief.

She resolved to put the betrayal and anguish in her past. Had she only read the letter this morning? She suddenly felt years older and very, very tired.

When the children arrived home from school, they began their homework, while Francesca cooked dinner mindlessly. Maria came that evening, and even helped with the children. "Louis and the children are going over to the Buchignanis for dinner tonight. I told Louis I needed to be here for you."

"*Grazie,* Maria, you are a true friend." Francesca kissed each cheek and led her into the kitchen for coffee.

It was three days later when Violet stopped by; unaware that Francesca knew her secret, she knocked on the door. She and Lauretta wore their masks as a continued safeguard against any flu that lingered.

Maria saw Violet heading toward Francesca's house from her front window and immediately went to meet her.

"Violet, Violet!" Maria yelled from the side yard.

"Hi, Maria! I have fresh baked bread," Violet greeted Maria.

"Violet, things have changed." Maria paused and looked away.

"What's wrong? Is there anything I can do?" she offered.

"You have done enough. I think you should leave," Maria said with a firm voice. "Francesca knows, she found a letter." Maria shot the evil eye.

The color faded from Violet's face, and she spun to leave. She stopped and looked back at Maria. "Tell her I am sorry," she whispered, as tears formed in her eyes.

Francesca pulled her hand away from the curtains and exhaled. Maria had saved her. She couldn't open the door. Francesca went to the sofa and lay down. She shut her eyes, pushed Violet from her mind, and recalled when Antonio had left Italy.

The lovers had stood under a shady allée of trees and held each other for what seemed an eternity. She studied every feature of his face before he bent to kiss her. After the kiss, Francesca crossed her fingers, and placed them over his lips, which simply meant, 'I swear on my life.' She promised her devotion, knowing there could be no other.

The screen door slammed just then, and she knew the children were home from school.

"Hello, Mamma! Did you have a good day?" Raffaele hugged her.

"Fine *amore,* how was school?" Francesca stood up from the couch and smoothed her skirt.

"I painted a cow today with my fingers," Raffaele said.

"How did you get a cow into the school?" Francesca laughed.

"Oh, Mamma, you are feeling better!" Raffaele hugged her waist again and ran to his room.

"Children, do your schoolwork. We will go to Giovanni's tonight for pizza with the Ginocchios, Francesca said.

"Yay!" Childish cheers, once so resounding and familiar, filled the house.

Maybe we will be okay, after all, Francesca resolved, touching her breast to feel her heart, still beating.

Remember, remember always, that all of us, and you and I, especially, are descended from immigrants and revolutionists.

— President Franklin D. Roosevelt

Chapter 21

Summer 1919

In June of 1919, the Versailles Peace Conference officially ended the war. To many around the globe, the cost of this war had been beyond counting. Lives were shattered, along with dreams, farms, homes, and jobs. Thanks to both the war and worldwide bout of influenza, many children found themselves orphaned. The war also brought scarcity of goods, and a rapid rise in the cost of living. Letters from home told Francesca of the deeper economic depression that had befallen Italy.

American soldiers who did not die in battle, or perish from the Spanish Flu or other foxhole maladies, at last returned home, many with injuries that would last a lifetime. After so much fear, pain, and sacrifice, the men came home to find a very different America. Along with the emerging question of women's voting rights, soldiers were dismayed to learn that it was now illegal to drink alcohol! The headlines screamed PROHIBITION, and bootleggers enjoyed a newly lucrative, but risky trade. Even in Lexington, owners of stills often fell victim to the thieves and the law.

Grief-stricken or not, life went on for most, and world instability contributed to the uneasiness of the Red Summer. Politicians and judges received deadly bombs in the mail, and the United States Government began to seek out anyone believed to be Bolshevik communists, anarchists, or socialists—anathemas to democracy and the American way.

In New York alone, officials rounded up more than five thousand Russians to be uprooted and deported.

A few weeks later, a horse-drawn buggy carried a bomb to Wall Street and killed more than thirty people. The blast was blamed on Italian anarchists.

If you did not display American flags from your house, you were frowned upon, or even accused of being one of the traitors.

"Francesca," Maria approached her in the front yard. "Louis picked up a few of these cloth flags for us. He thought it wise to hang them outside our houses." Francesca did as she was told and also removed the Italian flag she had stuck in a vase in the *salotto*. She quietly flew the green, white, and red flag from her bathroom vase—and never let a soul except her family enter.

After a few days, Francesca walked out on her front porch. As she peered down Lexington Avenue, she was awed by the transition. Her street, which at the time was predominantly Italian families, had been transformed into little America. For the moment at least, Italy had been carefully erased.

Francesca loved her complex new country, but she was aware of the prejudice and racism that came with it. She feared for what was left of her young family, as well as for her neighbors. She rarely left the house.

Louis and Maria stepped in to help when they could. Maria shopped for Francesca, and Louis took care of the business outside the house. Mr. Angelucci dropped off garments and accessories every Thursday for Francesca's masterful needlework. As always, the creative work was a balm for her mind. Maria came to visit Francesca every day to reassure her that life was still worth living.

The gloom of the Red Summer slowly waned, and Americans of all ethnicities returned to some degree of normalcy. There were still some Americans who felt as if they needed to express extreme opinions but, overall, in Lexington, things seemed to be back to business as usual.

In January of 1920, as the Progressive Era waned and the Prohibition Era took hold, Francesca spent hours working on custom garments and accessories, improving her craft with each commission. She increased her prices and felt more independent and artistically confident than ever before, though she still longed for Antonio's admiring and encouraging compliments.

Maria interrupted all thoughts of Antonio as she burst through the kitchen door. "Francesca! Margarita says she will watch the children tonight, and you will step out with me and Louis. We won't accept no!" With Francesca sputtering objections at her heels, Maria ran upstairs and looked through Francesca's armoire for her prettiest dress. "Wear this scarf with the sequins and colorful beads, and you will be the toast of the town!"

"I don't know, Maria," Francesca hedged.

"Oh, come on! There is a new dance hall opening tonight," Maria urged. "I can't wait to dance and mingle. Louis says he will dance with us both!" Maria picked out a bright red dress and red dress shoes and said, "It is time to get you out of this cave, my friend. You need to resume living!" Francesca looked less than enthused.

"Listen to me, *sorella!* The Phoenix Hotel has opened a café called The Red Room. We will stop off there before cutting a rug or two at the dance hall. C'mon—get dressed. You need a proper meal, and it will be fun!" Maria laid the dress on the bed and gave Francesca a stern look.

Margarita Buchignani walked across the street right on time to watch the children. As soon as she revealed a tin of pizzelles that she had just baked, the children followed her like eager little lambs to the backyard. The delicate waffle cookie had snowflake impressions and Mrs. Buchignani had dusted them with confectioner's sugar, a rare treat in the last year or so. The children were in great hands.

Louis took Maria's hand and hooked his arm through Francesca's, and the three of them took off down Lexington Avenue.

A typical man, Louis excitedly talked about baseball, "Can you believe Babe Ruth has been traded to the New York Yankees for $125,000?"

Maria rolled her eyes. "Louis! Do you know what we could buy with that kind of money? I could have another *bagno*."

"If I could hit a baseball like that, we would!" Louis laughed.

"Speaking of up north, I heard the craziest thing happened in Boston!" Louis slowed his pace so the ladies didn't have to scurry. "A large six-story tank exploded—full of more than two million gallons of molasses!"

"Oh my, two million gallons? I hate even a spoonful of molasses!" Francesca scrunched up her face.

"Some lad came into the market today and said a forty-foot wave lapped over Boston's north end and killed twenty people or more!" Louis pointed to the imaginary wave high above their heads.

"What a horrible end! How do you begin to clean that mess up?" Maria shook her head, "May God rest their souls!"

"I have no idea. Wait for rain? In some areas the molasses was three-feet deep—a sticky flood. Very bizarre," Louis replied.

They continued down to Main Street, each thinking of molasses running like a slow river through city streets. Francesca glanced up, noticing the flashing marquee at the Ben Ali Theater where a crowd of people lined the sidewalk, waiting to get into the motion picture house to see Mary Pickford in *Rebecca of Sunnybrook Farm.* Lexington was clearly alive once more with people and friendly chatter.

As they entered the hotel, Francesca felt that same sense of profound loneliness that had washed over her often since Antonio's death, harder to wipe away than even a tower of spilled molasses. Looking around at the lively people and lovely setting, Francesca could imagine Antonio's excitement and how he would wrap his arm proudly around her, introducing her to everyone and patiently helping her with English words.

She shook off the memories and smiled gratefully at Maria. "Thank you so much for bringing me here. It is quite lovely. You were right—I needed this."

She noticed that the ritzy hotel lobby flaunted many large, fluted columns that held aloft a high coffered ceiling. Tufted velvet and leather couches and settees overflowed with guests, filling the venue with laughter and conversation. They entered the newly refurbished café with its walls painted a flattering ruby-red, and they were seated immediately.

A few ladies stopped to admire Francesca's peacock scarf. They were in awe of the detailed needlework and delicate embellishments she had woven into the fabric. She'd chosen threads colored in brilliant azure, emerald green, and golden shimmering yellow. After several had inquired where such a beautiful item could be purchased, Francesca had a sudden idea for Mr. Angelucci at the clothing store.

Not one to notice fashion, or ladies' chatter in general, Louis said, "After dinner, we will take the trolley over to Chair Avenue. That is where the old brewery was, and it has now been converted into a big city dance hall—a much better use for it if you ask me! Ladies, I'm ready to cut a rug!"

"Sounds exciting!" Maria grabbed Francesca's arm and gave it a happy little shake.

Francesca wasn't quite comfortable without Antonio, but she had a dear friend at each elbow, and for now, that was enough. They placed their drink orders: lime rickeys in highball glasses, without gin, of course, and a sweet tea for Louis. Over their meal, they discussed the Eighteenth Amendment and the prohibition of alcohol. Louis had kept his and Maria's grape vines well-tended and healthy. They had a stockpile of homemade table wine in their basement, and made plenty more when the ban on alcohol took effect. *What fool in government thinks he can keep an Italian from his wine?*

Eventually, as was usually the case in Lexington, the talk turned to horses. "The city is talking about building a new racetrack," Louis groaned. "Did you know that the first horse race ever held in America was run right over there on Fifth and Race streets. And now they want to just tear it down and move it out of town toward Versailles. Antonio would be appalled, rest his soul. Is nothing sacred these days?" Louis sipped on his iced tea as he stealthily admired a young lady strolling past. Maria quickly pinched the underneath of his arm just enough to get her message across, and he sheepishly directed all his attention back to where it belonged.

The trio dined on lemon basil salmon, filet mignon, and pork tenderloin with applesauce. They did not pass plates for sharing like in the more carefree days before the plague. The uneasiness of that time would take months, and even years, to shed.

After dinner, they hopped on an electric streetcar guided by a grid of overhead cables, and enjoyed the clanging bells, city lights, and cool evening air all the way to Chair Avenue.

The empty brewery had been cleverly converted for a dance party. Multi-colored paper banners streamed down from the rafters and looked to Francesca like billowing rainbows. Hundreds of revelers crowded the dance floor, bouncing and twirling in a colorful frenzy to the beat. An eight-piece jazz band playing on a makeshift stage sounded exactly like postwar America itself—raucous, irrepressible, and freshly reborn.

As more partygoers stopped to compliment Francesca's peacock scarf, the more excited she became about her possible future project. Just as Vincent had also described in his letter, Francesca's hand-fashioned scarf was the hit of the evening, and the envy of many.

"I told you it was gorgeous," Maria whispered as the raving compliments piled up, from men and women alike. The overwhelming validation steadied Francesca's resolve and imbued her with the confidence she needed. With ideas swirling like embroidery floss tossed into a cyclone, Francesca was suddenly anxious to get home... and begin.

The next morning, the residents of Lexington Avenue and all of Lexington awoke to the shocking headlines about a robbery at the James E. Pepper Distillery. Masked men had emerged from the Town Branch Creek, overtaken the guards, and conspirators had taken off with the deceased colonel's prized bourbon. Not surprisingly, Italians were blamed.

Louis protested, "We wouldn't steal bourbon! For God's sake, blame the Irish!"

It seemed like in every major city, Italians couldn't manage to stay off the front pages. Many in America began to think that Italians had infected America with rampant criminality. After all, Prohibition was enforced to reduce crime, violence, and corruption. Everyone who had a bootlegger or a recipe still drank, of course. Bathtubs became basins to mix alcohol, glycerin and juniper juice, and steel hip flasks became standard accessories under coats and skirts. Even flappers in flirty bobs and swinging fringes happily slipped bootlegged flasks into their knee-high boots!

Prohibition gave life to underground gin joints. One spoke softly at these 'speakeasies,' and if you did not know the required password, the night beat cop could probably tell you. Once inside, people drank and danced the nights away.

The stock market had finally rebounded after the Great War to an all-time high, and it seemed most everyone had extra money to spend on every kind of frivolity.

Francesca's favorite Horace quote, embroidered on a *fazzoletto* she'd made for Antonio as a teen, was just perfect for these days: '*Carpe diem, quam minimum credula postero:* Seize the day, put no trust in the morrow!' Not only were people thoroughly seizing the day, they were seizing the nights, too!

While American men had been off at war, women had been needed at home to fill sudden workforce vacancies. This newfound freedom and confidence gave many women the courage that was needed to leverage one of the most significant moments in American history. After years of struggle from suffragists and the harsh insults and obstructions of those opposed, on August 26, 1920, the Nineteenth Amendment to the United States Constitution enfranchised white women with the right to vote. It was a new day for women in America—in almost every way – including fashion choices.

Like so many, a scandalized Pope Benedict XV wanted to ban the 'immodest' apparel of the time. But women had begun to take control of fashion, and their choices were here to stay. Women cut their hair into the fashionable and feisty Eton crop and skirt hems were raised to below the knees, making life much easier for working women—and much more fun for flappers.

Dance halls became an even more popular and pervasive form of entertainment out on the town, and a sassy dance out of North Carolina called the 'Charleston' took hold everywhere. One needed unstructured clothes to dance, and breathe, as freely as men.

Flappers preferred dresses that were ultra chic and elaborately embroidered in rich colors. Some had lavish gold metal thread, sparkling sequins, and glass beads that caught the light as they shimmied their way straight into magazines, newspapers, and fashion history. Revelers often chose coordinating feathered headbands to help them bob and weave in the madcap *joie de vivre* of the day. Men wore an improbable and light hearted pairing of raccoon skin coats and straw hats. For many, life was good, spirits soared, and everyone seemed to have the time of his – or her – life.

One of Francesca's favorite new poets, Madeline Ida Bedford, summed up the zeitgeist for many women who had stepped up while the men went to war. It is hard to pass on finer things – like freedom – like fun – once you have had a taste of them.

Munition Wages

I Earning high wages?
Yus, Five quid a week.
A woman, too, mind you,
I calls it dim sweet.
Ye're asking some questions –
But bless yer, here goes:
I spends the whole racket
On good times and clothes.
Me saving? Elijah!
Yer do think I'm mad.
I'm acting the lady,
But – I ain't living bad.
I'm having life's good times.
See 'ere, it's like this:
The 'oof come o' danger,
A touch-and-go bizz.
We're all here today, mate,
Tomorrow – perhaps dead,
If Fate tumbles on us
And blows up our shed.
Afraid! Are yer kidding?
With money to spend!
Years back I wore tatters,
Now – silk stockings, mi friend!
I've bracelets and jewelry,

Rings envied by friends;
A sergeant to swank with,
And something to lend.
I drive out in taxis,
Do theaters in style.
And this is mi verdict –
It is jolly worthwhile.
Worthwhile, for tomorrow
If I'm blown to the sky,
I'll have repaid mi wages
In death – and pass by.

The following Thursday morning, when Mr. Angelucci dropped off a stack of fresh handkerchiefs for monograms, Francesca gathered her courage and broached her idea for custom fashion accessories. The new ladies' fashion, she said, was calling out for her lively handiwork. Mr. Angelucci knew Francesca's customer base was rabidly loyal, and he told her he would be proud to sell her work, as much as she could produce. The two shook hands, agreed on terms, and Francesca's nascent artistic enterprise began.

Francesca set to work reinterpreting dresses she saw in magazines. They were simple frocks with dropped waists. She adorned them with a variety of colorful embroidered birds and flowers, whatever caught her fancy. Rosa and Ella loved modeling and helped in any way possible, cutting patterns, stringing beads, and sweeping up scraps. Raffaele read to Matteo and loved sorting colorful threads for his mamma. They had their own little production in the *salotto* that spilled into the dining room and kitchen. It seemed laughter and purpose were returning, at last, to 246 Lexington Avenue.

As the few remaining autumn leaves fell to the ground, a Western Union telegram messenger arrived at the door. Francesca noticed the words *EXTRA RUSH* and signed her name shakily, praying that everything was okay with Mamma and Papa. The envelope was postmarked November 21, 1919.

Dear Mrs. Francesca Bucci,

I hope this telegram finds you well. Recently I met Vincent and Anna Marcello at a dinner party in Manhattan. Anna was beautifully adorned with one of your handcrafted accessories bearing the most remarkable peacock design. I, in that moment, become an instant fan of your work, and am prepared to offer you a generous salary if you will consent to produce your designs for me. I will send a package of materials for your exclusive use and the courier will send my offer for you to review.

If you choose to join the House of Chanel, I will send for you in one month and we will meet at Ehrich Brothers in NY. I would be pleased for you to stay as my guest at the Vanderbilt Hotel. I should want to include a few of your

designs at this spring fashion shows in NY and Paris, if terms are agreeable to you. I hope for a long and mutually beneficial creative association.
   Sincerely Yours,
   Gabrielle Chanel

Flushing all the way to her hairline, Francesca whooped at the top of her lungs and ran with the telegram to Maria's house. With barely a knock, she rushed in and thrust the telegram at her surprised friend. Beaming with joy, she asked, "Maria, how would you like to go to New York City with me?"

In shock, Maria read the telegram. And read it again. Becoming less stupefied with each reading, she screamed at last, "Francesca, that is *Coco*! From our magazines!" Hugging her friend, she laughed, "If I'm going to New York with you, I'll need you to spruce up a few of my dresses. And I'd like one handkerchief to say, 'Proud as a Peacock'!"

The End